HENRY HOLT AND COMPANY • NEW YORK

Henry Holt and Company, *Publishers since 1866*
Henry Holt® is a registered trademark of Macmillan Publishing Group, LLC
175 Fifth Avenue, New York, NY 10010 · mackids.com

Library of Congress Cataloging-in-Publication Data

Names: Lai, Remy, author.
Title: Pie in the Sky / Remy Lai.
Description: First edition. | New York : Henry Holt and Company, 2019. | Summary:
   Knowing very little English, eleven-year-old Jingwen feels like an alien
   when his family immigrates to Australia, but copes with loneliness and the
   loss of his father by baking elaborate cakes.
Identifiers: LCCN 2018050006 | ISBN 9781250314093 (hardcover) | ISBN
   9781250314109 (trade pbk.)
Subjects: | CYAC: Immigrants—Fiction. | Language and languages—Fiction. |
   Schools—Fiction. | Belonging (Social psychology)—Fiction. | Cakes—Fiction. |
   Baking—Fiction. | Single-parent families—Fiction. | Australia—Fiction.
Classification: LCC PZ7.1.L228 Pie 2019 | DDC [Fic]—dc23
LC record available at https://lccn.loc.gov/2018050006

Our books may be purchased in bulk for promotional, educational, or business use. Please
contact your local bookseller or the Macmillan Corporate and Premium Sales Department
at (800) 221-7945 ext. 5442 or by email at MacmillanSpecialMarkets@macmillan.com.

First edition, 2019 / Designed by Carol Ly
Colors by MJ Robinson
Printed in the United States of America by LSC Communications, Crawfordsville, Indiana

ISBN 978-1-250-31409-3 (hardcover)
3 5 7 9 10 8 6 4
ISBN 978-1-250-31410-9 (paperback)
1 3 5 7 9 10 8 6 4 2

For Mama

1

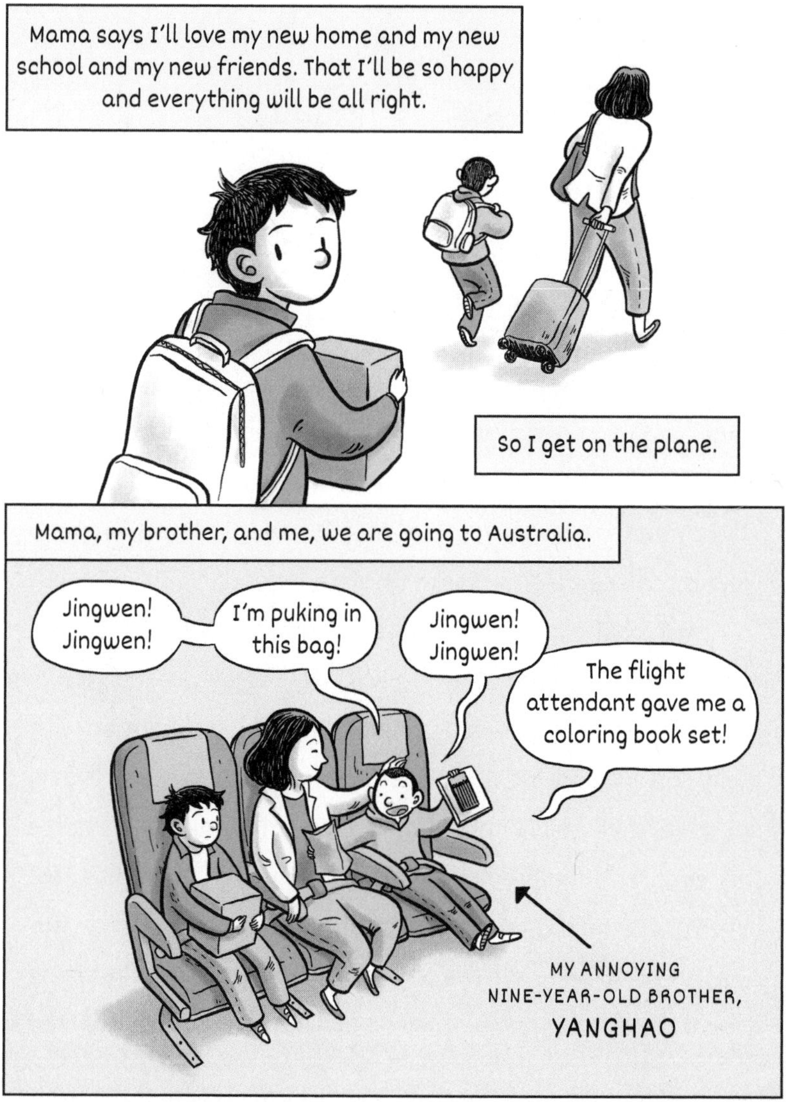
Mama says I'll love my new home and my new school and my new friends. That I'll be so happy and everything will be all right.
So I get on the plane.
Mama, my brother, and me, we are going to Australia.
Jingwen! Jingwen!
I'm puking in this bag!
Jingwen! Jingwen!
The flight attendant gave me a coloring book set!
MY ANNOYING NINE-YEAR-OLD BROTHER, YANGHAO

I look. The wing of the airplane slices through the fluffy cloud like a knife through cake. Sometimes, when the plane leans enough, I catch glimpses of the ocean. It's as blue as the sky. Only the clouds make it clear that the sky is the sky. Then Yanghao sticks his oily face to the window, and my view is replaced by the back of his giant head.

I turn to the box on my lap. It's pink and looks like a plain old box from a mom-and-pop bakery. The cake inside looks like a plain old cake iced with plain old cream and topped with plain old strawberries. But it's the most special cake. Not a special of my family's cake shop back in my old home, because this cake isn't on the menu. My family usually only has this cake on our birthdays, but my grandmother made an exception. Ah-po handed me the box of cake through the window of the taxi and said, "Jingwen, you'll be so happy over there that you'll need to celebrate with this cake." Goes to show that old people aren't wise about everything.

A long time ago, which really isn't that long ago but seems like from a time when dinosaurs roamed, I asked Ah-po if she and Ah-gong were coming along to Australia. She replied, "If we both go, who'll run our cake shop?"

"Our cake shop will never ever close," Ah-gong said, even though that day was a Sunday and our shop was closed, like on all Sundays. I asked him what if a giant meteor was hurtling toward Earth, or King Kong was on a rampage, or chickens became extinct so there were no eggs for cake making. He handed me an egg cake and told me to eat it while it was warm. Old people are sly at shutting kids up.

"We're too old and set in our ways," Ah-po said. And that was that. Once old people use age as a reason for anything, a kid can never come up with a reply that's good enough. But she and Ah-gong truly did look sad that they weren't coming. I wanted to tell them everything would be all right, but instead, I just split the tiny egg cake in half and watched short ribbons of steam rise out of it.

Ah-gong had the final word. "It's so far away. It's too long a flight."

Of course, because Ah-gong is old, he is right, and this flight I'm on is definitely too long. Not just because of the thousands-of-kilometers distance.

Hours that seem like centuries later, Yanghao's still going, "Looklooklook! A bathroom on the plane! Looklooklook!"

A shadow falls over the cake. I look up. A flight attendant is standing over me.

It's the first time someone directly speaks to me in English. It sounds like Martian.

Oh wait, I think I caught the word *"please."* But *please* what?

"Jingwen." Mama puts a hand on my arm. "The flight attendant wants to store the cake in the overhead compartment. We're about to land."

I close the box and hand it to the flight attendant.

Mama says, *"Thank you,"* and I think the flight attendant replies, *"Welcome,"* but I'm not sure. The word is lost in some other words.

Suddenly it feels like I've been frozen in this sitting position for days. My back is tired, and my knees are sore. I straighten my legs, but my feet knock the seat in front of me. A woman's face appears in the gap between that seat and the one next to it. She glances down at my feet. I squirm.

The cabin turns dim, and the plane shakes like I'm in my family's Honda CR-V back home, driving our way along a street that's more potholes than road. My ears hurt again like they did when the plane took off. I tell myself that everything will be all right, pinch my nose, and blow. Pop! Then the plane lands with a jolt like when our CR-V goes over a speed bump too fast.

Before the seat belt signs are switched off, people get up to retrieve their stuff from the overhead compartments.

Mama follows, standing on tiptoes to reach for Yanghao's and my backpacks and her handbag. She hands me the pink box.

Yanghao climbs over the seat dividers toward me.

I don't want everyone on the plane to stare when he cries, and Mama will make me be a good older brother anyway, so I pass the box over. "Don't drop it," I say. Then I shout, "Don't run! Don't be a silly booger!" as he skips ahead of Mama and me down the rows of seats.

I've forgotten that little brothers only do the opposite, and I should've told him to drop the box, run like a wild moose, and act like the biggest booger. I'm stepping off the soft carpet onto the clickety-clackety floor of the rectangular snake that connects the plane to the airport when he says, "Ah!"

The next thing I hear is a plop!

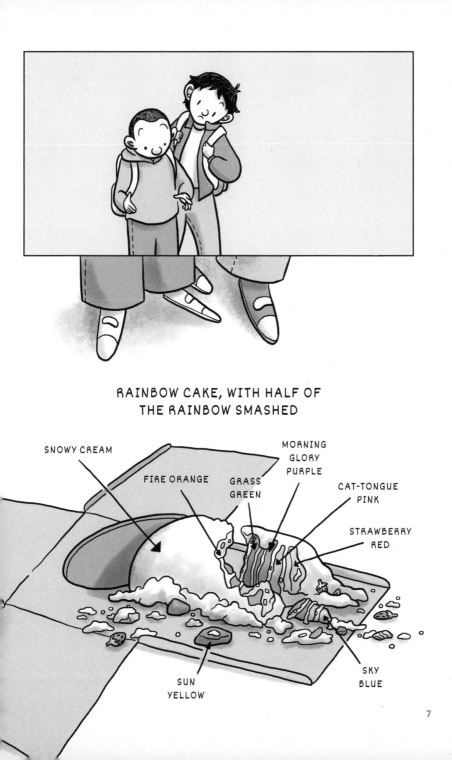

RAINBOW CAKE, WITH HALF OF
THE RAINBOW SMASHED

SNOWY CREAM

FIRE ORANGE

GRASS
GREEN

MORNING
GLORY
PURPLE

CAT-TONGUE
PINK

STRAWBERRY
RED

SKY
BLUE

SUN
YELLOW

All I can do is stare at the rainbow cake and let ridiculous thoughts run through my brain. Maybe it's an omen, that we shouldn't have stuck with the plan and come to Australia.

I want to yell at Yanghao, kick him when Mama isn't looking. He'll tattle, but it'll be worth it. I also want to join his concert of tears, wails, and snot. But then I hear the people around us—those in front of us who have turned back upon hearing Yanghao's cries, those passing by us, and those stuck behind us.

I'm on Mars.

Two months later, I'm still on Mars.

If I say that to Yanghao, he'll say, "We're on a bus."

Because he's only nine and still annoying.

If I say I'm on a bus on Mars, he'll say, "We're on a bus in Australia."

If I say we're on bus number 105 to *Northbridge Primary School*, which is in Australia, which might as well be Mars because to me English still sounds like an alien language even though we've been here for two months, and so everyone else is an alien and he and I are the only humans, he'll say, "Jingwen, you're a booger." That's what he always says when he runs out of lame comebacks.

So I say nothing. I just want to get us to school. Not because I'm a weird, school-loving kid, but because that's my responsibility. During our first week of school on Mars, Mama rode the bus with us. One week of training for me to memorize the way: a fifteen-minute walk from our apartment to the bus station, followed by bus number 105, get off after nine stops, and arrive at *Northbridge Primary School*; do the reverse for home. Yanghao doesn't need to do anything except follow his big brother like a rat following stinky cheese. Which is a bad analogy since I smell okay.

This going to school and back by ourselves is a big deal. Back in our old home, Yanghao and I never went anywhere beyond our own street without a parent or grandparent. I can also tell it's a big deal from the way Mama took a million pictures of Yanghao and me on this journey through the sub-urbs. Well, not a million, because the memory card on our secondhand digital camera can't store that much. But there are more pictures than anyone needs of Yanghao and me in our new uniforms, with our new backpacks, standing outside our apartment, waiting for the bus, tapping our cards to pay the bus fare, standing by the school gates, et cetera, et cetera. We were going to get the pictures printed and mailed by actual mailmen to my grandparents since they don't do emails. So I smiled like a clown in those pictures. Which is also a bad analogy since clowns are freaky. Nobody would paint such big smiles on their faces unless, inside, they are terribly sad.

The bus turns a corner, and Yanghao leans into me. "Look-looklook," he says, elbowing me even though he's already gotten my attention. "Cake!"

"So what?" I say. "Have you never seen cake?"

Yanghao makes his are-you-for-real face. Which I guess I deserve because back in our old home, far away from Mars, our family's cake shop occupies the front part of our house, the part that should have been the living room. We see cake every day, every minute, every second, even in our dreams. If there's an apocalypse and we all turn into zombies, while everyone else is stumbling around looking for brains, my family will be the odd ones craving something different.

Yanghao elbows me again and points to the box the alien is holding. "It's from *Barker Bakes*."

"Stop pointing," I say, stealing a glance at the alien in a more polite and less obvious way. On the box is the café's logo—a whisk lying on its side. That's where Mama works. At the café. Not in the logo. Or the box. I need to specifically point out that my mother doesn't work in a logo or in a box, because I've been hanging around my little brother way too much these past two months since we came to Mars—on account of our having made zero friends—and he'd have definitely joked, "Mama works in the logo? Or in the box?" and then laughed so hard snot would shoot out of his nose.

Mama says he's funny; I say he's cuckoo.

The bus screeches to a stop.

Yanghao leans into me too much, much farther than the bus's jerkiness would have made him.

The crowd of aliens on the bus has herded Yanghao and me to where we can't reach a seat's grab handle or anything to stop us from falling. The hanging loops don't count—I can't reach them even if I jump. Yanghao definitely can't reach them. He's short for his age because he used to get cooties that suck the blood you need to grow tall.

He and I domino into the alien with the cake.

The alien turns around and looms over us.

I can't guess what he's saying. The bottom half of his face is covered by a forest that muffles his voice. There's no way to tell if his tone is be-careful-you-naughty-boys or no-worries-all-good. He's wearing big, thick glasses, and I can't see if his eyebrows are angry or not. I want to tell him he should forgive Yanghao and me because back in our old home, far away from Mars, we never took the bus, only our Honda CR-V. Not that we're rich, but back there, the buses don't go everywhere and they come about once every hour instead of every fifteen minutes like here on Mars. And those buses aren't air-conditioned, and the seats smell like blue cheese, which I've never seen or eaten but have been told reeks of stinky feet. Plus, there are pickpockets. At least that's what my grandparents told Yanghao when he whined some time ago about how it was unfair he wasn't allowed to take a bus. He wasn't dropped on his head as a baby—I don't think so—but he'd watched an episode of SpongeBob SquarePants where there's a red bus that looks like a lobster, which was why he wanted to try it himself—and then he was disappointed to find out the real ones don't look like lobsters.

I'll explain all that to the alien, and he'll understand.

Yanghao elbows me—I swear, one more time, and I'll chop off his elbow. He grins sheepishly. "Luckily he didn't drop the cake."

I'm still sore about that rainbow cake, but Ah-gong once said it's good to let things go. Besides, the bearded, bespectacled alien is still staring at me.

I say, "Pretend we're talking."

Yanghao gives me his are-you-for-real look again. "We are talking."

"You know what I mean. Is he still watching me—don'tlooknow!"

"How can I know if he's watching you if I can't look?"

"Okay, look—but secretly."

"Jingwen . . . he's staring at you . . ." he says in what is supposedly a scary voice. "His eyes are bulging. He's gritting his teeth . . ."

The thing about Yanghao is, he doesn't know when to stop. For anything. He's always eating too much, always singing too loud, always crossing the line from a bit annoying to so annoying I have to thump him. And when he lies, he goes on and on, and I know he's trying too hard to convince me.

"His fists are clenched. His beard is trembling. His—"

"Riiight." I turn to see what the bearded, bespectacled alien is actually doing. That's when I spot the girl standing next to him. She's in a *Northbridge Primary School* uniform and about my age and staring at me. She notices me noticing and quickly looks at her feet.

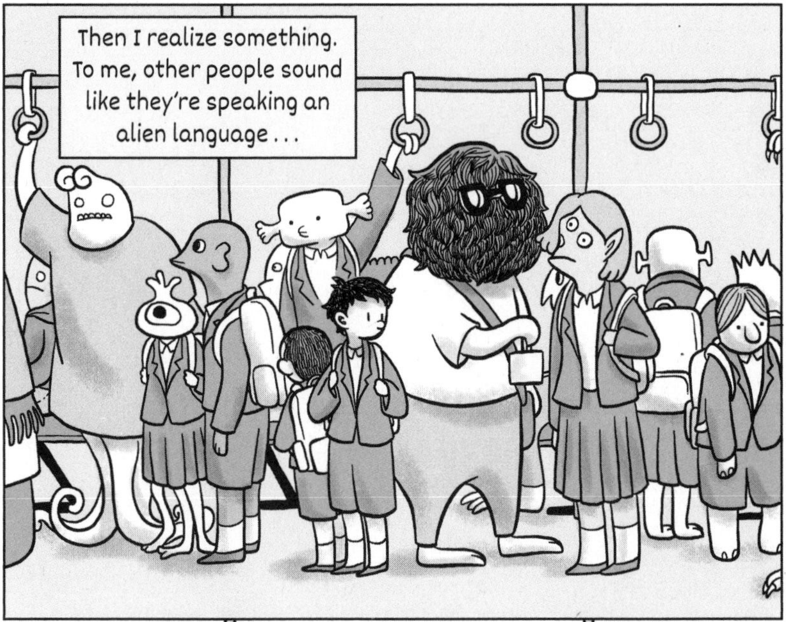
Then I realize something. To me, other people sound like they're speaking an alien language . . .

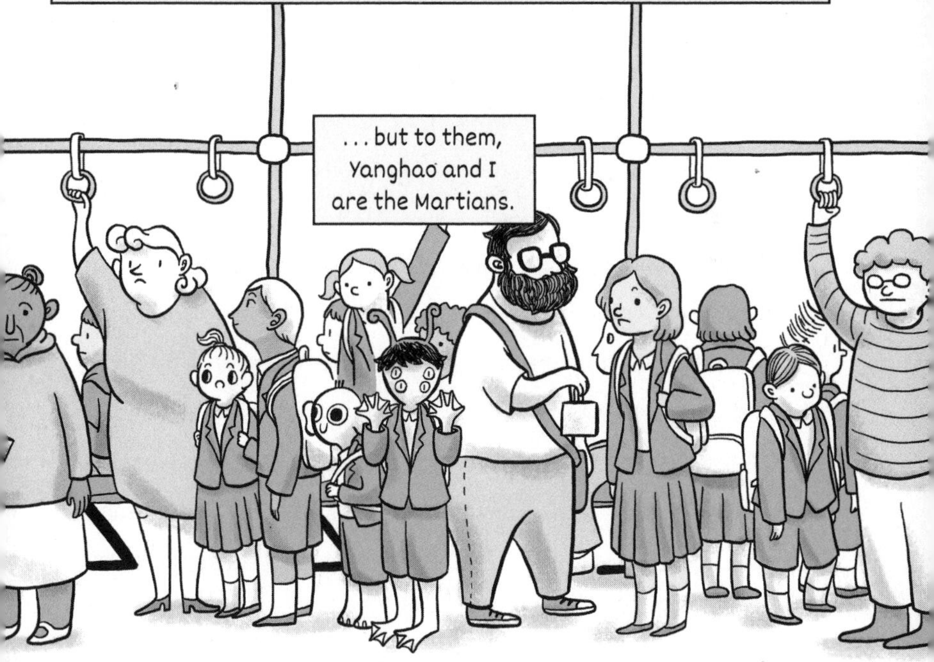
. . . but to them, Yanghao and I are the Martians.

The second time I was told we were moving to Australia, Mama broke the news by taking Yanghao and me to the special café that we'd only ever visited on weekends before.

I already knew a little bit about Australia because of the first time I was told we'd be moving there. Papa announced it over dinner. He showed us a book called *Welcome to Australia*, which had plenty of pictures of koalas and kangaroos.

Later, when I'd assumed that the first move to Australia was canceled, one of my classmates told me he was moving there. Turned out, he'd been having daily after-school English tutoring for a year. By the time he got to see the koalas and kangaroos in the flesh, I bet he knew more than just *"apple"* and *"thank you"* and *"pie"* and *"sky"* and *"bathroom."* But I didn't tell Mama that I should first attend a year of daily English tutoring, not even after I got over the shock of her announcement.

Reason one: I'd much rather spend my time after school doing anything else in the universe.

Reason two: Mama believed I was a genius who'd pick up a new language in a snap of the fingers. I was happy she thought I was a genius, and moms know everything, so maybe I was a genius and didn't know it. I promised myself then that I'd work hard at English so she wouldn't be disappointed. But in the two months we've been here, I've found that learning English is probably like learning to unicycle—possible, but you fall a lot along the way.

Reason three: Mama said Yanghao and I would love our new home and our new school and our new friends and we'd be so happy and everything would be all right.

At that café, I felt like I was being squeezed from all sides, like my skin was a onesie two sizes too small for my body, but I wanted to believe the last reason so badly I ignored the my-skin-was-too-small-for-my-body feeling and didn't ask all the questions I wanted to ask.

Now, on the bus, I'm getting a similar feeling. The bus is shrinking, or all its passengers are mushrooming into giants, or both. Everything is closing in on me. I squirm, but my elbow jabs someone who says, "Ouch!" and when I turn to make sure I haven't jabbed anyone in the eye, my backpack swings into someone who says, "Ow!"

Everything will be all right, Jingwen. Everything will be all right.

But the horrible feeling gets stronger and unbearable. It's no longer a too-tight onesie but something worse.

I squeeze past arms and backpacks to get to the back door of the bus. "Come on, Yanghao!"

Somewhere behind me, Yanghao shouts, "Wait, Jingwen! What are you doing?"

I don't stop. The humans glare and cluck their tongues at the two little aliens barging through.

When I reach the door of the bus, I have no idea how far we are from school. I'll never tell Yanghao this, since he'll tattle to Mama that he's afraid I might get us both lost: I never count the nine stops from the station to school like Mama taught me to. Many students from the school take this bus.

All I have to do is relax and let the crowd of students jostle me and Yanghao off the bus, through the school gates, and down the hallways, like we're tiny fish in a giant school of fish.

"Are we there yet?" Yanghao calls out. A second later he pops out of the tight bunch of people, like a slippery pickle popping out of a Macca's cheeseburger. "Macca's," I recently learned, is the Australian way of saying McDonald's.

"Not yet," I say. "But now we'll be the first to get off when we reach the stop."

Jingwen, you're a booger.

I keep staring out the door. After what seems like ten centuries, students who are seated get up and I know the next stop is it. I tap my bus card on the machine. It makes a series of loud beeps instead of just one, which means my bus card is low on value and I need to refill it soon, and everyone on the bus now knows that. With each beep, the python squeezes tighter.

When the door finally opens, I burst out like a baby calf shooting out of a mother cow's bottom. I don't mean to be disgusting, but animal documentaries are all I have to watch on TV here on Mars. There are other shows, of course, including ones we also have back in our old home, like SpongeBob SquarePants but in Martian, Ben 10 but in Martian, Pokémon but in Martian . . . Same but different.

Yanghao and I can't follow all those shows in Martian. He doesn't mind being bamboozled, because he's only nine. But I'm already almost twelve and too old to fumble through life, so I'd rather not make myself feel stupid by watching something I can't understand that everyone else can follow. So I watch the animal shows. Both aliens and humans don't know what the wolf is howling or what the meerkat is chittering, so it doesn't matter that I can't understand what the voice-over man says or that I probably get a few details wrong.

Yesterday's documentary was about a lamb who thought it was a dog. Since I didn't catch a word of Martian uttered on the show, I don't know how the lamb ended up living with a few golden retrievers in someone's house in the city. But it did everything the dogs did.

Most importantly, its bleat sounded almost like a dog's bark.

The golden retrievers didn't even know the lamb wasn't a lamb. Maybe they knew—no one will ever know for sure—but they treated the lamb like it was one of them. Not an outsider. Not an alien. That's what I have to do to not be an alien among the humans. I have to speak the same as them.

I hurry across the school courtyard, Yanghao close behind me. *"I want my birthday cake!"* he yells, nearly giving me a heart attack. He's been parroting the Martian phrases he's managed to catch from TV, mostly from SpongeBob.

Yanghao laughs so much he can't walk properly and is zigzagging down the hallway like he's dizzy. Other students dodge and sidestep and roll their eyes at him.

I leave the nincompoop and climb up the stairs. My classroom is on the fourth floor, while the nincompoop's is on the first.

On our first day at *Northbridge Primary School*, Yanghao skipped excitedly away from me toward his class. But an hour later, he was right outside my class, crying so hard he couldn't breathe. He wailed that he didn't understand anything anyone said, and nobody understood him, and he didn't even know how to tell his teacher he wanted to pee. His teacher escorted him to my class and talked to me.

Yanghao and I simply followed the teacher to the nurse's office. We were left sitting on a bed that looked like a hospital bed until Yanghao calmed down. The same thing happened for the next four days. I missed most of my classes. Not that it mattered, since I didn't understand anything. Every night for that whole week, Yanghao cried to Mama about not understanding English. She always promised the same thing.

Everything will be all right.

On the sixth day, when Yanghao wasn't delivered to my classroom, I figured he'd realized crying wasn't going to change anything. We're stuck among all this English. Or maybe, just maybe, he believes Mama is right. Everything will be all right.

I peer down the stairwell and watch Yanghao make his way to his class. His shoulders are still shaking with laughter. I guess everything has gotten more all right for him.

For me, everything is still far from all right.

On my first day, my classmates spoke with me. Or spoke at me.

They must have thought I was one quarter snobbish and three quarters weirdo. No one has really spoken with or at me since, but most of them are nice enough to nod or smile when they run into me. I only ever dare reply with awkward smiles that must make them think I've just come from the dentist and can't feel half of my face.

I have to make an extra effort to talk to my classmates. Actually talk. In English. Instead of nodding or shaking my head.

Learning English could be fun. It can be a game, kind of like the one Yanghao and I used to play, where we took turns throwing a die. Whoever had the bigger number got to imagine one awesome transformation onto himself, like a set of Wolverine's metal claws, or the Powerpuff Girls' flight. At the end we'd have a duel with our imaginary powers, and then Yanghao would lose and cry and tattle, and Mama would scold me for making my little brother cry. Maybe learning English can be like that game, except the transformation is in reverse—my alien form will morph into human form as my English improves. My antennae will shrink first, then the webs between my fingers, and slowly, I'll be less of an alien to everyone else.

And in this game, I get all the turns and nobody cries.

When I get to class, if a classmate smiles or nods at me, I won't even try to say *wassup*. Because I don't know what it means, even though everyone says it. There's no such word in the dictionary. Maybe I'm spelling it wrong. Anyway, most of the time when a student says *wassup*, the reply is quite long. If someone gives a many-words reply to my *wassup*, I'm doomed.

I'll just say *hi*. That's the easiest word.

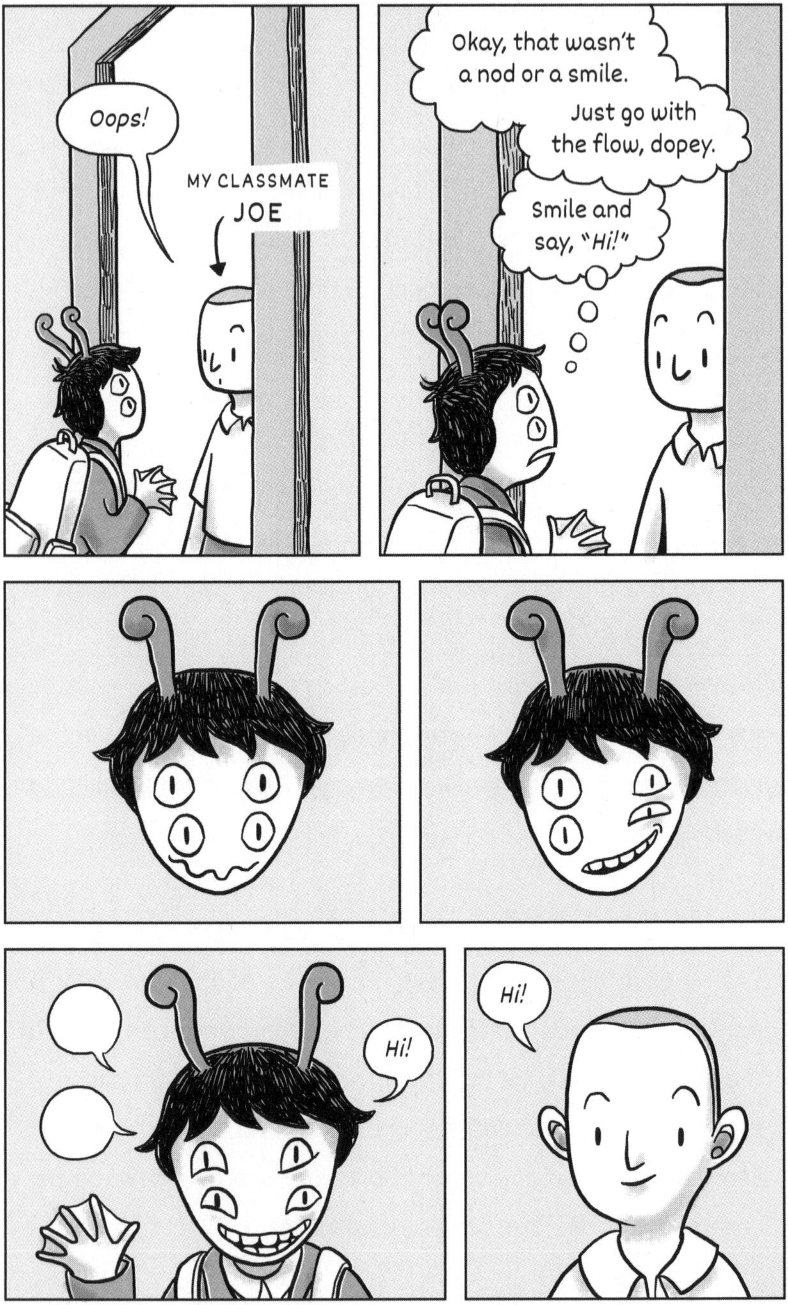
Oops!
MY CLASSMATE JOE
Okay, that wasn't a nod or a smile.
Just go with the flow, dopey.
Smile and say, "Hi!"
Hi!
Hi!

After last bell,
I'll say *bye* to Joe.

Miss Scrappell is already in the classroom even though the bell hasn't rung. Her name is pronounced like "*apple*"—as in *a is for apple*—but I think she's more like a *u is for umbrella*. Every time she turns back and forth between the blackboard and the students, her long skirt flares out, like an umbrella twirling and twirling. She teaches English and math. Back in my old school I had only one teacher who taught all the subjects, but here in *Northbridge Primary*, I have separate teachers for science, social studies, physical education, arts and crafts, and music. I sit in the same classroom all day while the teachers take turns dropping by for half to one and a half hours. I don't know which I prefer, one teacher who knows everything about me, all the bad grades and talking in class, though I don't have to worry about that now, or several teachers who don't know everything about me but who might be gossiping about me in the staff room.

I'm supposed to start sixth grade in Australia since I graduated fifth grade last year, but the principal of *Northbridge Primary School* reckons my English is poor, so it's easier for me if I repeat fifth grade. I asked Mama why Yanghao didn't have to repeat a grade. She said fourth-grade English was simple enough that he could catch up. I huffed—okay, threw a little tantrum—at having to sit through math and science lessons I already knew, but now I'm grateful for the principal's wisdom. If fifth-grade English was a language of Mars, sixth-grade English wouldn't even be from Venus. It'd be from Pluto, which was once a planet in our solar system but was later kicked out. Which is information I already learned in my old school but will probably have to relearn here.

Miss Scrappell writes something on the board.

I jot down "*adverb*" in my notebook. When I get home, I'll look it up. But for this whole class I'll be totally confused, then I'll be bored. I thought my old school was boring, but turns out, not understanding anything makes school 400 percent more sleep-inducing.

Luckily my desk is by the window. In the courtyard, there are three giant trees and fifteen tiny shrubs. A ratio of one to five. It's comforting to know I still know math. The school's maroon gates are a fence of spears that trap me within its grounds. Beyond them is a row of shops.

The leftmost is *Birds of a Feather Café*. At first, I was confused.

Why would birds drink coffee? Or was it a place where people brought their pet birds and the people would drink coffee while their birds chirped? But I read farther down below the definition of "*birds*" in my dictionary and found the idiom *birds of a feather*, which refers to people who are alike. Disappointingly, it isn't a special bird café. Just a regular café with a special name.

Happy Tails Vet is right next door. As soon as I knew what a *tail* was, I could guess what "*vet*" meant. Plus, people with dogs on leashes and cats in crates walk in and out of there. Some of the dogs have those big lampshade things on their heads. My cat, Mango, who's being taken care of by Ah-po and Ah-gong now that I'm here, doesn't like vets. He'll turn from the laziest cat in the world who only ever moves upon hearing the clinking of his dinner bowl into a murderous moggy with only one mission: destroy the world.

MANGO → HISS! SWIPE!

Jim's Laundry. I guess that potbellied guy who closes the shop at noon for an hour every day is Jim. He always has his lunch at *Birds of a Feather Café.*

Northbridge Pharmacy. The first word is made up of two words but doesn't actually have a meaning. It's a name—the same one used for my school. The dictionary told me the meaning of "*pharmacy*," but I'm not sure I got its pronunciation right. According to the dictionary, it's *fahr-muh-see*. Why, then, is it spelled with a "*ph*" instead of an "*f*"? Martian makes no sense.

Northbridge News Agency. This one is a no-brainer because of the newspapers on display outside.

Cherry on Top. It's a splendid name for a cake shop. But my favorite is still *Pie in the Sky*, the name Papa planned to give his cake shop in Australia. Papa's English was only slightly less terrible than mine, but he knew a *pie* is not a *cake*. It's just that he had a friend who spoke fluent English who told him the meaning of the idiom *pie in the sky*—an impossible dream.

Papa wasn't worried about English at all. What was supposed to happen in our first plan to move to Australia was that he'd make cakes at *Pie in the Sky* while I'd attend my new Australian school and learn English. Every day after school, I'd teach him all that I'd learned and help out in the shop.

My nose burns. Thinking about Papa a second too long always does that. The first year he was gone, my nose was permanently red like I was a clown, so I tried really hard not to let him pop into my head. I got so good at it that in the past year, I haven't even had to try. He appears in my thoughts so rarely that when he does, all I want is for him to stay. Until my nose acts up.

I rub my silly, silly nose and open my dictionary to look up "*adverb*." I need to work harder at English. I don't want to be an alien among humans.

> *adverb: a word or phrase that modifies the meaning of a verb*
> *phrase: a small group of words*
> *modify: change*
> *change: make or become different*
> *different: 1. not the same 2. separate*

I pause the flipping of the dictionary to silently curse

Mama. Wait, I take that back. If you curse your parent, silently or not, when you die and get reborn, it'll be as this:

I don't know yet if I believe in reincarnation, but until I decide either way, it's better to be safe. So I'm displeased with Mama. She got Yanghao and me an English–English dictionary each. Supposedly the best way to learn a language is to use it a lot. If having to look up a million English words to learn the meaning of one is not using English a lot, please just let King Kong trample all over us now.

separate: existing or happening independently or in a different physical place

I don't know what *"existing," "independently," "different,"* or *"physical"* means. I'm just going to assume and hope that *"different"* in this case means *"not the same."*

verb: a word or phrase that describes an action
describe: give a detailed account of in words
detailed: having many details

detail: a fact

fact: a thing that is known to be true

account: description

description: see describe

Ah . . . An *adverb* is a word that says something about an action . . . I think?

I look up. Miss Scrappell has written:

The little turtle crawls slowly.

Adverb? Little or slowly?

I know what "*little*" means because Mama introduced Yanghao to our neighbor as my *little* brother. I know "*turtle*" because Yanghao watches *Ninja Turtles*. I have no idea where I learned the word "*crawl*." I think "*slow*" is the opposite of "*fast*," but I check the dictionary to be sure.

slow: **1.** *not fast* **2.** *not exciting* (I know this means boring) **3.** *taking a long time to understand things* **4.** *of a clock or watch, showing a time earlier than the correct time*

For meaning number four, I don't know what "*earlier*" and "*correct*" mean, but a turtle isn't a clock or a watch. So the answer to Miss Scrappell's question is *slowly*.

Miss Scrappell says something, and several hands shoot

up. She looks around and catches my eye. She smiles at me. I look away even though I'm pretty sure I have the right answer.

She says, "Ben."

The boy next to me clears his throat. He's the quiet type, like me, and is rarely called upon by teachers and never volunteers answers either. I know his name only because I heard other classmates call out to him.

The adverb is slowly.

Miss Scrappell replies, "*Good.*"

I shout, *YES!* Except it was only inside my head. Just to find out the meaning of a single English word, my brain worked like I was inventing the computer, but I got Miss Scrappell's question right. The webs between my alien fingers are disappearing.

5

I must be at least one fiftieth human now. If I keep working hard at mastering English, and study it for ten hours a day, I'll achieve total and complete transformation after forty-eight to seventy-two days. I know those numbers because I once Googled how long it takes to learn a new language. That was after the first time I was told we'd be moving to Australia, a year before the second time. The first time, it was Papa who told me.

That was why I couldn't have the new computer I asked for. So, on our prehistoric computer, I Googled. This research took a long time since the old machine was so slow, and that blue spinning wheel on the screen is really there to hypnotize you into forgetting you're waiting, and then you turn into a fossil.

Miss Scrappell's English class runs for one and a half hours, five times a week. That's seven and a half hours a week learning English, not the ten hours a day Google recommends, so it will take me longer: sixty-four weeks to ninety-six weeks, or one year and three months to one year and eleven months.

It will be one year and eleven months before I look at least passable as a human. I pick the longer studying time for myself because I'm a realist.

Being an optimist and a realist at the same time is very hard. But today's triumphs with the *hi* and the *slow* make me 70 percent optimist and only 30 percent realist, so I'm going to keep trying.

During lunch, I usually stay in the classroom while all my classmates gallop to the cafeteria or the courtyard for noisy activities. I'll eat the food Mama packs for me—today's is fried rice with fried prawns—while gazing out the window at the other kids in the courtyard below. I play a game of fishing. The fish I try to catch are words the other kids yell.

Catching those words between peals of ha-ha-ha is a feat. Then I guess the spelling and check my dictionary for the meanings. Another thing I've learned besides all those words is that during recess, kids swear a lot.

I'm still too much of an alien to eat lunch in the cafeteria, so I'll wait until I've leveled up in English. And honestly, my brain's already fried from doing all that English work, and it's only half past eleven. For recess today, I'll just try to catch more words.

By ten to twelve, ten minutes before recess ends, I've caught these words:

Booger! (It's funny that "booger" is an insult here on Mars, just like it is back home.)

Darn!

Heck!

I also caught another word, which sounded like a swear word, but I don't understand how it could be one.

If only I'd caught more, but I hope my catch has helped

me lose another alien feature. Maybe it's my fourth eye, but I can't tell. All my eyes are on the same face and can't see one another. I head to the bathroom for a mirror.

I'm also in the bathroom because no matter how I look outside, inside, I still have the bladder of a human. Before anything else, I check the toilet bowl for snakes, just like my friend Xirong back at my old school told me to. He once saw a story on the news about a man in Australia who sat down without looking and paid a painful price. Now that we're here, whenever I go to the bathroom, I always think of my friend.

As I'm about to step out of the stall, I hear two boys come into the bathroom.

That, I caught. All the words.

"*Joe, shut up,*" the one who said *booger* hissed.

Joe, the boy I said *hi* to. I should have recognized his voice immediately. It's loud and clear and unmistakable like a crow's caw. Joe often makes my classmates and even teachers laugh. Now he's using me in one of his jokes. And he's using my *hi* against me.

But what Joe said was kind of true. If he hadn't said those words s l o w l y, they would've been gobbledygook to me.

There's a flurry of whispers. They must have figured out someone's in the stall. More whispers, followed by rubber soles frantically squeaking against tiles. Then, the creak of the bathroom door. The thunk of the door. Silence.

When I finally step out of the stall, I move like a robot—
turning on the tap, holding my hands under the water, pumping the soap dispenser, rinsing off the soap.

Once I get out of the bathroom, I'll head straight for my
desk. I'll work on the problems in my math textbook. I know
numbers. They're the same in all languages.

Everything will be all right.

I'll keep busy.

That way, I won't think about what I just heard.

Or worse, feel it.

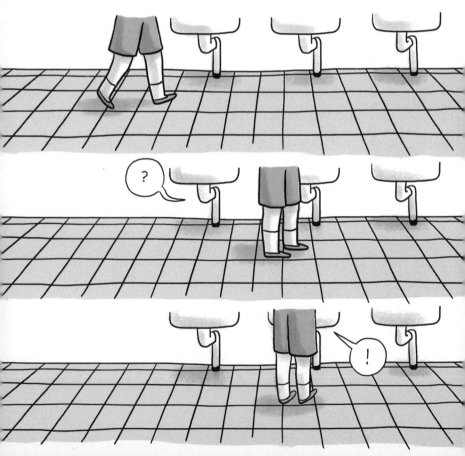

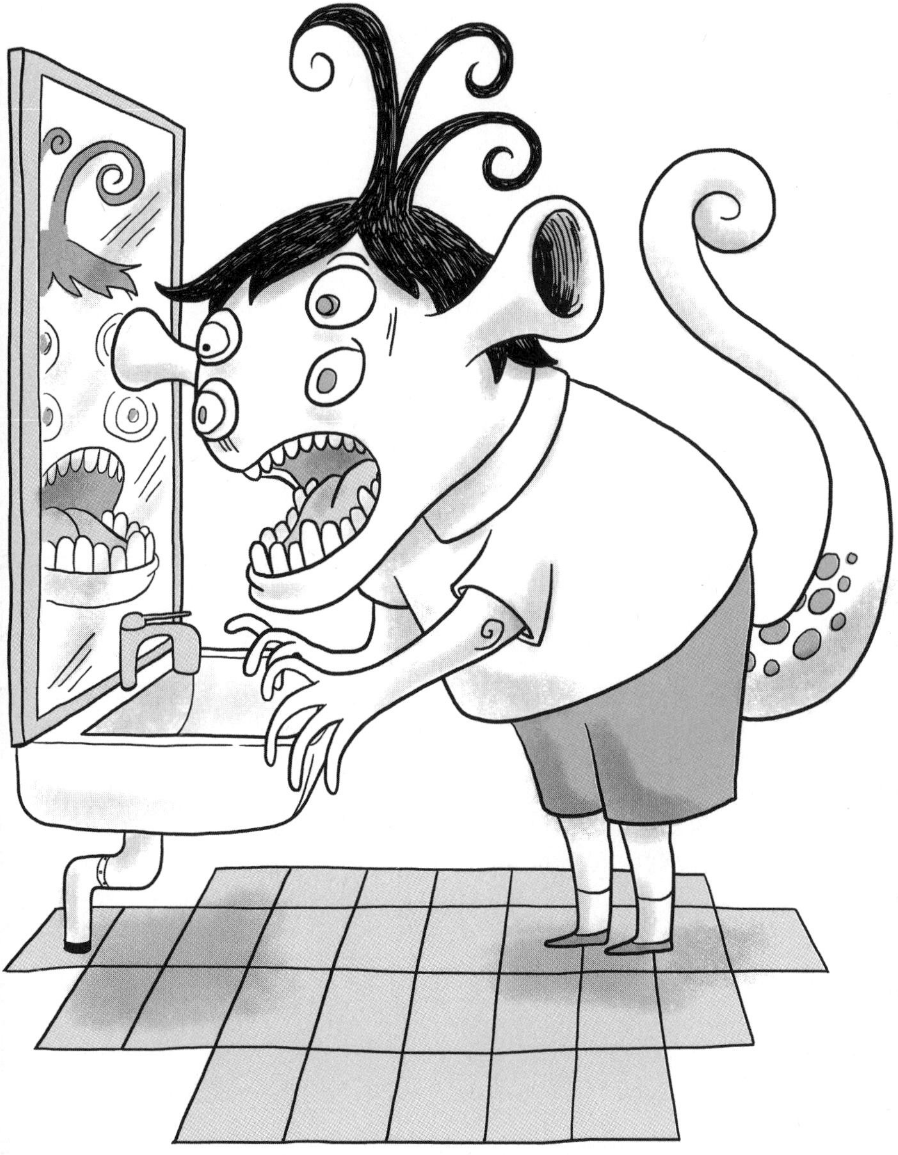

I don't want to play this game anymore.

7

When I step out of the bathroom, Joe and Max are at the water fountain nearby. They pretend not to see me. From the corner of my eye, I see them punch each other's arms. I hurry into the classroom and plop myself down at my desk. Too-happy ha-ha-has are still roaring from the courtyard below.

Once, I gulped down Papa's whole cup of coffee and spent the day in a fuzzy buzz. Now it feels like that. I'm not thinking about what Joe said but thinking about it at the same time.

In that whirl, I catch a glimpse of the cake shop *Cherry on Top* out the window. I imagine a cake. On a cake stand. What kind of cake? A cake with Nutella cream frosting. The cake on the cake stand is on a table. I'm there, too, looking proudly at the cake. Someone else is next to me. Papa. He's looking proudly at me. This is real. Not an imagination. A memory. We did make that cake together. It was practice. For *Pie in the Sky*.

My family's cake shop doesn't sell fancy cakes that have multiple layers or cream fillings and frosting, only simple cakes made mostly from flour and beans. But Papa said *Pie in the Sky* would be different. It was usually on Sunday afternoons when the shop was closed that he could squeeze out some free time, and we would practice.

And blueberry cheesecake.

Triple cookie cake.

Almond chiffon cake with caramel sauce.

Apple mille-feuille.

Neapolitan mousse cake.

White chocolate Swiss roll.

Pear tarte tatin.

On these Sunday afternoons, Yanghao sometimes joined in, but he always ended up abandoning us for a storybook. Mama popped into the kitchen from time to time to clean up the mess Papa and I made. Ah-po and Ah-gong peeked in to watch us, too. Mango had to be chased out of the kitchen often. Mostly it was just Papa and me. Papa and me making cakes. Papa and me with big smiles on our faces, the smiles he said cakes always bring.

But.

Papa, you and I.

We'll never have our *Pie in the Sky*, will we?

It was one year and eleven months ago, wasn't it?

A car smashed into your car, didn't it?

You died, didn't you?

Every time my memories about Papa come, I welcome them. And every time they hurt me, even after so many times, I'm still surprised. Like a clown in a circus who keeps stepping on a rake and getting whacked in the face by the handle.

I rub my nose and cover my ears to block out the sounds of the happy students in the courtyard. Soon the end-of-recess bell rings, and my classmates come running back in, including Joe and Max.

I should be thankful they didn't mean for me to hear all those things. But it's very hard to tell myself optimistic mumbo jumbo when the reality is *crap*.

I can't escape this *crap* either because here comes Mr. Fart marching in to start his science class. His real name is Mr. Hart. I don't know what I'm more upset about, the *s l o w*, or that I'm so upset about the *s l o w* I can't even secretly congratulate myself again for coming up with that nickname.

Without even greeting the class, Mr. Fart clops down the rows of desks, sounding like a horse in a hurry, and passes out papers from a stack in his hands. He does it so quickly he looks like a ninja throwing deadly stars. He might as well have been, because the papers turn out to be the homework we handed in yesterday, the one that was only ten multiple-choice questions but had taken me three hours to translate. I'm hoping for a pass.

I scored three out of ten.

"Jingwen," Mr. Fart says, "*read question six.*"

He hates me. Why else would he keep calling on me? My reading slows down his class to slower than a snail going uphill carrying a pebble on its back. Surely he can tell by my sweatiness and my twitchiness that I'd choose death by a thousand cat scratches over reading aloud.

I try to read Mr. Fart's deadpan face for clues about whether I was saying the words right or wrong, but I get nothing. Only his fingers furiously tapping on his thigh tell me to hurry up. Then I get a whole other kind of message from someone else. Max, who sits a few rows ahead and to my right, is looking at me.

Time.

Stops.

He quickly looks away. Just like that girl on the bus.

I whip my gaze back down to my textbook so fast I probably need one of those protection-from-vampire-bite neck braces.

Whenever Mr. Fart makes me read, a couple of classmates steal glances my way. Which I think is reasonable since they must all be confused. I don't even know what I'm blathering; how could they? Most of my classmates are kind enough not to openly gawk at me.

But maybe I'm wrong. Maybe they're all like that girl on the bus. They all think I'm an alien. Maybe they're all like Joe and Max. They all think I'm s l o w. I'm stupid. I'm a joke.

Jingwen,
there's more.

MR. FART

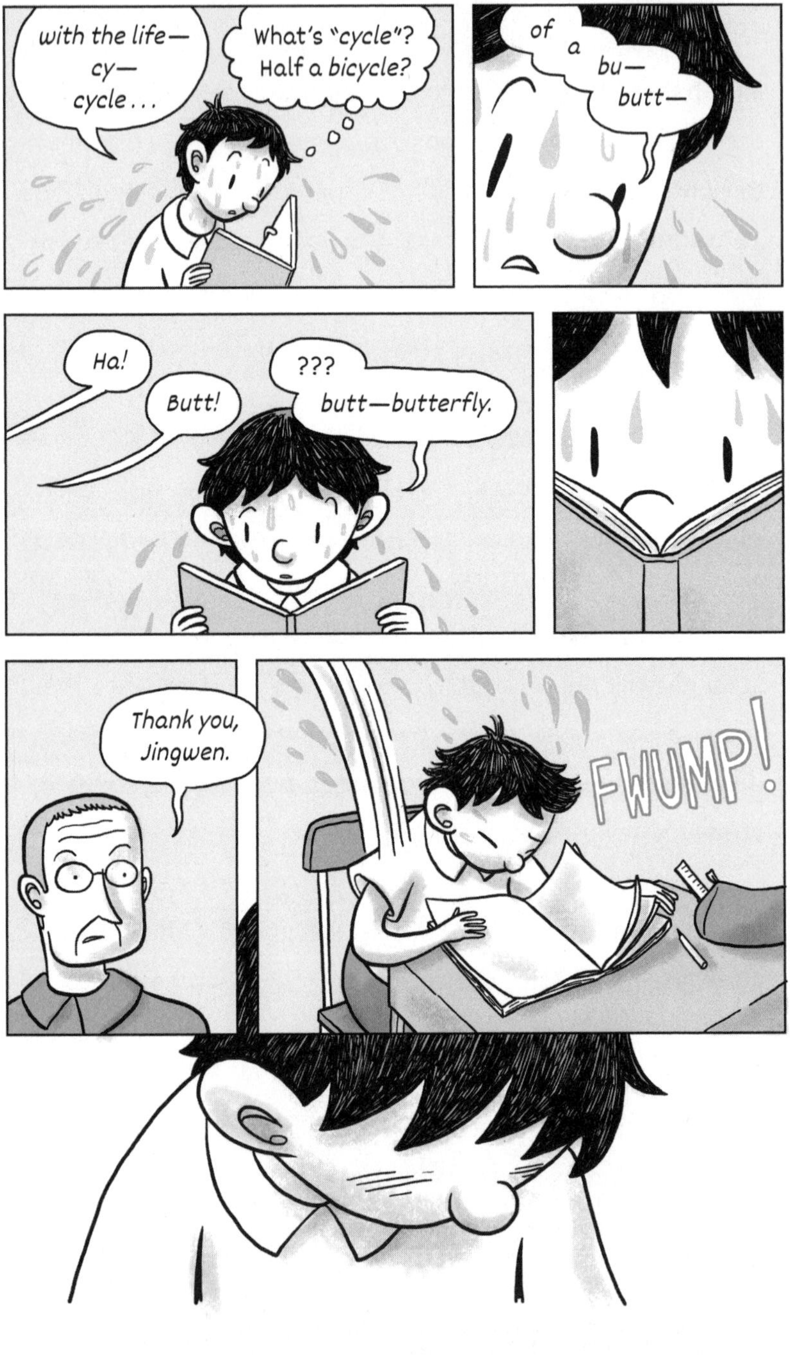
with the life— cy— cycle...
What's "cycle"? Half a bicycle?
of a bu— butt—
Ha!
Butt!
??? butt—butterfly.
Thank you, Jingwen.
FWUMP!

I can't see what everyone else is doing, but I feel hot like a fireball. Must be everyone's eyes burning holes into me. So that I don't drown everyone with my sweat, I concentrate on the words on my textbook.

Suddenly, all the Martian words on the page morph into words I know.

I close my eyes, but the hundreds of *s l o w* s are now in my head.

Come on, Jingwen. Think of something else. A cake. Sponge cake. Two layers. With Nutella filling. Slathered in Nutella cream.

In my mind, this cake drops from above. When it lands in the middle of my mind, it doesn't smash into bits. Instead, the hundreds of *s l o w* s are scattered away. So I think about carrot cake with cream cheese topping. And chocolate raspberry torte. And blueberry cheesecake. Until all the *s l o w* s are replaced by cakes.

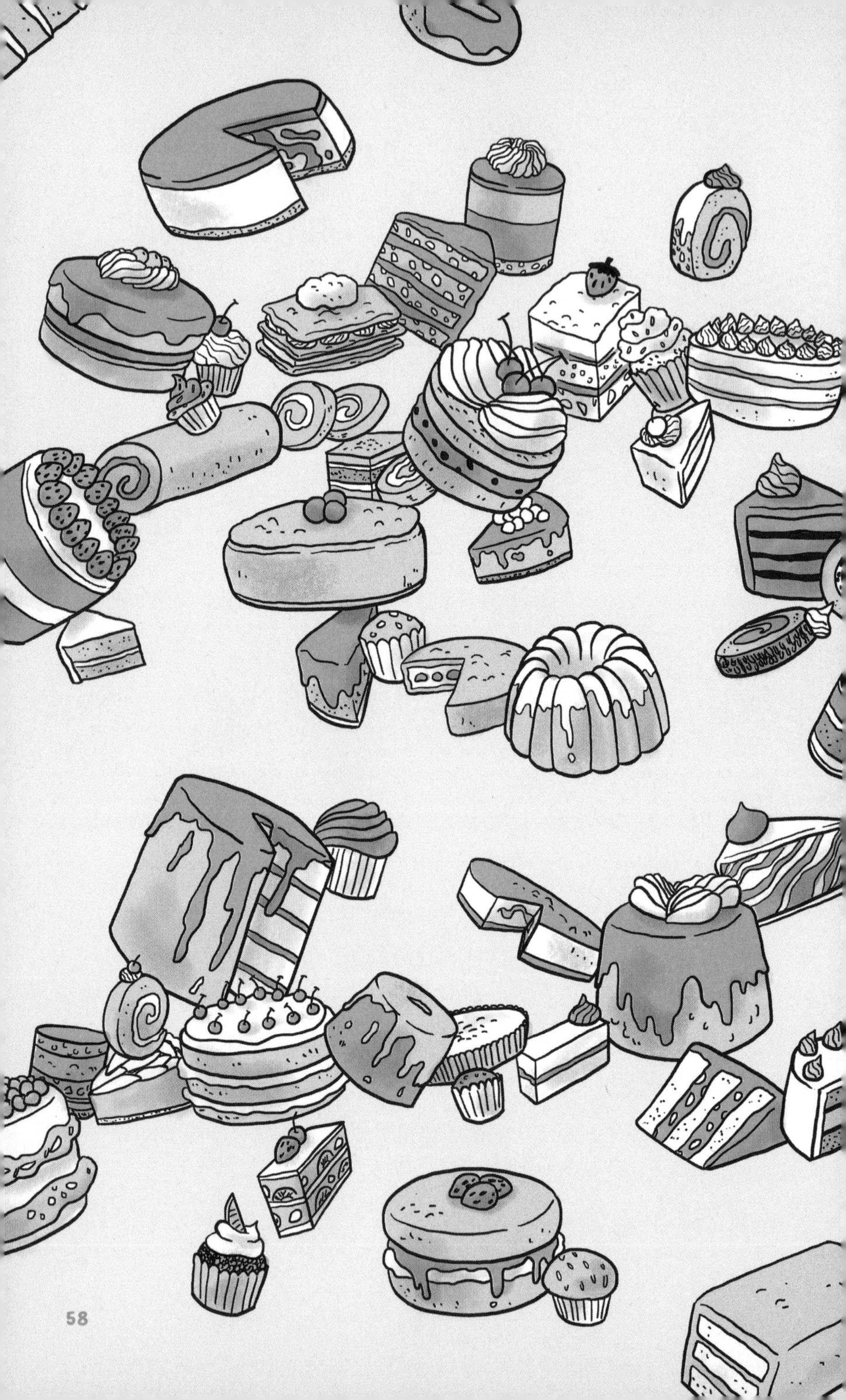

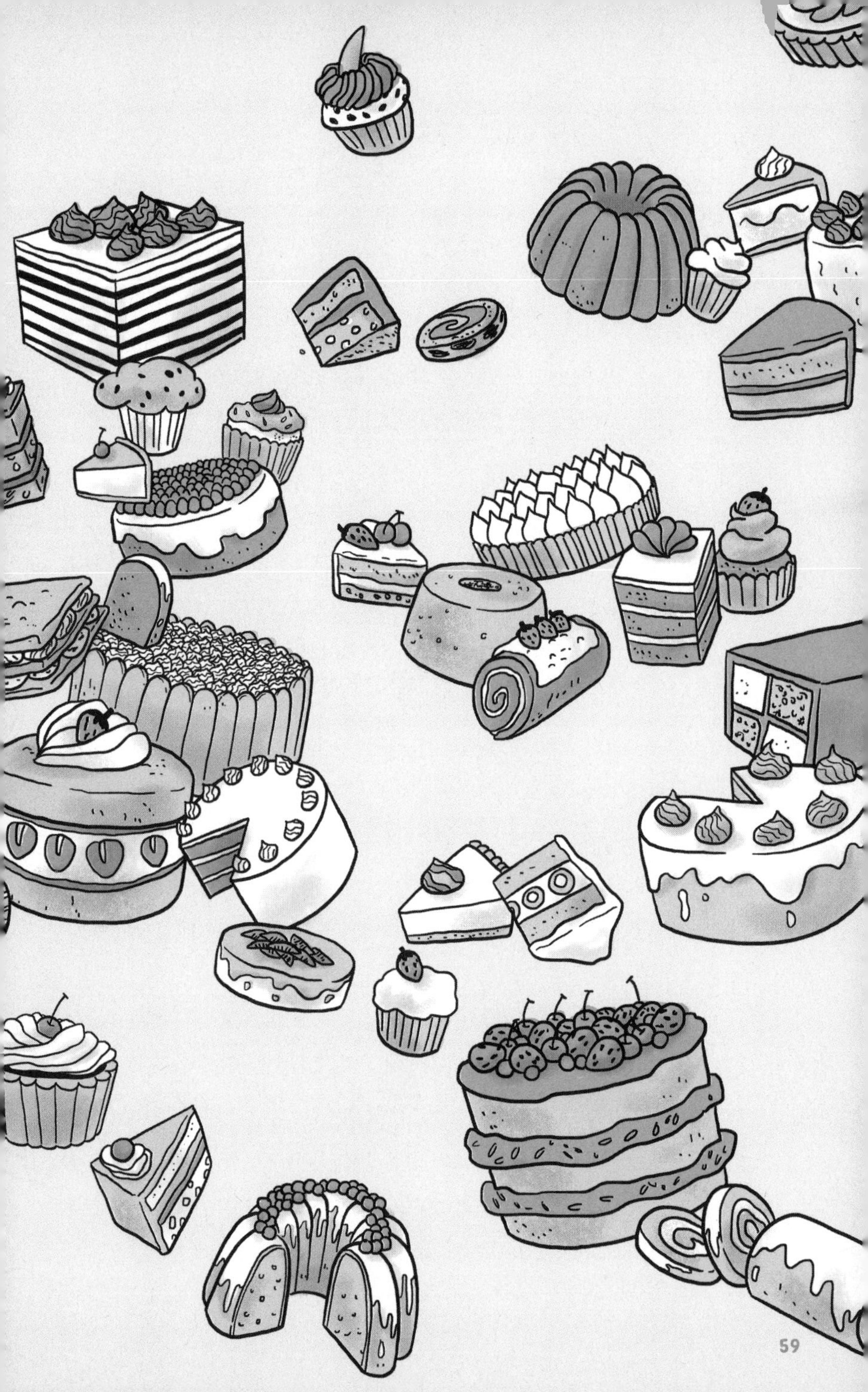

Before the *s l o w* incident, before I found out I was the alien, the dismissal bell was like the song of a bird. It signaled the end of six hours of prison, and that was when all my class-mates were happiest and most generous with their smiles and byes. They said *bye* and *see you* to everyone and anyone, including me.

Now that bell is ringing, and it sounds like the hissing noise Mango makes when I pat her a second too long. I keep my head down and pack my bag, shielding myself from my classmates' smiles and *bye*s and *see you*s as they step out of the classroom. Once I leave, they'll probably make jokes about me behind my back, just like Joe. They're not my classmates. They're my classmates-not-friends.

I don't want to have to come back to a classroom where I spend thirty hours a week knowing it's the scene of a horrible crime.

I rearrange the contents of my backpack like I'm com-pleting a ten-thousand-piece puzzle of the desert. The last boy to leave before me is Ben. As he turns to leave, his eyes catch mine. I'm frozen, like the time Mama caught Yanghao and me with our grubby fingers deep inside a tin of chocolate malt powder. I could look away, and everything would be just like it is now, or I could say *bye* and risk being made fun of, maybe even called *s l o w*, but there could also be a miracle and we could end up as best friends. This is a very, very big and important decision!

Ben smiles. And walks out.

All that's left in the room is silly, silly me. The only sound is my sad, sad sigh.

I wait a few more seconds before putting on the most organized backpack owned by an almost-twelve-year-old ever. But at the door, I run into Miss Scrappell.

By the way her tone goes up at the end of her sentence, I can tell it's a question. Plus, she's still looking at me as if expecting an answer. But what's the question? Should I reply *yes*? Or *no*? What if it isn't a *yes*/*no* question?

She talks some more, and my head's whirling with so much confusion I'm about to spin away into space. But then, as if she realizes what's going on in my brain, she puts a hand on my shoulder, gentle like Ah-po's kisses on my forehead yet firm enough to put my feet back on the ground. I catch the last bit she says: *"All right?"*

I know *all right*. I nod.

She gives me two thumbs-up. "Good."

Whatever the question was, I must've answered it correctly. I zoom off before she can ask me any more mystery questions.

In the hallway, English-that-sounds-like-Martian words echo off the walls and swirl round and round, hammering on my brain like techno music.

Mama promised everything would be all right . . .

I recite the nine-times table in my head to stop thinking about anything else. Nine. Eighteen. Twenty-seven . . .

Ninety-nine. One hundred and eight . . . I burst through the main door. Across the courtyard, standing at the gates, is Yanghao. As other students swarm past him, he shuffles his feet, his lips curled tight as if he's trying not to cry. He's swimming in his uniform, and his backpack looks like an oversized turtle shell. He looks so tiny and sad I want to put him in my pocket.

Whatever brotherly kindness I feel toward Yanghao is smashed and replaced by a brotherly desire to punch him. I rummage in my bag for my bus card as I hurry toward the stop. I hear the roar of the engine.

And . . . we miss the bus.

Yanghao stomps his feet. "Now we have to wait for the next one—"

"No talking."

"What—"

"Just be quiet." I pretend that *Jim's Laundry* across the road has a very interesting rack of coats, but I'm actually trying to spy from the reflection of Jim's big window if those students still at the stop are gawking at Yanghao and me. Or worse, using their phones to take a video of us speaking what to them is gibberish. To make matters worse, I won't even know if Yanghao and I have gone viral for the worst possible thing ever, since we don't have a computer—the one back at our old home was too heavy to lug all the way here, and we still can't afford a new one. As for cell phones, Mama says I'm too young for one. Funny how I'm suddenly too young when according to Mama, I've always been old enough to know better. By funny, I mean annoying.

"You're a booger, Jingwen." Yanghao pouts.

I say in a low voice, "You could have taken that bus. I didn't ask you to wait for me."

"Of course I can't. Mama doesn't let me go anywhere by myself. I'm only nine."

The truth is, he's almost ten and doesn't dare go any-where by himself. "The next one is in fifteen minutes. It's not a long wait," I say, even though I wish I could teleport right back to our apartment. Or even better, our old home. But if I'm wishing for impossible things, I might as well wish for a time machine, too. I wish to be beamed back to Sundays at our old home when Papa was still around.

Mondays to Saturdays, sometimes he'd be on the road in our CR-V to deliver goods, but most of the time, he'd be at our cake shop, bent in front of the oven pumping out cakes, stuck on the phone taking orders, hunched at his desk doing some kids-should-stay-out-of-this paperwork. But come Sunday, whenever there wasn't businessman stuff left over, he was Papa.

He'd take the whole family to the pool, the bookstore, or a restaurant. But the Sundays I liked best, not counting when Papa and I baked *Pie in the Sky* cakes together, were the ones when he drove the family all the way to the beach. Those several hours in the car, everyone all together in one place, our CR-V chug-chugging along as if everything would stay like that forever . . .

Why am I being forced to play this alien-morphing game? What are those students staring at? Yanghao being his usual booger self? Or Yanghao and me being aliens?

If those students are staring because Yanghao is a booger, there's nothing I can do about it. You can't choose your siblings. And it's been almost ten years, so I'm immune. If they're staring for the other reason, we can fix that. I'll tell Mama we should go back to our old home. We can make everything all right.

Or as all right as it can be without Papa. Sunday beach trips won't be the same without him, but at least I could collect seashells like I used to.

Mama's pockets would be so full and heavy that her skirt no longer fluttered in the wind. Only the hem of her skirt flapped meekly. When she wore jeans, her pockets would be so tight with seashells she waddled instead of walked.

Now I'm the one waddling from carrying too many seashells in my pockets, thanks to the extra heavy *s l o w* seashell. I can't wait to get back to our apartment and complain to

Mama about my nemesis, Joe. I won't say a word about Papa and *Pie in the Sky*, because she'll get upset. The last time I mentioned him, she hardly talked for a whole day. It was a weekend, and she spent it cleaning the whole apartment, including Yanghao and me; if you had run a finger along us, we'd have squeaked like a Palmolive plate. But I can tell her all about my Yanghao-and-I-are-the-aliens theory. Her face will screw up with concern, which is similar to the look she makes when she smells something stinky, and in an instant I'll feel lighter, as if my troubles are seashells she can carry for me.

Yanghao finally stops swinging around the pole, but now he's stumbling about because he's dizzy. The eyes of the other students are on him. When he finally finds his footing, he says, "Jingwen, can we stop by—"

"No talking."

His lips remain jutted out like a duck's bill all through the bus ride, which is good because that way he can't spout gibberish. No one on the bus stares at us.

After the bus pulls into the station and we've hopped off, I lean into him and say, "Your face is going to get stuck that way." My voice is drowned out by the ruckus of the crowd at the station. "Ugly monkey-duck face."

He points to the opposite direction from home. "Can we go to the grocery store? Please, Jingwen?"

"Mama said to go straight home."

"Just really quickly. I won't tell her you let me stop by the store. I won't tell her you made us late. We'll say the bus was late or something. Pleasepleasepleaseplease."

"I don't trust you. You're a tattletale."

"I'm not." He grabs my arm and swings it like we're best friends merrily, merrily, merrily skipping down a lane. "Please, let's go to the grocery store. I want to get gummy snakes. Pleasepleasepleaseplease."

Two policemen in dark blue uniforms pass by, each carrying a paper cup of what must be coffee.

"Yanghao, if you don't do as I say, I'll ask those policemen to catch you and throw you into jail."

Yanghao grins. "You're lying. You don't know how to say that in English."

He's got me there. "I'm going home. Bye." I stalk off.

As expected, two seconds later . . .

It's a fifteen-minute walk from the station to our apartment. On rainy days, Yanghao and I take the connecting bus, but most days we walk because we want to pass by *Barker Bakes*. We won't see Mama there since she's home at this time of the day, and even if she's at work, she'll be hidden in the kitchen. Still, we like to peer into the window. Inside, there's a long display case filled with rows and rows of cakes. Black Forest cake, Oreo cheesecake, red velvet cake, mud cake . . .

Yanghao presses his forehead against the window. "Mama said one day she'll have a cake in that display case."

"Really? I didn't know she wants to make such cakes."

"What's wrong with those cakes? They look yummy, even though they look small from here."

"The cakes at *Barker Bakes* are very different from the ones she made back at our shop," I say.

CAKES SOLD IN MY FAMILY'S CAKE SHOP
BACK IN OUR OLD HOME

EGG CAKE

PAPER-WRAPPED MINI SPONGE CAKE

RED TORTOISE CAKE

SESAME BALL

NEW YEAR CAKE

STEAMED PROSPERITY CUPCAKE

STEAMED RICE CAKE

RED BEAN PANCAKE

Yanghao drools, and I pull him away from *Barker Bakes*. He skips ahead of me. There's another reason he prefers the walk. He always thinks there's a chance I might one day, by some miracle, let us stop at the playground. He's 0 percent realist and 200 percent optimist. Mama says Yanghao's persistent; I say pigheaded.

At the playground, there are many kids wearing *Northbridge Primary School* uniforms. I recognize only one of them—Ben. He sits on the swing reading a book, paying zero attention to the other kids screaming and running around like monkeys who ate too much candy. Yanghao's like them, bouncing on the spot next to me and whining, "Justfiveminutes."

But something else catches my attention. Two kids on the airplane-shaped tower are staring at us. I grab hold of Yanghao's backpack and pull him away from the playground.

"I want to plaaaaaaay . . ."

What do those two kids watching us think Yanghao just said? I am an alieeeen? I am a giant turd? "Mama said to go straight home."

I don't loosen my grip until we reach our apartment building. If he runs now, at least I can honestly tell Mama I did bring him home. But he doesn't run off, because he wants to do something that he still finds exciting after two months: he rummages in his pocket for his key fob, which he holds up to the black box by the glass main door. The box beeps, and the door unlocks with a loud clack. He sprints inside. "Last one in is a slow turtle!"

I take my time to check the mail. Next to the building door, built into the wall, is a big metal box that's made up of rows and rows of small metal boxes. Ten mailboxes for the ten apartments in our five-story building. We get a heap of flyers and brochures for restaurants, plumbers, and real estate agents, but my friend Xirong's reply hasn't arrived yet. Snail mail is annoyingly s l o w—there's that word again. Handwritten letters should be illegal unless you're six or younger and writing to fairies or Santa Claus, or unless you're over sixty. Which I probably will be by the time Mama gets me a computer.

I use my key fob to enter the building and find Yanghao hopping up the steps one at a time with his feet together. Hop! Hop! Hop! I'm curious if he can keep this up all the way to the fourth floor.

From upstairs comes a loud creak, like a cat's wail, followed by a loud bang. I curse. That's our next-door neighbor Anna's door, which Mama told me has a spring so it automatically shuts. The story is: One time, Anna forgot to close the door, and her cat escaped from her apartment, and then, when someone opened the lobby door, it slipped out. It was many weeks before Anna got a call from the pound, and she had to pay hundreds of dollars to break her cat out of there. No one in the apartment building complains about the noise because Anna doesn't leave her house that often, she's old, and old people can get away with anything, and because of the cat story.

I really, really don't feel like dealing with Anna today.

"*Good afternoon, Anna,*" Yanghao wheezes.

"*It is warm today, isn't it?*" Anna talks like a robot, each English word pronounced clearly, with a pause between words, and every word that ends with a "t" is uttered with an exaggerated sound like the farting noise buses make when they pull in and out of stops.

Yanghao glances at me. I shrug. "*It warm today,*" he says.

"*It is warm today,*" Anna corrects.

"It is warm today," Yanghao repeats.

I wish the sun would burn out right now and bring the Earth back to the Ice Age just so we can skip this conversation.

Anna looks at me. I smile like a clown, then squeeze past her up the narrow stairway. She smells flowery, unlike most grown-ups I know. Mama, Papa, Ah-po, and Ah-gong smelled like cake.

"Wait! Jingwen!" Yanghao scurries after me, his footsteps sounding like a round of applause.

When I open the door of our apartment, Mama has her head in the fridge. Unlike our old house, this apartment is so tiny that from where I stand, I can see most of it. Which isn't much.

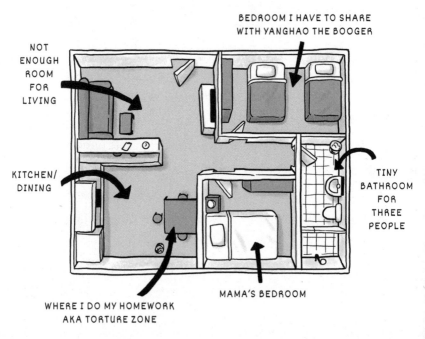

NOT ENOUGH ROOM FOR LIVING

BEDROOM I HAVE TO SHARE WITH YANGHAO THE BOOGER

KITCHEN/ DINING

TINY BATHROOM FOR THREE PEOPLE

WHERE I DO MY HOMEWORK AKA TORTURE ZONE

MAMA'S BEDROOM

Mama straightens up, and her glasses turn foggy. "How was school, boys?"

She doesn't ask why we're late, and I'm not silly, so I don't bring that up. "School was the worst," I'm about to whine, but Yanghao barges past me, yodeling, "English is too hard, Mama."

He flops onto the sofa. Mama hands him his staple drink—caramel-flavored milk that comes in a little box with a little straw—and sits next to him, putting an arm around him.

I frown. But she's too busy peeling Yanghao's backpack off him to notice. I squeeze my eyebrows together. Her eyebrows scrunch up as if in reply. But she's not looking at me. She's rubbing Yanghao's prickly hair, which has to be kept short because of the same cooties that made him puny. I slouch.

Instead of telling me I'll be stuck as a humpback if I don't stand right, she says, "Everything will be all right."

"No, Mama. It's been two months, and nothing is all right!" I'm about to scream, but I spot letters on the coffee table. They're from Ah-po and Ah-gong. I tear open the one addressed to me.

In my last letter to Ah-po and Ah-gong, I told them I hoped they were able to handle pumping out all those cakes for the family cake shop on their own. In their reply, they wrote they've hired a diligent young baker, so everything is swell. Under their signatures is a PS: "Over there in Australia, you're the man of the house, Jingwen. Take care of your mother and little brother."

I'd give anything to not have to be the man of the house. But I'll try, even if I'm only almost-twelve. I've always looked out for my little brother, since it's one of the unspoken rules of the universe, and all the adults ask me to, but I'm not sure how I'm to take care of Mama. Maybe make her tea in the morning. Except she always gets up before me.

"What about you, Jingwen? How was school?" Mama asks. As if she's suddenly very heavy, she sinks farther into the sofa. I want to give her the seashells of trouble that are weighing down my pockets, but she's already taken the ones in Yanghao's and put them in hers. Adding any more might make her so heavy she'd fall through the seat. For now, I should try to carry my seashells in my own pockets.

Her eyebrows smooth out, and she smiles. "I'm glad." She grabs her chef uniform that's draped over the kitchen stool. "Now I have to get to work. Make sure your brother takes a shower. I've made dumplings and noodles for dinner. They're in the fridge. Heat them up in the microwave and make sure your brother finishes his, and do your homework. I'll see you in the morning." She picks up her handbag from the sofa, kisses Yanghao and me on the tops of our heads, and disappears out the door.

I sigh. Mama's shift at *Barker Bakes* runs from 4:30 P.M. to 3:30 A.M., so when Yanghao and I get home from school at about half past three, we only have her for less than an hour before she has to go to work. Back at our family's cake shop, she used to work long hours too, but because the shop occupies the front part of our house, she was always just a few steps away if I needed to ask for help with my homework or complain that Yanghao was being a turd.

"Jingwen, was school really all right for you?" Yanghao asks, slurping the last of his caramel-flavored milk.

Even if it wasn't, can Mama help me? Will she do my homework for me? Can she attend class for me? Speak to my teachers for me? Take my exams for me? What good will telling her do?

I flip through my dictionary for the millionth time in the last five minutes. In my old school, I learned all about photosynthesis, so I bet I know all the answers in my science homework . . . if only I knew what the questions were. Imagine if Sherlock Holmes was asked to look for clues not with a magnifying glass but with old people's reading glasses, like the ones Ah-po, Ah-gong, and Anna wear. English is my old people's reading glasses.

SpongeBob's and Yanghao's laughter booms from the living room, disrupting my train of thought for the thousandth time. If only our bedroom were big enough for a table so I could do my homework in peace there, but I have to set up camp in the kitchen, on a square table that butts against the wall. Why is Yanghao laughing, anyway? It's not like he can follow what SpongeBob is saying. Even though English-speaking SpongeBob looks the same as the one on our TV back in our old home, they're really different, and I can't stand this one who makes jokes I don't understand.

"Yanghao, take a shower," I yell.

"Five more minutes."

"That's what you said a million minutes ago."

"No problem-o!" SpongeBob says.

"No problem-o!" Yanghao mimics.

I storm over to the coffee table, grab the remote control, and press mute.

"Poo face!" Yanghao shouts. "What did you do that for?"

"You don't even understand what you're watching."

"Of course I understand. I'm smart."

"Liar." I march back to the dining table. "Don't laugh so loud. I'm doing homework."

I continue trying to do my homework. Yanghao has made me forget what I just read about *stomata*. It's hard, holding on to the meaning of *"stomata"* while also holding on to the meanings of other words I've just learned from the same sentence, which are *"explain"* and *"function."*

It's like trying to be that clown I saw in that circus in a big tent in a big field that Papa and Mama took us to a long time ago. As a tiger jumped through a burning hoop, the clown juggled five balls in the air. I imagine myself as that clown.

I give up. Randomly, I circle B from the multiple-choice answers, then move on to the next question. Which I don't understand either.

Urgh! I throw my dictionary open. *"Photo-Photosyn-Photosynthesis* . . . URGH! I toss it onto the table. "Yanghao? Want to play cards? Board games? Anything?"

There's no reply. I crane my neck to look for him. He isn't in the living room, and I can't hear the trickle of the shower. What trouble is he getting into now?

I find him in Mama's bedroom, sitting cross-legged on the floor, reading one of Mama's cookbooks. Next to him is Mama's suitcase, opened. On the suitcase handle is the sticker tag with the bar code and our flight number to Mars. I ask him why he made a mess and why he's reading a cookbook.

"Because you don't let me watch *SpongeBob*. And I have to find something else to do. And I found Mama's cookbooks. And I'm reading them because I don't have my storybooks. Because they're all back home. Because the plane didn't allow us to take more than thirty kilograms of things each. Will you make me a cake?"

"Ask Mama to make it this weekend."

"Can you make it for me now?"

"I don't know how."

"But Ah-po and Ah-gong taught us."

"They let us mix batter and play with dough. Quit stalling. When I'm done with my homework, you'd better be in the shower." I wag my finger as I march out of the room.

"That gives me plenty of time, then. A forever of time."

If he weren't such a crybaby, I'd have punched him, because the truth hurts and it shouldn't hurt only me. I return to the kitchen and pick up where I've left the *photo-photosun-photosyn—*

I conk my head against the table repeatedly. It doesn't matter if I permanently damage my brain. I'm already *s l o w*.

Conk! Conk! Conk!

S l o w. S l o w. S l o w.

If only Mama could tell I was lying about how my day went. If she'd pressed a bit more, I would have told her everything.

Conk! Conk! Conk!

S l o w. S l o w. S l o w.

My head hurts.

"Jingwen?" Yanghao sounds close by, just outside the kitchen.

There's no reply.

I look up to find him neither in the kitchen nor the living room. Come back, Yanghao. Come back and annoy me. Argue with me. Make me procrastinate doing this homework that I'll fail anyway. Call me a booger. I'll punch you. You'll kick me. We'll fight. You'll cry and threaten to tattle. I'll be angry, and my brain will be filled with revenge schemes. Which are better thoughts to have than all these *s l o w* s swirling around in my brain.

Just then, there are creaks—probably Yanghao's bed—and then footsteps pitter-patter down the hall. Yanghao's head pops out from behind the wall. He stays there staring at me like a spooky, little kid ghost.

"Stop creeping me out—"

Before I finish, he's already by my side, his finger on a picture in the cookbook that's already on the dining table. "I want to eat this."

TWO LAYERS OF SPONGE CAKE

NUTELLA CREAM

NUTELLA

Nutella cream cake. The *Pie in the Sky* cake that made me feel better this morning. And now, just when I'm feeling lousy, Yanghao pesters me to make it for him. It can't be a coincidence. It's Papa sending me a message through the universe. Or it's just the universe finally not being a poo face.

Cakes always bring smiles, after all.

We're so excited about the cake we forget to turn our shoes upside down and tap-tap-tap them before putting them on. It's actually a matter of life and death. Poisonous Australian spiders like to hide in shoes. People with bigger feet and shoes have to watch out for not only spiders but also snakes.

"After we've made this cake," I say as I lock the apartment door behind me, "you're not to annoy me again. I need to finish my homework. And on our way to the grocery store, and then back home, we're not stopping at the playground. Not for five minutes. Not for one minute."

Yanghao runs down the stairs. When he gets a flight of steps ahead of me, and out of my reach, he shouts, "You're such a nag!" Then he zooms off. The slapping of his shoes echoes all around the stairwell, totally out of beat with the horrible made-up song he's belting out. "Cake cake caaake caaaaake!"

I'm so going to regret this.

We have the ingredients for making a basic sponge cake at home, because Mama bought them to make cake "this weekend," but she's always tired when "this weekend" rolls around. The Nutella cream cake also needs heavy cream and Nutella. We have Nutella at home, of course—who doesn't?—except it's down to the last couple of spoonfuls.

"Hurry up, slow turtle," Yanghao keeps saying to me as we make our way to the grocery store by the bus station. I'd have shut him up, but his eagerness means he doesn't ask to stop at the playground. When we approach *Barker Bakes*, I stop him. Mama won't be at the storefront, but it's better to be safe. If she sees us sneaking out to buy stuff to make a cake in an oven by ourselves, there will be an apocalypse.

"Who's the slow turtle now?" I continue running all the way to the grocery store. I'm not going as fast as I can, of course, because I don't want to lose Yanghao and get a scolding from Mama.

At the grocery store, Yanghao goes nuts over Nutella. The recipe calls for a total of one cup of Nutella for the cream frosting and the filling, but he insists on buying the biggest tub on the shelf.

Since Mama pays for everything whenever we go any-where, and I don't have to buy lunch from the school cafeteria, my allowance has been untouched for two months. Which makes me at least as rich as a billionaire's butler. But that doesn't mean I want to spend ten dollars on one kilogram of Nutella when the three-dollar-and-seventy-cents jar is enough.

"No," I say, and grab the smallest jar.

"But I want to buy the papa Nutella."

I almost drop the jar in my hand. No one has said "papa" out loud for a very long time. "What—" I start, but choke.

The biggest Nutella is the papa Nutella.

PAPA NUTELLA

MAMA NUTELLA

BIG BROTHER OR SISTER NUTELLA

BABY NUTELLA

He clutches Papa Nutella to his chest. "I'll finish whatever we don't use for the cake, Jingwen. I promise. Buy Papa Nutella, please?"

I walk away. "I'm going to get the heavy cream." If he says "Papa Nutella" one more time . . . don't know what I will do, but it won't be good.

Luckily, Yanghao doesn't mention "papa" again, and we go to pay. As the cashier scans our items, she scans Yanghao and me too. Then she looks around to see if any of the grown-ups nearby is with us. I quickly hold out the money. She eyes me suspiciously, but then Yanghao flashes his Colgate smile at her and she chuckles and takes the money from me.

All the way home, Yanghao skips ahead of me. From time to time, he turns and yells, "Slow turtle!"

When we reach *Barker Bakes*, he waits for me so we can do our stealth dash past the café again. "This is so fun!" he says, colliding into me as we hide behind the mailbox.

We take a peek at *Barker Bakes*.

There are three kinds of lies: kind-intentioned lies told to avoid hurting others' feelings, lies of omission where you simply leave out certain facts, and lies told to benefit yourself while harming others. What I told Mama, about school being all right, was a kind-intentioned lie, which is the least bad type of lies. My kind intention was to make Mama happy, and the lie worked.

So I don't understand why seeing Mama happy doesn't make me happy.

Maybe when Mama says everything will be all right, she means for her. Everything will be all right for everyone except me.

The deities, or the universe if deities don't exist—but don't tell Ah-gong I said that—if they could read my thoughts, they'd probably say, "Look at that evil boy who doesn't want his mother to be happy. Let's hex him. May he miss all his buses and may all his socks have holes."

I like my socks without holes, so I try to get more excited about making a *Pie in the Sky* cake. If I'm happy, then I won't be jealous that Mama is happy. But by the time Yanghao and I get home, I'm still feeling like *crap.* Even Yanghao dropping the one-kilogram jar of Nutella on his foot doesn't make me smile. Without a word, I rummage in the bottom cabinet in the kitchen. There are mixing bowls, cake pans, and cooling racks—things Mama lugged all the way from our old kitchen but hasn't used in this new kitchen. I glumly take out what I need for the Nutella cream cake. Yanghao tries to help.

"Why?" He clambers down and hands me the tiny container of baking soda.

"Because you'll make a mess, and then I'll have to clean it up. Also, you're too little to be near the hot oven." I step onto the stool and exchange the baking soda for baking powder.

He sticks his finger into the jar of Papa Nutella. "Jingwen, do you know what time it is?"

I look at the clock above the TV. "Quarter to six."

"You're wrong."

"Can't you read time?" I say. "The small hand is between five and—"

IT'S CAKE TIME!

14

"Gross!" I say, screwing the lid back onto the Nutella jar. "I don't want to eat your germs."

"Everything's going into the hot oven anyway. All the germs will be dead."

I ignore him and start mixing the ingredients, and he pesters me to let him help. The smart aleck turns out to be the GREATEST HELPER in the whole universe.

Once I take over, things go a lot more smoothly.

Yanghao blows a raspberry, but he also folds his arms. While I continue whisking the eggs, sugar, and butter, he sings that silly cake song over and over.

I place a hand over his mouth. "Shush."

Something wet touches my palm. "You licked me? GROSS!" I yell, but he just continues belting out his cake song.

I move on to sift the flour mixture into the egg mixture while at the same time gently using a spatula to fold.

"Don't you know how to mix?" Yanghao says. "Do like this." He makes quick, forceful circles with his arm.

"I'm not mixing, but folding. You have to do it gently until the wet and dry mixtures are just combined."

"Who says?"

"Papa." I haven't said that word in a long while. It sounds familiar and strange at the same time. Like a shout and a whisper. A cry and a laugh.

Papa and I were making this exact same cake when he told me that when you whisk eggs and sugar together, you are whisking air into the mixture. That's how the mixture ends up three times bigger than when you started.

"So when you add flour to this egg mixture," I tell Yanghao what Papa told me, "you need to do it gently so you don't squish all the air out. Otherwise, your sponge cake won't be fluffy."

"Oh," Yanghao says. "I didn't know."

I pour the batter into the round pan. "It's called folding."

"I mean I didn't know this cake we're making is on the menu for *Pie in the Sky*."

My heart skips a beat. No one has ever mentioned *Pie in the Sky* since the accident either.

"Ah-po told me that was what you and Papa did in the kitchen on Sundays. But I don't remember what cakes you and Papa made. I only remember they were yummy. Is rainbow cake on the menu?"

"No. Rainbow cake is too simple for *Pie in the Sky*." I slide the pan into the oven and sit in front of it.

Yanghao plops down next to me. "Too simple?"

"Yeah. All the cakes of *Pie in the Sky* are more expensive because they have things like cream and chocolate and fresh fruit."

He rubs his head. "Rainbow cake has cream and fresh fruit."

"Yes, but—the thing is—" I don't know how to explain it to him. "*Pie in the Sky* cakes are more difficult to make because of the layers and the techniques."

"Rainbow cake has seven layers. Nutella cream cake has only two."

"Yes, but Nutella cream cake has chocolate, in the Nutella."

He sits upright, all excited. "So do all the *Pie in the Sky* cakes have chocolate?"

"No, but— You— I don't— You're giving me a headache. Rainbow cake is not on the menu of *Pie in the Sky*, okay?"

"But we don't sell rainbow cake in our shop either."

"Because the layers and cream and fruit make it too fancy and expensive for our shop back home."

He squints at me. "How can something be too simple and too fancy at the same time?"

"You'll understand it when you're older—" I gulp. I hate it when grown-ups use that line on me. Am I all grown up now? Am I going to start getting all hairy all over?

Yanghao calls me a booger, but nothing more, and we sit there watching in silence as if the oven were a TV and the rising cake were a cartoon.

After fifteen minutes, he points to the oven door. "The cake's rising." I slap his hand away before he touches it and burns his finger. He pokes my cheek with his finger that's teeming with germs. "A mosquito landing on your cheek."

"Ow! Another rule: Don't poke me in the face or anywhere else. Or I'll cut off your finger."

"I'll tell Mama you cut off my finger, and she'll kill you." He smirks, then suddenly, the corners of his mouth drop and his eyebrows squeeze together like two caterpillars kissing. He looks straight into my eyes and he says, "I know how the rainbow cake can be too simple and too fancy at the same time."

I let him talk.

"Let's say I'm wearing a short-sleeve shirt. With buttons. And jeans. And I tuck in my shirt. That outfit is too fancy for that birthday party you had in our old school when you were ten years old—"

"Oh." I didn't know he remembered that party.

"But it's too simple if I'm going to the birthday party of the Queen of England."

I. Have. No. Words.

He opens his mouth to say something else, and it's fifty-fifty on whether it'll be something genius or something cuckoo, but he clamps his mouth shut, then his nose twitches like a rabbit's. I catch a whiff of what he sniffs. Three little ingredients: eggs, flour, sugar. They have hardly a smell on their own, but when together and baked . . . I close my eyes and see Mama and Papa in our old kitchen.

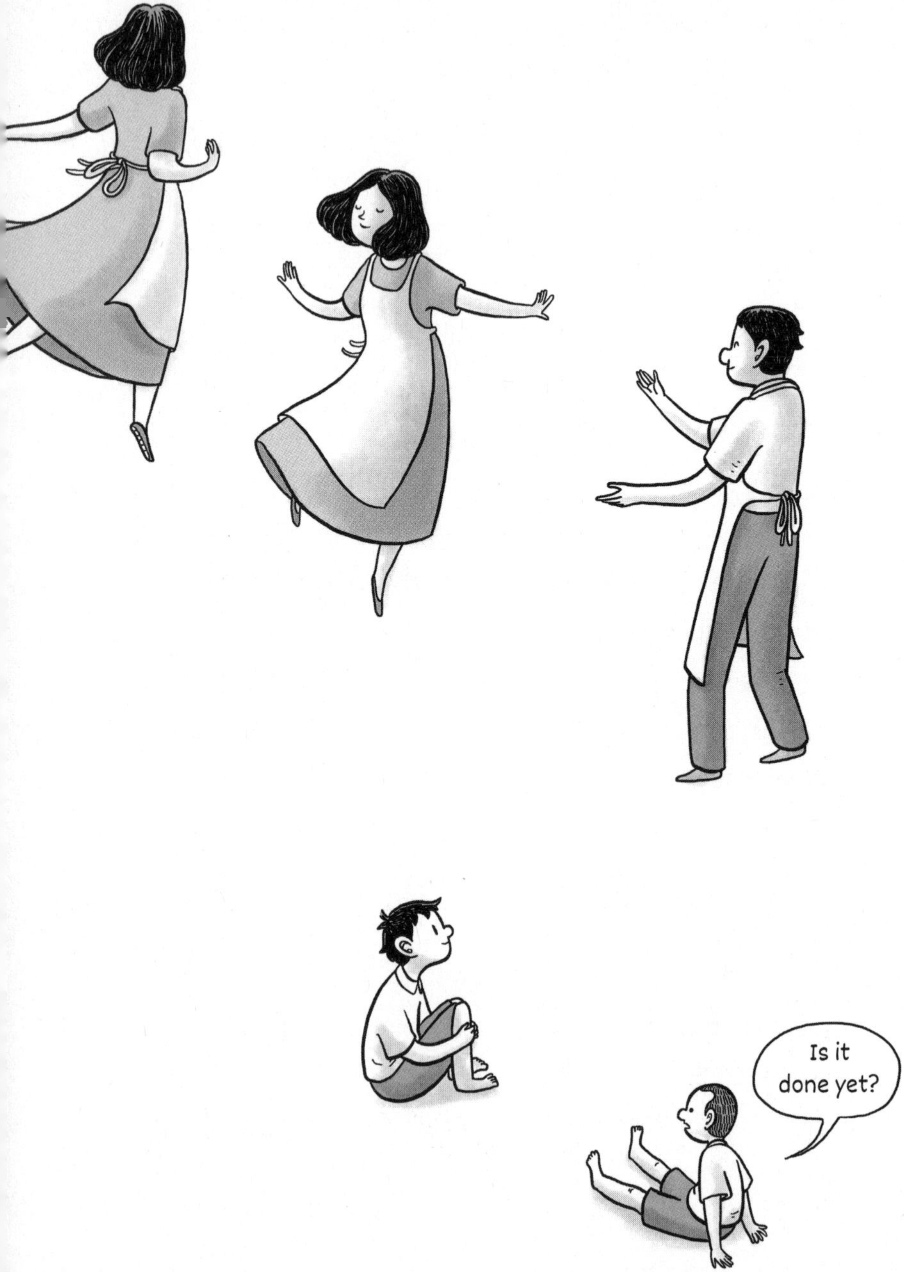
Is it
done yet?

The sponge cake has turned golden brown. I pierce a tooth-pick into the middle. When the toothpick comes out clean, Yanghao hoots—the sponge cake is ready. I slip on Mama's oven mitts and hustle Yanghao out of the kitchen. "Another rule," I say. "Yanghao's feet must be on the carpet and not on the tiles. Unless Jingwen says he can enter the kitchen."

"Why?"

"For your safety. Remember whenever the grown-ups took cakes out of the oven, we had to stay on the doormat in the corner of the kitchen?"

Both corners of his lips curl up like he's the Grinch, then he lifts a foot. His foot hovers over the tiled floor—exactly what he and I used to do back home, except in our old house, we didn't have carpets, just tiles. I hiss, and he stomps his foot back down on the carpet.

I'm right back in our old kitchen, Papa right next to me. I watch him take out the pan of sponge cake we've just folded together.

The cake is stuck. When I turn the pan over on a cooling rack, the cake won't drop. "Uh-oh. We forgot to oil the pan."

"Oh no!" Yanghao crosses into the danger zone.

"Step back! The carpet rule!"

He marches back into the safety zone and crosses his arms.

I ignore him and run a knife around the cake to separate it from the pan. It works. But the sides and the bottom of the cake are pockmarked. "It looks like it's been eaten by mice."

"Doesn't matter," Yanghao says. "We're going to cover it in lots and lots of Nutella cream, right?"

"Right." I start on the Nutella cream. "When the Nutella cream's ready, the cake should be cool enough to slice."

Jingwen . . .

What other cakes are on the menu of *Pie in the Sky?*

I swallow. "There's tiramisu—"

"Is that the one Ah-gong said can make you drunk?"

"One of the ingredients can make you drunk, but very little is added into the cake. You'd have to eat maybe a hundred cakes to get drunk. Besides, the one for *Pie in the Sky* doesn't have alcohol. Just coffee."

"What other cakes are there?"

"Chocolate raspberry torte—"

"What's that?"

Torte is a type of cake that uses only a little flour.

It has ground nuts like almonds instead. In a chocolate torte, there's a lot of chocolate, too.

Yanghao smacks his lips. "Tell me another cake."

"Neapolitan mousse cake." I wait, but he only looks at me. "Well?"

"I know that one. It's like Neapolitan ice cream, the one with three flavors. Chocolate, vanilla, and strawberry. Another cake."

"Blueberry cheesecake."

"Another cake."

I bet he doesn't know this one. "Apple mille-feuille."

He scrunches up his face. "Apple what?"

Hah! "It's the most difficult cake on the menu."

It's from France, and it has caramelized apples sandwiched between many layers of puff pastry.

That's the kind of pastry in a croissant.

"Croissants are yummy!" Yanghao groans. "Talking about those cakes makes me so hungry I'm going to faint."

The Nutella cream is fluffy and ready, so I hand him the cream-covered whisk. "Don't faint. Lick that."

As he licks and slurps, I work on the cake. While I'm a professional at dividing a cake into equal pieces, I stink at sawing a cake horizontally into two layers. One layer ends up much thicker than the other, and their surfaces look like giant rats have been gnawing at them.

"Cover it with more Nutella," Yanghao says.

Slathering the chocolaty goo on sponge cake isn't easy. With each swipe of the spatula, more and more big cake crumbs stick to the spatula. I have to use up the whole jar to finally cover the top of one of the cakes. Before I can say no, Yanghao picks up the other layer and drops it over the Nutella-covered one. Blobs of Nutella squish out. Even though

I say, "No no no!" Yanghao runs his nose-digging finger along the side of the cake, one whole round, to wipe up the excess Nutella. Then he licks his finger as if it were an icy pop.

"It's not batter," he says. "I'm not breaking your rule."

Surprisingly, he doesn't stick his fingers in the Nutella cream when I slather it all around the cake and when I pipe swirly cones on top.

"Cut me a big piece. Bigger than my face," he says, even though the whole cake itself is the size of his face.

"Will you be able to finish your dinner?"

He doesn't even think before answering yes, so I cut him a regular-sized piece and tell him it's a bigger piece. He's so mesmerized by the Nutella he doesn't notice. After he scarfs it down in about two seconds, he helps himself to five more pieces.

The last slice of
Pie in the sky cake.

I can't bear to eat it.

All that while I was telling Yanghao about Papa, my nose didn't burn. Somehow, the sweetness of the cakes takes away the bitter sadness. Somehow, sometime during the cake making, some of the seashells in my pockets disappeared.

My thoughts are interrupted by the sound of Yanghao lick-
ing his fingers. He's standing outside the kitchen, having
another round of Nutella feast. I pinch the back of his collar
and haul him into the bathroom. Luckily, he doesn't throw his
I-hate-showers-and-my-sweat-smells-like-perfume tantrum,
although he does start singing his silly cake song again. As he
scrubs off his Nutella mask and gloves, I scrub his shirt with
hand soap at the sink.

"Caaaake! You're so chocolaty and pretty . . . ," he sings in
the shower.

After I throw his cleanish shirt into the laundry hamper,
I lay down a set of his clean clothes on the toilet tank. Just
then, the phone rings. I run out and glance at the clock. It's
half past seven and Mama's break time, which is when she
calls to check up on us.

"Hello?" As usual, Mama asks me what we are doing, and
I say, "Yanghao's taking a shower. After that, he'll have his
dinner."

I say nothing about the cake. Technically, I'm not lying. I'm
just leaving out the truth.

"Make sure your brother finishes his dinner," she says. "Is
that him singing? What's he singing?"

"A nonsense song." Which is the truth.

"Have you finished your homework?"

"Ah." I haven't thought about homework and school and being an alien and Joe and Max and Mr. Fart and s l o w. Not since I decided to make a cake. "I'll finish my homework, Mama."

Mama reminds me to heat up dinner for Yanghao and then we say good night. I know I should feel a little guilty that I sort of lied to Mama, but I don't. Yanghao and I had fun. I temporarily forgot that I'm on Mars, that I have no friends in school. Yanghao and I got to talk about Papa. I got to remind Yanghao of things he's forgotten about Papa, things I'm afraid I might forget myself.

Besides, Mama's also having fun at *Barker Bakes*.

I said I'd only make one cake.

But what if . . . what if Yanghao asks me to make another?

What if it's the only way to stop him from crying?

What if cake is like the oxygen helmet that I need to survive on Mars?

That's when I realize Yanghao is no longer doing what he thinks of as singing. He isn't making any noise at all. I hurry back to the bathroom to make sure he hasn't fainted in the shower from too much cake. He hasn't, but he's not moving. He just stands there, the water rushing down on him. Is he feeling queasy?

He sighs too heavily for someone so small and steps out of the shower. "Jingwen, I wish . . . I wish I could eat all the *Pie in the Sky* cakes."

"You—You can buy those cakes, you know," I say. "*Barker Bakes* probably has some of them."

"It's not the same." His voice is muffled because he has a towel around his head, and he's wiping his hair vigorously.

My heart is a balloon, and each THUMP is a puff of helium. "What's not the same?"

Yanghao says, "It's just not the same."

"Jingwen." He pulls the towel off his head. "Would you make all the cakes? Pleasepleasepleaseplease."

Never have I loved my brother and his little-kid ways more than at this very moment.

"Pleasepleasepleaseplease—"

"There will be more rules. We'll write them down so you remember. You have to do everything I—"

Before I finish, Yanghao bounces out of the bathroom, wearing only his underwear, shouting, "*Caaaaake! Caaaaake!*"

Following his yells and the trail of puddles he left behind, I find him in Mama's room, jumping up and down on her bed. I toss his T-shirt and shorts at him. "Put on your clothes, wild monkey."

But he leaps off the bed and out of the room. I lie down on Mama's bed and breathe deeply.

Am I really going to make all the *Pie in the Sky* cakes? Eleven more cakes. That will be many, many more lies of omission to Mama. This could be a recipe for disaster.

It's then that I notice the bare wall above the bed.

In our old home, above Mama and Papa's bed, there was a photograph of them on their wedding day. The frame was gold. Before we left for Australia, I'd gone room to room in my old house, drinking in everything. I didn't know when I'd be back. When I got to Mama and Papa's room, I saw the photograph was gone.

I assumed Mama had taken it to hang it up in her new bedroom in this new apartment. Has she forgotten to hang it up? Has she forgotten Papa?

I won't. I will make all the pies. All the pies in the sky.

But the next morning, Mama asks, "Why does it smell like cake?"

I choke on my congee breakfast. I cough and cough, long after I've cleared my throat. Last night, I washed everything that was used in the making of Nutella cream cake. I didn't think smell would be what gave our secret away. Yanghao can't help me because he's still in our bedroom, packing his schoolbag.

What should I tell Mama? Maybe that Anna likes to bake, and the smell of Anna's cake always drifts over to our apartment.

Luckily, Mama is distracted by something else. "Did you finish your homework?" she asks as she opens the fridge.

"Yes." It's the truth. Last night, I returned to my homework and played eeny-meeny-miny-moe with the multiple-choice questions.

But Mama doesn't say, "Good." Instead, from the fridge, she takes out a plastic container half filled with noodles, as well as half a dumpling. "Who didn't finish his dinner?"

"Not me," I say.

Just then, Yanghao appears.

"Yanghao," Mama says, "why didn't you finish your dinner?"

"I wasn't hungry."

Of course he wasn't. He spoiled his dinner with half a Nutella cream cake that was as big as his face.

"How come?" Mama asks.

Yanghao turns to me, his eyes wide. What should I say? Yanghao had a tummy ache. He had too many gummy snakes. Oh no. Too much time has passed since Mama asked the question. Hurry, come up with an answer. Before she turns suspicious! Yanghao is a booger, Mama, who knows why he does things? He—

Yanghao?

Jingwen made a cake.

Yanghao. You. Are. Such. A. Booger.

The rule among siblings is that the older one is always the guilty one. Because the older one, in any and all circumstances, should know better than the younger, clueless one.

So Mama scolds me. I hang my head and pretend I'm truly sorry, but I'm actually shooting daggers at Yanghao from the corner of my eye. He innocently and noisily chews his breakfast. As if congee needs chewing.

"What were you thinking, making a cake by yourselves? What if you burnt yourselves?" Mama shoots off her questions so fast I can't get an answer in. "What kind of cake was it? What's so delicious that you can't wait until I'm free this weekend?"

"It was Nutella cream cake, Mama," Yanghao says softly. "It was yummy."

She stops her interrogation and sighs. "I said I'll bake a cake for you boys, so don't make one by yourselves. I'll make one next weekend, all right?" Then she says I'm not to touch the oven or the stove ever again, not without her permission and supervision. If I disobey, she'll have Anna babysit Yanghao and me every day after school. I imagine that horrible what if.

speak like me, Jingwen.

I wince. Several hours of that per day, five times a week. No, thanks. I already get enough of feeling stupid from school.

Yanghao, too, has his face scrunched up like he's eaten an orange gummy snake—the worst of them all.

I want to tell Mama how fun last night was, how I forgot for a moment all about failing school and failing at friendship. But before I can, she says—

Someone could get hurt, Jingwen.

I remember when I was five and playing roll-down-the-hill with Yanghao. It was a game where we lay down on my bed hugging each other, and we'd roll off my bed onto Yanghao's trundle bed below. We rolled, rolled, rolled, until the back of Yanghao's head smashed right into the corner of my bed. There was no wound and no blood, but he cried and cried. When Mama rushed in and asked what was going on, I said Yanghao wanted my toy, but I wouldn't give it to him, and she believed me. Shortly after, Yanghao said everything was spinning, and he started walking funny, like after I spun around on the spot a hundred times and made myself dizzy.

Only at the hospital, after Yanghao was wheeled off to get a picture of his brain, after Mama cried a lot, after Ah-po and Ah-gong prayed to the deities a lot, after the doctor told us Yanghao had a bruise on his brain but would be fine and did not need surgery, just a lot of rest and quiet time, only after all those things did I tell Papa what happened. He didn't scold me.

I used to love the walk to the bus station with Mama.

This morning, all I can think about is the *crap* that's waiting for me in school. I won't even have making a second *Pie in the Sky* cake to look forward to. Time will move so s l o w l y. Glaciers. Snails. Getting old enough to do anything anytime you want.

Then it's rewind and replay for tomorrow. And the day after. Forever and ever.

Last night was the happiest I've been since we landed on Mars. I wasn't doing cartwheels when Mama said we were going ahead with the move, as if it didn't matter to her that Papa wasn't coming along, but I thought I was okay with it. I thought I was okay these last two months. Sure, sometimes I felt terrible, like the thing with the aliens and with Joe, but life is like a packet of gummy snakes—there'll always be the sour orange ones nobody likes. But maybe I haven't been okay for two months. Maybe I've been . . . distracted.

THE FAREWELL GIFTS
FROM MY OLD CLASSMATES

THE FLIGHT,
WHICH WAS MY FIRST
AND ONLY ONE

THE KANGAROOS AND
KOALAS AT THE ZOO

THE NEW SCHOOL WITH
THE NEW UNIFORM THAT
DOESN'T SMELL LIKE CAKE
BECAUSE THE NEW HOME
DOESN'T SMELL LIKE CAKE
ALL THE LIVELONG DAY

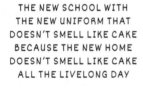

THE POLICE CARS THAT LOOK
THE SAME AS THE TAXIS

Mama, Yanghao, and I reach the bus station, and the bus is already boarding. A queue of passengers snakes into it. Yanghao and I wave good-bye to Mama. Once we hop on, I hiss, "Booger! Why did you tattle?"

"You didn't—"

"Shhh! Don't shout." I glance around to see if anyone is staring at us. Luckily a group of noisy students drowns out Yanghao and me.

He whispers, "I wasn't shouting. And you didn't tell me I couldn't tell Mama."

He's right. It's my fault. I should have told him outright. It's common sense that we have to keep the cake making a secret from Mama, because back at our old home, when Yanghao and I helped out at the cake shop, we were forbidden from touching the stove or the oven. But my little brother doesn't have common sense on account of my doing everything for him.

More passengers board the bus and jostle us toward the back. "But," I whisper, "what about when we passed by *Barker Bakes* on our way to and from the grocery store? Why did you think we hid behind the mailbox?"

His lips form a perfect O. "I was following you. I thought we were playing a game."

It's not fair. He should have said something wacky; then I'd have the right to call him a booger.

"Jingwen, can we make one more cake?"

My eyes pop out. I don't want people staring, so I pop them back in. "Be quiet," I whisper, but what I really, really want is for Yanghao to shout, "It's CAKE TIME!"

In my classroom, I slump at my desk, Mama's cookbook open in front of me, and stare at the triple cookie cake that I won't get to make. Someone says, *"Cakes?"*

I look up to see Ben. He just arrived and is settling into his seat. His eyes are on my book.

Cool! I'm *cool*! Okay, he might be saying that cakes are *cool*, but at least I know being called *cool* is a good thing. When I first heard the other students saying this to one another, I wondered if this was what everyone here did in the summer, because Australian summers are hot like hell, so people went around wishing everyone was cool.

But is Ben like Joe? Is he going to laugh at me behind my back? I think I said *cakes*, but maybe I said it wrong and to him it sounded like *eggs*.

I steal a glance at Ben. He's writing in his homework book while my other classmates-not-friends race around like monkeys. I know how most of my classmates-not-friends divide themselves into cliques of two or more. Lisa with Rani. Ravi with Christine. Pete with Shafiq. Joe and Max. Back in my old school, it was Jingwen and Xirong. But Ben doesn't seem to have any twenty-four-seven friends, just for-the-moment friends. There's no clique he hangs out with day in and day out. He seems to flit from group to group, but he's welcomed by them all.

At least he has branches to perch on. Meanwhile, I'm a bird that can't find land. When I spot a tree, I try to land, but all the other birds there are chirping.

I try to drown out that chirping by singing Yanghao's cake song inside my head. But soon "Caaaake! Caaaake! You're so yummy!" is replaced by Mama's voice: "Jingwen, don't ever touch the stove or the oven again."

I try to shake Mama's voice out of my mind, but she keeps yammering on.

"Jingwen, you're older, and you should've known better."

I'm not even twelve.

"Jingwen, someone could get hurt."

No, I'm old enough to make sure Yanghao won't get hurt. That's why I made up the rules.

"Jingwen, everything will be all right."

You've been saying that for two months.

"Jingwen, we're moving to Australia."

We shouldn't have! We shouldn't have!

"*Crap!*" says Ben, interrupting my playlist that's titled Jingwen's Stinky Life on Mars. He shakes his pen vigorously and then presses it hard into his notepad, but it's out of ink.

Those two simple words surprise me so much I can't think of the Martian words that mean "you're welcome." He doesn't say anything else to me, not until Mr. Fart's class.

Mr. Fart asks me to read aloud. I'm sweating so much I probably need a blood transfusion. I'm on the first word, and I'm already stumped, even though I'm sure I've come across this word before.

Words not sticking in my brain reminds me of last weekend, when Mama finally had some free time and took Yanghao and me to Underwater World. Lots of glass and lots of fish. There was a section with a shallow aquarium where you could touch different kinds of starfish. As instructed by the man in charge, and translated by Mama, I placed one starfish on my upturned palm. Yanghao did the same. After a few minutes, we were told to turn our palms back over, and according to the man, the starfish would stick to your hand.

THUNK!

My starfish is like English to me. It never sticks. I'll come across a word and try to store it in my brain, but the next day my brain will have kicked those words out, just like this word that Mr. Fart is still waiting for me to read. He's clearing his throat like he needs a soothing lozenge.

I croak, *"Des-Des-Des—"* and my tongue freezes when I catch Joe staring at me. He notices me noticing and quickly turns back to the blackboard.

"Describe," someone to my left whispers. I turn to see Ben with his nose in his book. Was it Ben? What did he say? Can he repeat it?

Before Mr. Fart can ask me to read the next question, I plonk back down and bury my nose in my book. Luckily he has mercy on me today and doesn't continue my torture, moving on to addressing the class. I want to say *thank you* to Ben, but he doesn't look my way, and I don't dare to even whisper to him. No point risking drawing Mr. Fart's attention back to me. But I really hope that Ben is nothing like Joe.

Mr. Fart says something about *homework*. Now, that's a word I hope my brain forgets.

There is one word I don't want to forget even though I don't know its meaning yet. I look up *"metamorphosis"* in my dictionary.

Turns out, it's just a fancy-pants way of saying a very big change. Which in Mr. Fart's class, refers to a tadpole changing into a frog.

I wonder if there's a fancy word that means a very small change that feels really big.

19

"What's wrong with your face?" Yanghao asks when I meet up with him at the gates after school.

"What?" I pat my cheeks. "Is there rice on my face?"

"No. You're smiling."

It has turned out to be a surprisingly good day. Cakes make me happy. Not just because they taste good, but they also bring me good luck. I don't know why, and I don't know how. But cakes are magic. Okay, maybe not, but cakes bring smiles, just like Papa said. The day he told me that, I'd been sulking. I don't remember why because I was little, but it was probably all thanks to Yanghao. He must have stolen or destroyed something of mine. Papa asked me if I knew why he liked cakes.

Because we sell them for money to buy toys.

Ha!

Yes, but also, when someone is feeling sad, they can't help but smile at the sight of a cake.

But, just this morning, Mama said no to cakes.

Even though she's the one who put me here on Mars in the first place.

I'm not unreasonable. I don't expect Mama to turn back time to before she decided to move to Australia without Papa. Anyway, if she could turn back time, I'd make her bring us to a time before we were without Papa. I don't expect her to wave a magic wand and make everything all right. But she could let me have one thing that makes some things all right. She just chooses not to.

I think these thoughts all the way home. I don't even

care that Yanghao's chattering away and elbowing me for a response and making everyone on the bus gawk at us. My jaws clench tighter and tighter, my teeth grit harder and harder, so much so that by the time Yanghao and I reach home, I need a dentist and some kind of jaw doctor.

As I'm fishing for my keys, I see the apartment door is ajar, then I hear Mama's snorting laugh. Yanghao hears it, too, for he sticks his head under my armpit and peeks in. I peer over his head.

Anna speaks too softly for me to hear, though I probably wouldn't understand her even if she were screaming. But Mama understands, and it must have been something funny because she laughs a whole-body kind of laugh, where you lean back and throw your head back.

I can't remember when I last laughed like that. Or when Mama last laughed like that.

"That must be Anna's cat," Yanghao whispers.

There's a fat cat on Anna's lap, its orange fur bright against Anna's dark blue pants. I wish that cat was the only thing I noticed, instead of Mama's laugh.

"Jingwen, the cat looks like Mango." Yanghao forgets to whisper this time, and Mama and Anna turn toward us.

"*You boys are home,*" Anna says.

"*Hello, Anna.*" Yanghao makes a beeline for the cat and strokes it. "*Cat.*"

"*That is right. Cat. Her name is Ginger.*"

"*I have cat,*" Yanghao says. "*He orange. Same to Ginger.*"

"*I have a cat, too,*" Anna corrects him. "*He is orange, same as Ginger. Now, how was school?*"

"*School is good.*"

"*School was good.*"

Yanghao cocks his head. "*Was?*"

"*Past tense,*" Anna says.

She launches into what I guess is a long, boring explanation about *past tense*, and I shudder. If I make more cakes and Mama finds out, I'll have to spend afternoons listening to that. I kneel down and very, very slowly untie my shoelaces. Mama has to leave for work in fifteen minutes, so Anna will have to leave then, too. If I have to pretend to undo a knot for fifteen minutes to avoid a conversation with Anna, that's what I'll do.

Luckily, Anna gets up, cradling Ginger over one elbow. She

says a string of Martian words to Mama. She isn't speaking haltingly like a robot. Does she think Yanghao and I are sluggish snails? Is that why she speak s l o w to us?

I only catch the last bit: "*Have a good evening, Meixin.*"

She then turns to Yanghao and me. "*Have   a   good   evening,   Jingwen   and   Yanghao.*"

"*Have a good evening, Anna and Ginger,*" Yanghao says.

She doesn't leave but looks at me, waiting for a reply.

Mama walks Anna to the door. I scurry away to the dining table and pretend to do my homework.

. . .

"Mama," Yanghao says as soon as Anna's gone, "can you make a cake for us?"

"You boys better not be making cakes when I'm not home," Mama says. "You hear, Jingwen?"

"My ears work fine, Mama." I press my pen into my book so hard the tip bends.

"I want a cake, Mama," Yanghao says.

"How about this weekend?"

He claps and hoots as if he's won the gold medal for Best Clown.

"What cake would you like?" Mama asks.

"How about Ah-po's cake?"

"What's Ah-po's cake?"

"The rainbow cake Ah-po made for us before we got on the plane," Yanghao says.

I feel like I've been kicked in the stomach by a clown's giant shoe. Yanghao has forgotten.

"The one Ah-po made for our birthdays," he continues.

Ah-po did make rainbow cakes for our birthdays, but only for the last two years. Because Papa wasn't around to make them anymore.

I listen closely.

"Rainbow cake?" Mama asks.

Mama, tell Yanghao that rainbow cake is Papa's cake. Tell him! Now!

Mama has forgotten Papa. Yanghao has forgotten Papa.

I want to scream that rainbow cake is Papa's cake, but Mama will get upset even if I whisper his name. Even though I'm angry at her and don't want her to be so happy, I don't want her to be upset either. I definitely don't want to be the reason she's upset.

But I can't let Yanghao forget. It's not his fault he can't remember. He was only seven when Papa died. Since Ah-po and Ah-gong are too far away, it's all up to me to fix this.

Last night, while we were making the Nutella cake, Yanghao asked me all kinds of questions about Papa. That's how I'll help him remember. With Papa's cakes.

I can't help but grin at how cakes truly are magic.

All I have to do is find a way to keep them a secret from Mama, to tell lies without lying.

Once Mama leaves for work, I say, "Yanghao, want to make a cake?"

He mutes SpongeBob, and I know I've got him. He hops into the kitchen, shouting a phrase he must have learned from Professor SpongeBob.

I'm ready!

But first, we need rules.

"You already told me the rules yesterday," Yanghao says, sitting down next to me.

"New rules. To make sure Mama doesn't find out, we'll keep the cake making super secret. She won't even suspect, so she won't ask. So we won't have to say anything." To make this cake, we have to tell lies of omission, which are barely even lies. I'm not telling them to benefit myself, but for Yanghao and Papa. And no one will get hurt. After all, nobody got hurt in last night's cake making.

Yanghao grabs the pencil from me and slides the yellow notepad toward himself. "I'll write."

"Fine. At the top, write 'Rules for Making Cakes.'"

He nibbles on the eraser end of the pencil. "Umm . . ."

"What? Don't you know how to write 'rules'?"

He flips open my dictionary and riffles through it. The pages rapidly turning sound like when Ah-gong counted the money in the cash register after the last cake of the day was sold. "*Rules!*"

I peek at what he's jotting down. "You're writing in English? Why?"

"Mama says if I use English more often, I'll learn it faster. So it's . . ."

I huff. "As long as YOU understand what you've written and follow the rules. Number one: Jingwen and Yanghao cannot tell anyone about the cakes.

"Number two: Jingwen and Yanghao have to finish dinner. Number three: Open all windows so the apartment doesn't smell like cake. This morning, Mama could smell last night's cake."

"*Cannot . . . tell . . . anyone . . . ,*" Yanghao murmurs as I carry out rule number three.

"Number four: After cake making, clean, dry, and place all the cake-making things back where they were—"

"Slow down, Jingwen." The dictionary flip-flip-flips furiously. "What's 'dinner' in English . . ."

"Number two already? That was quick." I look at Yanghao's Martian letters. It's very possible that he's actually writing "my brother is a tyrannical, odoriferous fart." If only I knew a long and difficult Martian bad word that he doesn't already know.

But I don't, so I make him add the rest of the rules I made up last night:

Number five: No sticking dirty fingers in the batter.
Number six: Yanghao is not to poke Jin in the face.
Number seven: Yanghao's feet must be on the carpet unless Jin says he can enter the kitchen.

When Yanghao finally finishes, he gives a big, tired sigh, and I'm glad English is tiring for him, too.

"Can we make rainbow cake?" he asks.

"We don't have the recipe. Is it in any of Mama's cookbooks?"

He shakes his head. If a cake is baked in an oven that's too hot, it'll rise too high, then collapse in the center before it's thoroughly baked. That's what Yanghao looks like now, with his head hung so low.

Of course there's no recipe for rainbow cake in those cookbooks. Our family's cake shop has been selling the same cakes since before I was born. Ah-po, Ah-gong, Mama, and Papa could make those cakes blindfolded and with one arm behind their backs. The recipes were passed down by word of mouth from my I-don't-know-how-many-great-grandparents all the way to my parents. I don't know why no one has bothered to type them up. Maybe if we had a better computer. Anyway, there are recipes not just for cakes, but for stews, sauces, and bitter herbal soups that can help you grow a new nose if you lose yours after a very bad cold, and of course, a recipe for the rainbow cake.

Yanghao slaps the dining table. "I know! We can ask Mama."

"Is your brain on vacation? She'll ask why we're asking, and then we'll have to tell her. Unless you want to lie?"

His reply is to bolt to the living room.

"Who are you calling?" I ask.

"Ah-po. To ask her for the rainbow cake recipe. What's the special international number we have to dial before the actual phone number?"

I snatch the receiver and slam it back down. "We can't call Ah-po."

"Why not?"

"International calls are very expensive. Mama says we can only call home if she's around. When the telephone bill comes, she'll know and will ask why."

I don't want him to cry, so I go back to the dining table and start writing on a new page of my notepad. "Let's write a letter. 'Dear Ah-po and Ah-gong, I'm having a great time in Australia.'" That's how I always start my letters to them. "'Would you please send me the recipe for your rainbow cake? Mama asks for it.'"

Yanghao cackles as if we've pulled off a great caper. He kneels on the other stool, his elbows on the table and his rosy cheeks cradled in his palms. "Tell Ah-po I say hi. Tell her we're making—what cake are we making?"

"Triple cookie cake. And, you foolish booger, we can't tell Ah-po that. She'll tell Mama. Go get a stamp and an envelope from Mama's room."

"You're the *booger*," he says.

"I know what that means."

You only know the bad words.

When he returns, I don't let him lick the stamp. But he doesn't throw a tantrum, only asks, "When will Ah-po reply?"

Ten to fourteen days for our letter to reach her, a few days for her to reply, and then another ten to fourteen days for her reply to reach us.

By the time the recipe arrives, I'll already have made all the cakes of *Pie in the Sky*, and the gray of my cloudy days will have turned into the colors of a rainbow cake. When I write back, "I'm having a great time in Australia," for once, it'll be the truth.

21

We mail Ah-po's letter on the way to the grocery store. This time, we take even greater care when passing in front of *Barker Bakes*. We thought of going across the road, but there isn't anything large enough—like that big red mailbox—for us to hide behind. Mama has never taken us via a different way to the bus station and grocery store before, and if I get us lost, I'll have double punishment: for not sticking to her directions, plus for secretly trying to make a cake. That equals Mama disowning me.

But I don't spot Mama laughing inside *Barker Bakes* today.

Yanghao and I buy flour, eggs, butter, sugar, chocolate chips, cocoa powder, and Oreo cookies and pack them into the two reusable shopping bags we brought from home.

We're getting ready for the Great *Barker Bakes* Dash again when someone calls out to Yanghao.

"Who's that?" I ask.

"Sarah. My friend."

At that moment, I spot my enemy. Joe. About to walk out of *Barker Bakes*.

I duck behind the mailbox.

Without a word, Yanghao darts behind me. When I peer around the mailbox, he follows suit.

Joe hangs around near *Barker Bakes*, eating a muffin. What's he doing here? I hope he chokes on that muffin. Not death by muffin, but so that he can't say *s l o w*.

"What? What is it?" Yanghao whispers, his head swiveling left and right.

A car pulls up next to Yanghao and me. Joe walks toward it. I propel Yanghao around the mailbox, risking our being seen by Mama. But I don't want Joe to see me hiding. He climbs into the car. When the car speeds off, I quickly pull Yanghao the rest of the way past the café.

"What exactly did he say?" he asks.

"Just something bad."

Yanghao scratches his head. "Are you sure? Maybe he wasn't talking about you."

"Of course I'm sure. He said my name."

He purses his lips and is quiet. Which for once I wish he weren't, because I need his chatter to stop me thinking about Joe. When Joe and Max caught on that someone had overheard them, I could've played along and laughed it off. This whole incident might not have exploded into this big thing where I'm hiding behind mailboxes. But there's an equal chance they might have thought it'd be okay to share the joke with everyone, and then everyone would tell it to my face for eternity, and I'd have to pretend for eternity that I found it funny, too. Being a laughingstock is the worst. If I think about it this way, hiding behind mailboxes doesn't seem so silly.

Yanghao finally says, "But . . ."

"What?"

"Don't be angry, Jingwen . . . but how could you understand what he said? Your English isn't the best."

I give him my how-dare-you look.

"I said don't be angry."

"Walk. Home. By. Your. Self." I bolt.

Surprisingly, he doesn't immediately run after me. It's several seconds before I hear his running footsteps and his yelling. "Jingwen! Wait for me!"

I don't slow down.

He runs sideways alongside me. "Sorry, sorry. We're still making cake, right? Right, Jingwen?"

That's a stranger-than-aliens thing that just happened: Yanghao saying sorry to me. Cakes have done that. But I hide my surprise and don't even look at him.

All right, Jingwen.

Rule number eight: Jingwen is always right.

I press my lips together tightly, but it's no use. A guffaw escapes, and Yanghao knows he's forgiven. He keeps yelling, "Hurry up, slow turtle!" as I check the mailbox. Just junk mail. Maybe my last two letters to Xirong got lost. It's a long way to get to him. Or he gave up handwriting, since his handwriting is like a doctor's chicken scratch, and emailed me instead. Maybe by the time his letter reaches me, cakes will have helped me make a friend, and it won't matter so much.

• • •

Back in our apartment, I'm laying out the ingredients on the dining table when Yanghao gasps. "Oh no. Jingwen, our clock's broken."

The clock says quarter to six. It's still light outside, and sunset is at seven. "What does our alarm clock say?" I ask. "Is it not quarter to six?"

Triple cookie cake looks complicated, but the three layers are made from the same basic butter cake recipe, only mixed with different flavors.

BUTTERCREAM
FROSTING

CHOCOLATE CHIP
LAYER

CRUMBLED OREO
COOKIES LAYER

CHOCOLATE
LAYER

Since we have only two round pans of the same size, we'll have to start by making two of the layers and then a third one.

"Is it a salty cake?" Yanghao asks, studying the ingredients on the table.

"What are you talking about?"

He points to Mama's cookbook, which is open to the recipe for triple cookie cake. "It says a teaspoon of salt for the butter cake and a pinch of salt for the buttercream filling. We already have much more than a teaspoon and a pinch at home. We didn't need to buy salt."

"I didn't buy salt."

He holds up the packet of sugar. "What's this, then?"

"Duh. Sugar."

He huffs. "This is salt. See this word? *S-A-L-T. Salt.* Sugar is *S-U-G—*"

"I know! I read wrongly because I was in a hurry."

Yanghao is about to call me a *booger.*

"It's not a problem. We'll use the sugar we have at home." I pour the jar of sugar into a bowl on the weighing scale. We're short by ninety grams. "It's not a problem. We'll go to the grocery store now and get more."

"Jingwen, remember, it's *SUGAR.*"

"One more word, and no cake for you."

He mimes zipping up his lips and follows me to the door.

A-Anna!

Where are you two heading?

Yanghao points to his head. "*Head?*"

"*Where are you two going?*" Anna asks.

I'm still translating in my head what Anna said when Yanghao replies, *"Grocery store."*

I flick the back of his neck.

"Ow! I wasn't going to tell her we're making a cake."

"Mama won't like our going to the store by ourselves either. We'll have to lie to her that we only went downstairs to check the mail. It's all your fault. Come on!" I hurry down the steps, but Yanghao doesn't move. He's watching Anna and picking at his pursed lips. Uh-oh. That's his I-have-a-ridiculous-idea-brewing-in-my-head look.

Before I can murder that idea, nail it into a coffin, and bury it ten thousand meters underground, he opens his big mouth. *"Excuse me, Anna."*

"What are you doing?" I hiss.

He pretends not to hear me. *"You have . . . sugar?"*

"Do you have sugar?" Anna shuffles toward her apartment. *"And yes, I do have sugar. What is it for?"*

Anna smiles and says some things, of which I catch zilch, then she steps into her apartment, leaving her door ajar.

"Where's she going?" I ask.

"She asked us to wait here. And you have to make me sweet tea so what I told her won't be a lie."

Less than a minute later, Anna emerges again. She hands Yanghao a big jar of sugar and launches into a speech in Martian.

"*Thank you*," Yanghao says.

Did he really catch that gobbledygook? I hustle him back into our apartment. "What did Anna say?"

"She said you're a *booger*." He laughs. He's the only one who thinks he's funny.

Less than an hour later, the kitchen is warm. A sweet smell of vanilla and butter lingers, even though I've opened all the windows. When I was younger, I was foolish. I complained everything I owned smelled like cake, from my hair to my school uniform to my books, and my friends had nicknamed me Smell Like Cake (not very creative, my friends). Mama, Papa, Ah-po, and Ah-gong would laugh. Papa would say these fragrant cakes were putting me through school and would put me through a better school in Australia, and when I grew up, I could get a good job—anything I wanted—and not have to be Smell Like Cake.

Now I'm taking extra deep breaths, trying to draw into my chest all the cake-smell molecules, like the dog at the airport that was supposed to sniff out bad guys.

Later, while we're waiting for the chocolate and Oreo butter cakes to cool and I'm whipping up the buttercream, I look up to see Yanghao picking at the crispy skin of the cake. "Hey! Stop that!"

"Mama and Papa always let me have the cake skin."

"Rule number nine: No picking of cake skin unless Jingwen says so," I say.

When it's time to flip the third layer, chocolate chip butter cake, out of its pan, I banish Yanghao to the carpeted area.

Just then, the phone rings. Before I can do anything, Yanghao picks it up. "Hello?"

I glance at the clock. Half past seven. Mama.

"You ask what I'm doing, Mama?" he says.

"Rule number one! Rule number one!" I hiss.

"I'm going to take a shower. After that I'll finish my dinner."

I could have kissed him if he weren't my little brother.

"See you in the morning, Mama." He hangs up the phone and says, "I did just like you said, Jingwen. I didn't lie, and I didn't break rule number one."

I know I should feel guilty about having taught my little brother to lie, even if they aren't really lies, but I'm not. Hopefully the deities—or the universe—won't send a bolt of lightning my way.

Heart. Uh. Tack.

I slap his arm. "Don't do that! What are you talking about?"

He points to the edge of the table close to the wall. A small patch of the red tabletop has been singed right off, and the very pale brown wood underneath is staring at us. "Jingwen, you forgot to put the cork mat underneath."

"Why didn't YOU remind me?"

"Because of rule number seven. I can't see what you do from all the way over there on the carpet."

I groan. Unless I can hide that scab on the table, our cake making is over. The past. History. A memory. "Hmm . . . Maybe . . ." I plonk my dictionary over the scab. "Problem solved."

"But, Jingwen, you can't leave the dictionary here forever. You'll need to use it in school."

I say, "I won't take it with me."

"Mama will ask you why you don't need it. Then what are you going to say?"

That when I try to use English, people laugh at me. That I need to make all the *Pie in the Sky* cakes because that's the only way it feels like I haven't abandoned Papa. That cakes make me less lonely in school.

I say, "Got a better idea, bald Einstein?"

He hurries out of the kitchen, then returns with a red permanent marker. He hands it to me. "You do it."

While I color over the exposed part of the table, he adds to *Rules for Making Cakes*.

Rule number ten: Jingwen is to ◖:▯ ⬠ 틴 ⬃ cake ◗𝕽

"That means, Jingwen," he says, "you're to remember to place hot cake pans and pots on a mat."

I'm so busy covering up our crime I don't call him an annoying smart aleck.

But the cover-up works. Sort of. Only if Mama looks very closely will she see that I'm a liar.

23

"Jingwen," Yanghao groans, "I'm going to—"

"Stop. Don't say you're going to puke. Don't whine. You have to finish dinner no matter what. We can't throw any food out. Our cake shop never threw away cakes, remember?" Back at our old home, on Saturday nights, before our weekly dinner outing, our family would drop by the temple with the week's unsold cakes. Mama always made Yanghao and me hand the cakes over to the temple warden, who'd thank us on behalf of the orphans who'd get to eat our cakes, which used to always make me feel a little guilty for still having parents.

"That's not what I was going to say at all." Yanghao pulls himself up.

I scream and roll away from the poison cloud. Then we laugh and laugh.

It really is more gross than funny, but all the blood in our brains has gone to digest the cake in our bellies. I've never had as much fun with him as the last two nights. Most of the time, everything we do together ends up with someone crying, usually him. Cakes make everything better.

But Yanghao and I so completely enjoyed last night's Nutella cream cake that we didn't think about how impossible it is to eat a full-sized cake in two days, plus all our meals. For our next cakes, we'll use math and division to make smaller ones.

Do smaller cakes equal smaller lies?

I like weekends because Mama doesn't have to work. Even though there'll be no cake making for two days, I don't have to tell Yanghao to take a shower or have his dinner or go to bed or make sure he doesn't somehow bang his head or break his toe. The heavy seashells that I carry in my pockets, the ones that are about looking after Yanghao, I pass on to Mama once Saturday comes.

And *Rules for Making Cakes* works. In the morning, as Yanghao and I force our oatmeal breakfast down our throats, Mama doesn't mention any cake smell in the apartment or suspect we're about to upchuck as our stomachs are bursting.

How did she know Yanghao and I made cake? The red we colored onto the table is still intact. We opened the windows.

We finished our dinners. We cleaned up. Then I see it, the evidence, the leftover eggs from last night. There the carton sits, on a shelf of the fridge door. Isn't there even more evidence in the cabinet? The leftover flour and vanilla beans and cocoa powder and icing sugar. Anna's empty jar of sugar. I glance at Yanghao, whose eyes are wide like he's looking at a ghost.

Me, I'm looking at hell. Not Mama's punishment, but the hell of not making the other ten *Pie in the Sky* cakes. "I—I didn't make . . . Nutella . . . cream . . . cake."

Mama closes the fridge. "Good." She grabs the bucket of cleaning supplies from under the sink and walks out of the kitchen. Yanghao wipes his forehead and mimes a "phew!" but I wait until she has turned into the hallway before thanking all of Ah-gong's deities.

I bought the same brand of eggs Mama always does, so she must have assumed she bought them herself. She's probably too tired to notice the little things. But then what made her suspicious?

"You lied, Jingwen," Yanghao whispered.

"I didn't. I said I didn't make Nutella cream cake last night. Which I didn't. I made triple cookie cake. From now on, all leftover cake-making ingredients must be hidden. Maybe behind your caramel-flavored milk in the fridge."

Mama always keeps the fridge stocked with those tiny boxes of caramel-flavored milk for Yanghao and me, but mostly for Yanghao. She never drinks them, so we should be safe.

When I hear the scrub-scrub-scrub of Mama cleaning the bathroom floor, I grab the leftover flour, vanilla beans, cocoa powder, icing sugar, and Anna's empty jar of sugar from the cabinet and run on tiptoes into my room. "Come on, Yanghao."

Some ingredients can be kept in my suitcase under my bed.

That's *rule number eleven.* Yanghao, keep a lookout for Mama.

I am!

We fly back to the dining table just as Mama appears. She yanks rubber gloves off her hands. "After you two have finished your breakfast, let's go to the library. I recently found out there's one a fifteen-minute walk away."

"Library!" Yanghao spurts clumps of oatmeal all over the table. "I can borrow books?"

"Of course. I'm sorry you couldn't bring your storybooks on the plane. But you can borrow so many more of them at the library. Reading is a very good way for you to improve your English, and storybooks are much more interesting than my cookbooks."

I choke. Yanghao kicks me under the table.

"Ah," Mama says, grabbing two glasses from the cabinet. "I forgot to pour you two some juice."

"Ma-Mama, how did you know we read your cookbooks?" I ask.

"You two—" She opens the fridge. "Another one here." She points to the fridge door; a cookbook lies wedged behind tall cartons of juice. "You two always leave them lying all over the house."

That giant booger Yanghao. Why did he put that book there? Rule number twelve: All cookbooks to be put away after use. We'll stack them on the coffee table.

Mama places a glass of orange juice in front of me. "That's why, at first, I thought you had made another cake."

I slurp my juice even though there's still oatmeal in my mouth. Mama said "cake." She didn't specify which cake. So

I can't say, "No, Mama, I wasn't making another cake." To me, that's a kind-intentioned lie, but Mama will think it's the worst kind of lie where someone gets hurt. I grimace and swallow. Oatmeal plus orange juice equals not delicious.

But Mama's still looking at me. Her hand is frozen, holding the juice carton. Why isn't she pouring juice for Yanghao?

I.

Like.

Books.

Mama pours the other glass of juice. "Very good, Yanghao."

It's the first time I'm grateful that Yanghao is an attention seeker.

The first thing I spot when we arrive at the library is not books. It's computers. Two rows of them. Angels sing in my head. I hurry to the only computer that's available. Yanghao tries to wedge himself next to me, but I don't scoot over. I move the mouse, and the aquarium screen saver disappears. A window pops up.

"*User . . . name*," Yanghao reads. "*Pass-Password*. What do they mean?"

Duh. My English is horrible, and I can guess what they mean. I turn to Mama, who's standing behind us. "I need a username and password."

"Let's ask the librarian."

I go with Mama and Yanghao to the long counter next to the computers. There's a woman with pink-rimmed glasses who I guess is the librarian. She's scanning some books like she's a cashier. She stops what she's doing and smiles at us.

Mama looks at me. She's not going to speak for me.

Yanghao's such a show-off.

Mama finally speaks to the librarian, after which she translates for Yanghao and me. Turns out, a library member can use the computer for a maximum of thirty minutes a day. Mama signs me and Yanghao up. We can't choose usernames, but we can choose passwords.

I log in.

Username: SL0052320W

Password: yanghaoisabooger19

Yes, I notice the username. *S l o w*. Ha. Ha. Good one, universe. But I'm lucky there's a computer available. Usually members need to book computer slots well in advance. I ask Mama how to book one so I know for next time, and she says online. Which is nuts. If I had a computer to make an online booking, I wouldn't have to go to the library to use a computer! Or, she says, the information counter is another option. Which is a bigger pile of nuts. Because I'll have to speak English with the librarian.

But anyway, there's no computer for Yanghao.

"Jingwen," Mama says, "you use it for the first fifteen minutes. Let Yanghao have the other fifteen minutes."

I give a giant sigh. "Fine."

Finally, Mama and Yanghao leave to look at books. It's been two months since I last logged in to my email, but I still remember the password. It's easy: "yanghaoisabooger" plus whatever year it is. I wonder how many emails from Xirong are waiting for me.

Two unread emails in my inbox. One is a newsletter from

my ex-school. Another is a mass birthday e-invitation from one of my ex-classmates who must have forgotten to take me off the class mailing list. As if I was never gone. As if I was never there in the first place.

I click delete, delete. Empty trash.

I guess Xirong's been really busy with school.

I Google videos of cats.

"*Please!*" Yanghao's squeaky voice pierces the library's peace. He's back at the counter, pushing a stack of books toward the same librarian with pink-rimmed glasses. As if he could understand any of those books. A few of the titles on the spines are simple enough—*Three Little Pigs, The Little Prince, Fantastic Mr. Fox*—but I don't know the rest. The librarian leans forward and speaks softly. I can't hear what she says. Wouldn't understand if I could, anyway, but Yanghao replies loudly, "*Yes!*"

I'm about to shush him when Mama goes over to the counter.

Yanghao's English sounds terrible. Sometimes the words crawl out slowly, sometimes jerkily, at other times they tumble too quickly. It's nothing like the smooth way Miss Scrappell and everyone else speak, not counting Anna, who speaks slow on purpose.

But he knows the words.

I leave the computer even though my fifteen minutes aren't up. Mama and Yanghao don't notice me passing behind them. I saunter along the shelves and shelves of Martian books. They threaten to collapse on me, so I jog away. Then I see *Cakes and More Cakes, Book of Sweets* . . . Most of the other titles, I don't understand.

I flip open *Cakes and More Cakes* and huff. Inside, it's mostly incomprehensible Martian words. I expected it, but I was hoping for a miracle. At least I can enjoy the photos of fancy cakes.

I tuck *Cakes and More Cakes* back into its place. "I'm hungry, Mama. That's all."

"We just had breakfast. You're growing up too fast. Don't you want to borrow any storybooks? Your library cards will come in the mail soon, but the librarian said you and Yanghao can borrow eight books each today."

Like I want to spend more time not understanding anything and feeling like I'm *s l o w*. "Yanghao can use up my eight."

"Come on. The kids' books are that way." She starts to walk away.

I've never seen her that way, looking like she doesn't know what to do. This is the first time I've disobeyed her. Sure, I've moaned and grumbled in the past, but I've always done what she asked. Watch out for your brother when you cross the road. Make sure your brother takes his shower. Remember what to do in an emergency.

Fighting with Yanghao doesn't count as disobeying because it's the rule of the universe that brothers will fight no matter what moms say. The few times I haven't done what Mama asked, she hasn't known that I've disobeyed. Like making cakes.

Meanwhile, Yanghao never does what she asks him to do. Stop running around near busy roads. Stop picking your nose. Take a shower. Stop flicking snot at your brother.

But she doesn't like him any less. So what does it matter if I bake behind her back? If she finds out, she'll punish me, and it'll stink to be me for a while, but in the end, it doesn't matter. She already likes me less. What matters is keeping the cake making a secret until I've made all the cakes.

I pull *Cakes and More Cakes* out from the shelf again and flip it open.

Mama says, "I'll pick out the books for you," and then the soft tep tep tep of her footsteps on the carpet disappears.

When I'm older, if I decide to be a pastry chef, I'll keep it a secret from Mama. I'll work in a cake shop but tell her I work in a bank or something. That's also what I told myself when I was little and still loved hanging out in my family's cake shop. I wanted to knead dough with Mama, cut cookies into shapes with Ah-po, slide the pans into the oven with Papa, pack all the baked goods into boxes and bags with Ah-gong, and taste-test all the cakes. I said I wanted to be like Ah-po, Ah-gong, Mama, and Papa when I grew up. That was before my classmates called me Smell Like Cake. That was also the year I wanted to be a rabbit, so my words should have been taken with a giant heap of salt. But Mama got all serious and told me no, I wasn't to toil away in a hot kitchen at odd hours.

But once Mama wasn't listening, Papa told me something else.

Jingwen, you can be anything you want. But promise me you'll study hard in school.

That way, you keep your options open. So that if you wanted to be a doctor, you could be one.

If you wanted to make cakes, you could.

Papa was so nice to me. Too nice.

Plop! A teardrop falls on the picture of *angel food cake* in *Cakes and More Cakes*. I shut the book and wipe my eyes on my sleeve.

Then I hear Yanghao yelling, "*SpongeBob SquarePants*!"

I peek through the gaps in the bookshelves.

I sidle up to Mama. "Can we go home now?"

25

All the way back to the apartment, Yanghao has his nose in *The Little Prince*, his pouty lips silently mouthing Martian words. Mama has to keep an arm around his shoulders so he doesn't walk into lampposts.

What a *booger*.

His nose is still in *The Little Prince* when we have dinner. Most of his rice ends up on his cheeks and on the table. I peek and see there are illustrations in the book. I bet he's just looking at the pictures. Then he scurries out of the kitchen and returns with his dictionary, the one with cartoon stickers all over the cover. Now he has his nose in two books. Double *booger*. Yet Mama looks at him as if he were Einstein.

After dinner, we sit in the living room and eat peeled and cut-up apples. I'm watching TV. Today's documentary is about two wolf cubs growing up, and then one of them has to leave the pack—or at least I think so. I'm not 100 percent sure, because when I say I'm watching, I really mean staring at the screen as Martian gibberish blares on. Yanghao is still *booger* Einstein. By the time I'm on my hundredth slice of apple, he's still on his first. I want to finish the plate of apples because they're turning brown, but Mama says to leave some for *booger* Einstein.

"*No! No!*" Yanghao says.

Is *The Little Prince* scaring him? Is it a horror book?

But turns out, he's just reading aloud. "*I don't want an elephant inside a . . . a . . . bo-bo . . .*"

"Jingwen." Mama waves me over. "Read with us."

"No thanks. An elephant inside a snake? What kind of prince is that? That book is for babies."

"Is not," Yanghao says. "But even if it is, I bet you won't understand it because *your English is bad.*"

I like my brother a lot better when Mama's not around.

"Yanghao, don't say that," Mama says. "It's harder for your brother because as you get older, it becomes more difficult to learn a new language."

"Then, is it really, really, really difficult for you to learn English, Mama?"

She chuckles. "I'm not that old. Besides, I learned a bit in school, and when I was learning how to make cakes a long time ago, my chef teacher spoke English. But, Jingwen, if you want to improve your English, you have to be more like your brother. You have to try to read and speak English."

I chomp on the apples like I'm a wolf tearing into its dinner. "Who says I want to improve my English?"

"How are you going to continue in school?"

I tried, Mama. I did.

"How are you going to make friends?"

It's impossible when I understand no one and no one understands me, when kids who don't know me think I'm stupid just because I can't speak their language.

Mama picks up the remote control and turns down the volume of the show I'm watching. "We're in Australia now, so—"

"Why are we even in Australia? Why did we still come here without Papa? Why did we leave him behind?"

Mama's lips turn into an O, which makes my lips form an O. I'm surprised she's surprised this is what I think. Then her O flattens into a long hyphen.

I've done it. I've upset Mama. I can't do anything right. I should say sorry.

I've always thought that maybe my brain is stupid for forgetting English words, but maybe it's actually genius level and knows something I didn't know I know until I said it out loud just then. Like in your unconscious or subconscious. Whichever. But my brain knows we shouldn't have come to Australia without Papa. It knows picking up English equals loving Australia equals abandoning Papa equals I'm a terrible, terrible son. After all, moving here was Papa's dream. It's not right we're living it without him.

26

On Sunday, Mama doesn't ask me to read or speak English. She spends the morning quietly scrubbing the bathroom, vacuuming every inch of the apartment, even the curtains, and she spends the afternoon cooking and packing our meals for next week.

I want to tell her about the cakes. When she took Yanghao and me to that café to tell us we'd be moving to Australia without Papa, if I'd been honest and told her we shouldn't go, she might have changed her mind. I should be honest now and tell her I'm making the cakes for Papa, and how that will help my English. Maybe she'll understand and even join in. I cross into the kitchen and peer around her at the noodles in the wok.

When I was little, I used to follow her around the kitchen, but I stopped when I was almost nine. Shortly after, I heard Mama say, "He used to follow me around everywhere." I froze and peeked into the shop. She was sitting behind the register, on one of the lawn chairs that had strips of colorful plastic wrapped around the metal frames. On warm days, you'd stick to the plastic and you'd have to peel yourself off the seat. She was talking to Papa, who was transferring fresh-out-of-the-oven, paper-wrapped sponge cakes from a tray into the display box. She sighed. "He's not little anymore."

What Mama and Papa didn't know was, I hadn't stopped because I'd grown up. It was because of what happened in my old school.

I was a completely different student back in my old school.

After that, I never followed Mama around the kitchen again. I was Smell Like Cake no more.

Something in the wok sizzles. Mama takes two steps to the fridge. I follow. She fetches a bottle of soy sauce and takes two steps back to the stove, but bumps into me. I step aside and bump into the trash can. Luckily it doesn't topple and spill. She says nothing. I get a box of caramel-flavored milk from the fridge as if that's what I've come to the kitchen for all along.

I linger in the kitchen. I'm going to tell Mama I'm sorry for last night and confess that I've been baking, but not just any old cakes—*Pie in the Sky* ones.

I can't bring up Papa. Mama's pockets are already full of seashells, and the biggest, heaviest ones are from me.

"Jingwen," Mama says, "stay out of the kitchen. Read the books I borrowed for you yesterday."

I step off the tiles and back onto the carpet. She'll never understand.

If she ever finds out about the cake making, even if I say all the best, most convincing words in the world, she won't understand. If she catches me, there's no second chance. I have to make quadruply sure I don't get caught. I have to lay down more *Rules for Making Cakes*.

I come up with another one just then. Rule number thirteen: All cake-making garbage to be thrown in the big Dumpster outside the apartment. Thank all the deities and the universe Mama didn't notice those empty jars of cream and Nutella and empty packets of flour and chocolate chips I'd so carelessly thrown into our trash can.

Yanghao's in the living room, still reading *The Little Prince*. This time, he doesn't read aloud. I plop down next to him, and I'm about to tell him to write down the new rule, but I catch a glimpse of an illustration in the book. It's a boy standing on a very small planet, which has tiny volcanoes and not much else.

"What's the book about?" I ask.

"A prince," Yanghao says. "The prince is from another planet, and now he's stuck in a desert on Earth, where he meets a pilot whose plane crashed in the same desert."

They're both trying to get home.

I smuggle Mama's cookbook to school again to study the recipe for the cake Yanghao and I are going to make after school. Carrot cake with cream cheese frosting.

Papa and I didn't make the *Pie in the Sky* cakes in any particular order, but he was an expert, so Yanghao and I should start with the simplest. Which we did, with the Nutella cream cake and the triple cookie cake. It was either a happy coincidence or the deities or the universe were helping us. Yanghao and I will build up our skills until we can make cakes of higher and higher difficulty level, like in a video game. The last one, the king of the cakes, will be the apple mille-feuille.

Without the book, the ten minutes before class begins would be torture. Having my eyes on the book means I don't have to stare at my classmates-not-friends chatting, joking, playing. Still, I can't help but take a peek.

I concentrate on the cookbook, feeling all jittery like I am a chicken about to be fed to those alligators. Luckily, cakes make something else all right again because once more, the book catches Ben's attention when he arrives in class.

"More cakes?" he asks.

I want to reply, *"Do you like cakes? What is your* favorite *cake? Do you like* carrot cake with cream cheese frosting?"

Ben smiles and then starts taking his books and pencil case out of his backpack. A part of me wishes he'd continue talking, but a bigger part of me is afraid I won't understand what he says, and even if I do, he probably won't understand my reply.

When Mr. Fart comes into the class, I'm curious if Ben will help me again while I'm reading aloud.

"Jingwen," Mr. Fart calls.

I'm about to stand, but he hands me the multiple-choice homework from last week, the one I did using eeny-meeny-miny-moe after making Nutella cream cake. I expect a big fat goose egg.

Surprise, surprise. I got three out of ten, which is the same score I got on my previous homework, which I spent hours on looking up the meanings of all the Martian words. All that hard work didn't matter.

Maybe things work differently here on Mars, because in my old school, I had to study like heck to change my C's and D's to A's. A few months before I turned ten, I asked Mama and Papa if, instead of a small celebration at home, I could have a birth-day party at school, like some of my classmates did. Mama and Papa agreed, but only if my grades improved. I'd never been a bigger bookworm than in those months, and it paid off.

But on this topsy-turvy planet, Newton didn't have an apple fall on his head. Not only because the gravity is much weaker, but also, all the apples have been used up by me to make apple mille-feuille.

Today Miss Scrappell teaches us about *adjectives*. I find the word's meaning by searching ten other words in my dictionary. But by the time I look back up at the blackboard, "*adjectives*" has been erased, replaced by another word, "*antecedent.*" If only she would talk much, much slower, or write out every single word she says, then I might have a chance to look up those words in my dictionary. I toss my dictionary to the edge of my desk and read the cookbook instead. I keep one ear on Miss Scrappell, listening for if she stops prattling gobbledygook or sounds like she's coming closer. But most of my attention is on carrot cake.

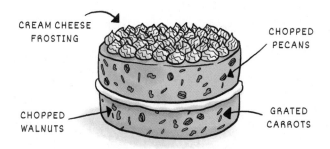

CREAM CHEESE
FROSTING

CHOPPED
PECANS

CHOPPED
WALNUTS

GRATED
CARROTS

Carrot cake with cream cheese topping was the first *Pie in the Sky* cake Papa and I made. I was nine and had been avoiding the kitchen and the shop because I didn't want to be Smell Like Cake at school. But then I saw Papa alone in the kitchen on a Sunday.

At first, it was the unfamiliar cakes that drew me to Sunday cake making, but later it was Papa who kept me there. I'd never hung out with him like that, just the two of us, and for once he wasn't in a hurry to pump out hundreds of cakes or didn't have to rush off to deliver orders or buy supplies. Still, each time after Papa and I made cakes, I acted like an ingrate and did something I shouldn't have.

Just the thought of it makes me feel warm all over like I have a fever. But I'm not ill. I'm ashamed of myself.

"*Jingwen*." Miss Scrappell walks toward my desk. I quickly slip the cookbook under my English textbook. A string of

Martian words rolls out of her mouth, but I catch only *it's been two months* and *Mr. Fart said*.

Whatever Mr. Fart said about me, it isn't a compliment. I should say, "*I am sorry.*"

She sighs and says something about *help*. Help about what, I need help to find out. "*What do you say, Jingwen?*"

What do I say about what? The weather? World news? My secret cake making? Probably none of those.

She smiles. "*Yes? No?*"

I have a 50 percent chance of being correct. "*Yes?*"

"*Good.*" She walks to the front of the class and says something. All at the same time, my classmates-not-friends flip their textbooks and concentrate on whatever page we're supposed to be reading. I flip my textbook to a random page and worry about what I just said *yes* to.

Yes, Miss Scrappell, I'll read the whole textbook aloud in front of the class.

Yes, Miss Scrappell, I'll be best friends with Joe and Max.

Yes, Miss Scrappell, I love it when people laugh at me.

I get to the school gates before Yanghao. As students trickle through, I keep my nose buried in the cookbook. A few of them glance at the book, surely curious about the non-English title on the cover. I quickly stuff the book into my backpack.

"Yanghao!" someone shouts.

Yanghao is skipping toward the gates, a girl close behind him.

SARAH

You're it!

He laughs, throwing his head so far back the silver filling on his back tooth is on exhibition for the whole world to see. The girl talks some more, but it's actually much harder to understand a little kid speaking English than an older kid. Although little kids use simpler words, they don't pronounce their words clearly, and they're always too excited and speak too fast. But Yanghao nods.

"Bye, Yanghao." Sarah skips through the gates.

When Yanghao and I ran into Sarah the other day, I assumed the most they'd ever said to each other was *hi* and *bye*. I was very wrong. If only I could speak with Ben the way Yanghao does with Sarah.

Yanghao spots me. His eyes flicker to the cookbook, and they light up. "What's today's cake, Jingwen?"

"Carrot cake with cream cheese frosting."

"Can I grate the carrots?"

I'm so surprised I only nod. My brother thinks vegetables are poison. "You don't mind eating carrot? What are you up to, Yanghao?"

"All the cakes you've made so far look a bit funny, but they're yummy. If it's not yummy, you have to finish it all yourself. But it'll be yummy because it's a *Pie in the Sky* cake, right? Papa knew what's good." With that, he skips ahead to the bus stop.

Papa didn't know I wasn't good.

Papa didn't know that each time after he and I made *Pie in the Sky* cakes, I'd stand under a very hot shower and scrub my skin really hard till it was red, and shampoo my hair three times till it was as dry and coarse as a broom. I was so clean even Mango didn't recognize my scent, and his eyes would bore into me as his tail twitched angrily. Worse, every night before school, I would hang my clean, dry uniform on a hanger outside my bedroom window to get rid of the smell of cake my uniform had absorbed while sunning dry in the courtyard behind the kitchen.

But that wasn't all the terrible things about me that Papa didn't know. After my teacher at my old school scolded me for being a hooligan while my father worked so hard, after my classmates sniggered about my being Smell Like Cake, I laughed it off. I wanted to burrow into a hole, but I laughed it off. Usually, telling the same joke over and over again very quickly makes the joke not funny. And it worked. Until a few weeks later. It was after school. I was heading to the school gates with Xirong and some other classmates to wait for our families to pick us up.

I hoped and hoped that Papa wouldn't call out to me or that my old classmates wouldn't recognize him.

I couldn't even be mad at Xirong, because he didn't know I hated that nickname. But the worst thing? I laughed along. I laughed at Papa.

I was wrong then, and I'm wrong now. Making *Pie in the Sky* cakes is not just about Papa's forgiving me for coming to Australia without him, but also about his forgiving me for being ashamed of our family's cake shop just because some kids at school called me Smell Like Cake, and for all the other bad things I've thought, said, and done. Once I've made up for all the wrong I did to Papa, my English will get way better, I'll have friends, and everything will be all right.

"Bunny and mouse caaaaake!" Yanghao sings, interrupting my thoughts. People at the bus stop stare at us.

I hiss, "Quiet! People are going to think you're cuckoo."

"Why? They can't understand me."

"That's exactly why they'll think you're cuckoo."

Rule number fourteen: After a trip to the grocery store, Jingwen and Yanghao are to hide all the ingredients in their schoolbags before they reach home.

Yanghao and I, with our backpacks filled with eggs, flour, carrots, cinnamon, pecans, walnuts, sugar, and cream cheese, rush home to make a bunny and mouse cake. But when we get there, another animal greets us: Anna's cat.

Somewhere in Anna and Mama's conversation of gibber-ish, Mama has agreed to let Ginger hang out in our apartment whenever Anna isn't home. "So the cat won't be lonely," Mama tells Yanghao.

Anna also brings a plastic tray with gray pellets, which Mama tells Yanghao is where Ginger does her business because Ginger is an *indoor cat*. When they all disappear to find the perfect corner in the bathroom for the tray, I quickly fish out the dictionary from my backpack and look up "*indoor.*"

Mango is not an *indoor cat*. He comes and goes like he's the king of the world and only returns when he wants ear scratches or food, though I'm sure he's eaten many mice while roaming the streets.

Yanghao is way too happy about this part-time pet and busies himself scratching Ginger's ears. He doesn't think about how it will disrupt our cake making. Anna says she'll come by later to pick up Ginger but doesn't say exactly when. If she comes while Yanghao and I are making cakes, even with the windows open, even if we don't invite her in and only open the door just enough to pass Ginger over, she'll smell the cake.

Once Mama leaves for work, I come up with a rule to solve this Anna trouble.

Rule number fifteen: Yanghao and Jingwen must always listen for the sound of Anna's door. When we hear it, Yanghao will immediately take Ginger back to her home, so Anna has no need to drop by ours.

Surprisingly, when I tell Yanghao this rule, he doesn't whine, "Why me?"

Maybe he wants to eat cakes so badly he doesn't dare annoy me, in case I stop making them. But I thank cakes for his obedience. He's basically my servant now.

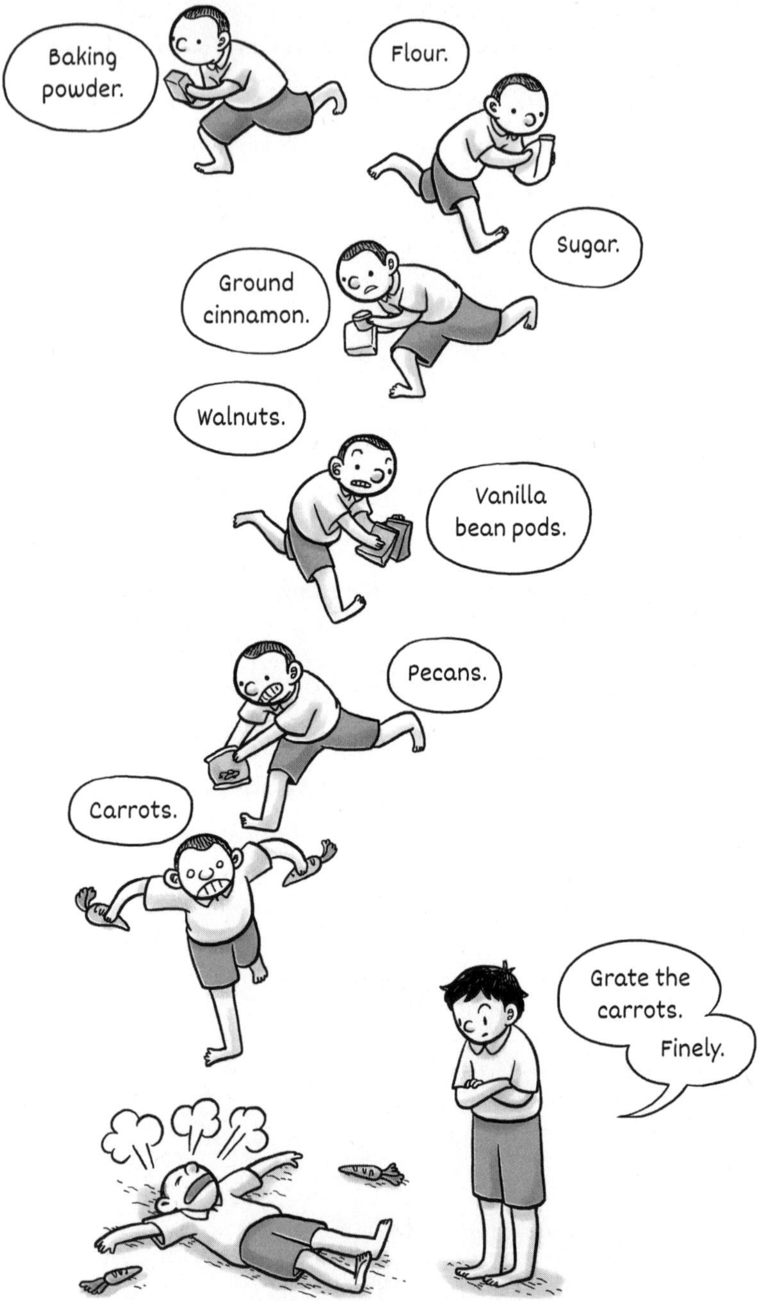
Baking powder.
Flour.
Sugar.
Ground cinnamon.
Walnuts.
Vanilla bean pods.
Pecans.
Carrots.
Grate the carrots.
Finely.

He also doesn't question me about rule number sixteen.

When the phone rings, I follow that rule by pushing all the cake-making stuff to one side of the dining table and replacing them with my homework stuff. Yanghao leaps to the sofa and switches the TV on. That way, when Mama asks us what we're doing, we won't be lying.

But tonight, when Yanghao picks up the phone, it isn't Mama on the other line.

"*Oh! My mother is not home,*" he says, and finishes the call with a bunch of other Martian words.

"Who was that?" I ask. "What was that last thing you said?"

"Some woman." He sticks his finger into the bowl of cream cheese frosting, breaking rule number five. "I said we're home alone."

I slap his arm away. "You told a stranger we're home alone? What if the stranger is a kidnapper or a burglar?"

He licks his finger, grabs the yellow notepad, and writes with the help of my dictionary.

I look over his shoulder. "*Rules for Making Cakes, number seventeen . . .* What does the next sentence mean?"

"Yanghao is not to tell kidnappers and burglars he and Jingwen are home alone."

Kidnappers and burglars are not things Mama has ever instructed me about in my lessons on Staying Home Alone for Good Sons Who Listen to Their Mothers.

I'll have to run over to Anna's house and tell her. She'll call the firemen.

I'll have to tell Anna, too, and she'll call the plumber. I'll then pay the plumber using the emergency money Mama stashed in the old coffee can in the kitchen cabinet.

But there's nothing about dealing with kidnappers or burglars or a little brother who has no common sense.

And there's nothing in Staying Home Alone for Good Sons Who Listen to Their Mothers about what to do when you eat so much cake that vomiting is very likely. I reduced the recipe to three quarters, but it's still too much carrot cake.

"We should have halved the recipe," Yanghao says as he stabs his fork into his third-to-last slice.

I want to puke.

My stomach's full, but not bursting. We haven't eaten cake for two days. "If I can finish it, then you can too."

"But I have a smaller stomach, and I finished a whole bag of gummy snakes—" He clamps his mouth.

"What? Why? When? Where did you get gummy snakes?"

He grins sheepishly, his teeth clumped with brown crumbs, and whispers, "I put it in our shopping basket, and you didn't see. Then I ate it all when you were pretending to do your homework while Mama was still home."

"Rule number eighteen: We can buy only ingredients for cakes, not gummy snakes."

His belly is so swollen from eating tons of cake that even without the button, his shorts stay up.

Yanghao and I crawl around searching for the button. After five minutes, he crawls over to me and burps cream cheese frosting in my face. "Jingwen, I can't eat any more."

"Rule number nineteen: Yanghao is not to burp in Jingwen's

face. And you have to finish your half of the carrot cake." I search under the table. "Take a break, Yanghao. Eat the rest of the cake later."

The front door creaks, and I look up from my button quest. The front door's open, and Yanghao's gone. So are two pieces of carrot cake. There's a much louder creak. Anna's door.

Crap! Crap! Crap!

I step outside and see Yanghao and Anna at her door. She holds a plate with two slices of carrot cake.

"What the heck, Yanghao?" I hiss.

"I'm not a booger. I didn't tell her we made the cake. I didn't say anything, but she assumed these are unsold cakes from *Barker Bakes*."

"What if Anna thanks Mama for the cakes?"

Anna is smiling, but her eyes ping-pong between us, as if she's trying to figure out what secrets we're keeping from her.

Yanghao grimaces. He really never thinks things through.

I sigh. "Rule number twenty: Yanghao is not to give cakes to anyone without Jingwen's okay. But after this, we might as well tear up those rules, because when Anna tells Mama about the cake, there'll be no more cake making ever."

He turns to Anna, waving his hands rapidly. *"Don't tell my mother."*

"Why not?" Anna asks.

"Because . . ."

Yanghao looks at me, but all I can come up with is one word: "*booger.*"

Suddenly he looks like he has a brilliant idea, and he turns back to Anna. "*Because you're fat!*"

If only I didn't know what "*fat*" means, then my eyes wouldn't have popped open so wide they hurt.

Yanghao must have also realized he's a booger, for his face reddens, and he clamps his mouth. Anna, too, looks like she can't believe anyone as blunt as Yanghao exists.

White lie? I must have heard wrong.

But Yanghao asks, *"White lie?"*

Anna replies in Martian, and when she's done, I elbow Yanghao. "Why isn't she angry?"

He shrugs. "She said I don't know how to tell a *white lie*. She said it's a lie you tell to save someone's feelings. She said Mama must have told us Anna has been trying to eat healthily for a long time because her doctor told her to."

He turns back to Anna. *"You won't tell my mother? About cakes?"*

Anna puts a finger to her lips. *"It's   our   secret."*

He turns to me. "Anna said—"

"I got that."

I'm on my hands and knees in the kitchen, searching for Yanghao's button and thinking about *white lies*.

The least bad type of lies, which is the kind-intentioned ones, is white.

The worst type of lies hurts others. When I get hurt, like when I scrape my knees, I bleed, so these lies must be red.

Lies of omission are when I say nothing, so they have no color. Maybe they're invisible and so it's totally okay to tell as many of these as I want.

I spot the button under the fridge. I stick my hand into that tight space and grab the button. As I pull my hand out, my palm scratches along something sharp under the fridge. "Ow!"

There's a long but shallow cut on my palm. Trickling out of it are teeny tiny drops of red, red blood.

By the next morning, the cut on my palm has almost completely healed. Even the scab is almost gone.

When I get to school, Ben and I have our routine *cakes* greeting, after which I don't expect to hear from him until Mr. Fart calls on me. My first class is Mrs. Lim's social studies. I've never understood what this subject is really about, because one lesson I'm looking at pictures of the polar caps melting and the next I'm recycling aluminum cans. But at least Mrs. Lim treats me very, very well. She never calls on me or even looks at me. I spend her class doing some math—dividing the recipe for our next cake, white chocolate Swiss roll, in half. That way, we won't have to give any to Anna and risk her mentioning it to Mama.

I'm halving the white chocolate when someone passes me a blue sticky note. The someone has adult-sized hands and wears a jade bracelet like the one Ah-po never takes off her wrist. It must be Mrs. Lim.

Slowly, I look up, trying my hardest not to grimace, because whenever I do, Yanghao always says I look like I'm making a someone-in-the-room-just-farted face. But Mrs. Lim has already walked back to the front of the room and is sputtering more Martian words to the rest of the class. All I catch are *tree* and *Thursday*.

I read her sticky note. Only these words are on it:

family tree

remember

This must be the *tree* that she's talking about and the one she kept mentioning in class last week, but I didn't *remember* until now since I have no interest in gardening. *Thursday* is only two days away. That's not much time to grow some kind of fruit tree.

As I reach for my dictionary to find out what kind of fruit *family* is, Ben slips me a note.

I must still be wearing my someone-in-the-room-just-farted face. I write *yes* and give him a big smile as I pass the note back to him.

I think that will be the end of it, but then Ben scribbles something else under my *yes*.

What kind of Swiss roll?

What is "*Swiss roll*"? What's Ben asking me? What kind of hairstyle? What kind of face? What kind of alien? I reach for my dictionary that's sitting at the edge of my desk but quickly draw my hand back. If I use the dictionary, Ben will know that I don't know some of the words he's written. It's no secret my English is horrible, but using the dictionary to understand a one-sentence note is like taking a megaphone and shouting, "Look at me! I'm *s l o w*! I'm *s l o w*!" What if he tells Joe and Max? I'm only 70 percent sure that Ben's nothing like them. But I want to talk to him like Yanghao talks to Sarah.

Ben slips another note onto my table: *Yummy?*

He must be talking about cakes, since that's all we ever really discuss with each other. He can't be anything like Joe. Cakes only bring smiles.

I decide to trust that cakes are lucky and reach for my dictionary. Turns out, *"Swiss"* has something to do with Switzerland the country. Maybe Ben thinks I'm from there. But before I flip the page to check *"roll,"* I see *"Swiss roll"* at the bottom of the definitions for *"Swiss."* Ben's talking about the cake that the cookbook is open to.

I double-check the spelling and write, *white chocolate.* Then I pass the note back to him.

He replies with *Cool!*

I write back, *Do you like cakes?*

Like? LOVE!

I want to ask him what's his favorite cake, but I have no idea how to say "favorite" in English, so I reply with:

Mr. Hart = Mr. Fart

He's definitely nothing like Joe.

Yanghao is a lot like the king of all boogers.

We're passing by the playground after our trip to the grocery store when he says, "Ten seconds!" Before I can figure out what he's talking about, he bolts up the plane-shaped tower. He disappears into the tube slide. I hear a loud CRACK and a second later, he swooshes out the bottom of the slide on his back. With his backpack on, he looks like an overturned turtle.

> I . . . forgot . . .

> in . . . my . . . bag . . .

Rules for Making Cakes number twenty-one: Yanghao is not to carry eggs ever again.

Later, the moment Mama leaves for work, I stop my award-winning acting as the most studious kid and fish out the ingredients—including a new, unbroken carton of eggs—from my backpack. But Yanghao stays put on the sofa, hypnotized by SpongeBob.

"Let's bake tomorrow," he says without taking his eyes off the TV. "I'm still full from yesterday's carrot cake."

"It's already almost twenty-four hours after. You'd have pooped all that out."

"I don't eat enough fiber."

"Carrot is fiber."

"Jingwen, you're a booger."

I don't need him to bake with me, so I start on my own. Brushing the rectangular pan with butter, weighing out sugar, sifting flour, separating egg yolks . . . I find out Yanghao's more of a hindrance than a help in cake making. The recipe's steps are suddenly done at the speed of light. When I take the cake out of the oven, the serial egg killer and greedy, lazy bum finally shuffles into the kitchen.

Turns out, I'm not as good at math as I thought I was. I used the wrong ratio for the ingredients.

Our third try goes perfectly.

I move on to cutting strawberries into halves.

"Why did Papa choose to put fruit on top of this cake? I thought he didn't like fruit," Yanghao says after he has written rule number twenty-two: *When Jingwen is using the knife, Yanghao is to keep his hands in his pockets*.

"What do you mean? Of course he liked fruit."

"But when Mama cut up fruit, he always ate only one piece and then told us to finish it all up."

"Ah," I say, surprised. I've never thought about this. "That was because we could afford only so much fruit, and he wanted us to have more."

"What other things did Papa pretend not to like so we could have more?"

"Fried chicken, BBQ pork, tea eggs . . ." These are things that I'm only now realizing, too. I prattle on and on. There are a lot of words I have to say about Papa, and Yanghao's the only one who understands them.

"I'm broke," I say, looking at my wallet, open and hungry like the beak of a baby bird. "Only two dollars left. My piggy bank is empty. You have to pay for the ingredients from now on."

Yanghao pauses midchew. White chocolate cream is all around his mouth like he's Santa. "I'm poor. My piggy bank is empty."

"How can that be? You've never paid at the grocery store ever."

"I pay at the school cafeteria. During recess."

"But Mama packs us lunch."

"I buy drinks and snacks."

I chomp on my last bite of Swiss roll. "No wonder your button popped."

Yanghao plops his last two slices of Swiss roll onto a clean plate. Even though we halved the recipe, he says he can't finish his and insists on going over to Anna's to share.

"What about the money for tomorrow's cake?" I ask. "It's tiramisu."

He shrugs. "We'll get five dollars each on Sunday. We can wait until next week to make tiramisu. It's not like it's an emergency." With that, he leaves me alone in the apartment.

But it is an emergency! I don't want to waste tomorrow,

Thursday, and Friday. The longer we take, the more time I'll have to think about Joe and Max and all the Martian words I don't understand, and the greater the chance Mama will find out our secret.

The ten dollars in total Yanghao and I will get on Sunday will be enough for only one tiramisu. Then we'll have to wait for the next Sunday for more money. One cake a week. Eight weeks for eight cakes. That's eight weeks of everything not being all right. This is definitely an emergency!

Emergencies remind me of Staying Home Alone for Good Sons Who Listen to Their Mothers.

I throw open the cabinet that has cans of tea. I grab the only coffee can, which is a bit rusty. Mama brought it from our old home.

Two hundred dollars of emergency money. It's shocking a plumber costs that much, but that's definitely enough for the remaining eight *Pie in the Sky* cakes that I have to make.

I tuck five ten-dollar bills into my wallet. It feels heavy. Not with cash, but with wads and wads of useless receipts.

I stash the coffee can back in the cabinet.

This is not stealing. This is borrowing for an emergency. I'll return it as soon as I get my allowance. I repeat these three sentences until Yanghao comes back and fills my brain with his chattering about Anna and Ginger.

"We can make tiramisu tomorrow," I interrupt him. "I forgot I still have money in my drawer." There's no point telling anyone about the emergency money.

Luckily, he hasn't found out about my loan. He's actually pointing at the burn mark on the table. Patches of the red ink have rubbed off. Slivers of light wood shine through.

I'd have killed him if my heart hadn't stopped.

"Better cover it before Mama finds out," Yanghao says.

When my heart starts pumping again and I'm resurrected from the dead a minute later, I get the marker and block out the spots of light.

33

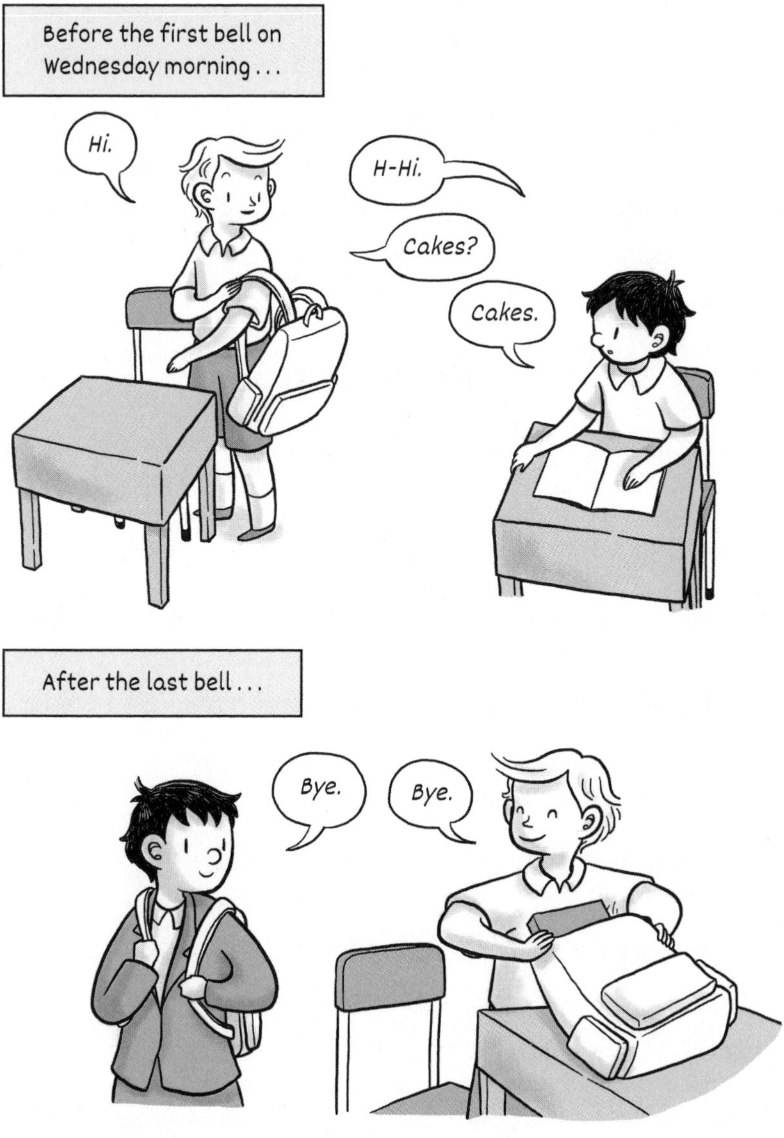
Before the first bell on Wednesday morning . . .
Hi.
H-Hi.
Cakes?
Cakes.
After the last bell . . .
Bye.
Bye.

While we wait for the bus, Yanghao drones on and on about Sarah. Sarah said this book is very good. Sarah said that movie is funny. Sarah said the sun rises in the east. I tell him to whisper, but then he sounds like a snake hissing and about to bite. People at the stop are staring. I tell him to shut it, or we're not going to get coffee for the tiramisu.

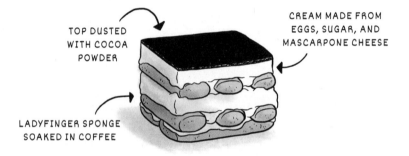

TOP DUSTED WITH COCOA POWDER

CREAM MADE FROM EGGS, SUGAR, AND MASCARPONE CHEESE

LADYFINGER SPONGE SOAKED IN COFFEE

We don't have any coffee at home. Mama doesn't drink it because it makes her hands tremble and then it's hard to make cakes. The grocery store has instant coffee, but Papa said tiramisu needs the best coffee, which the instant kind he usually drank is not. So he'd gone to that café, the one where Mama later broke the big news to Yanghao and me, and bought three cups of good coffee. He'd taken all of us along, too, and while everyone else ate their egg tarts, Papa and I watched the good coffee trickle out of a big, noisy machine.

I've spotted the same machine inside *Barker Bakes*, next to the display case, but getting the good coffee there is risky because Mama may find out, and then Yanghao and I will have to tell a real lie about why we bought coffee. Luckily, as we're standing in the bus station racking our brains, two policemen with coffee cups pass by.

I walk in the direction the policemen came from, and Yanghao follows. There must be another place that sells good coffee nearby. Sure enough, there's a little cart with the same noisy machine.

"*Espresso*," I say to Yanghao, handing him a ten-dollar bill. "Get three cups."

I could have bought the coffee, but the man behind the counter might ask why a kid is buying bitter black coffee, which isn't a crime, but then I'd have to reply in English. Besides, Yanghao is happy to do it. He skips all the way to the cart.

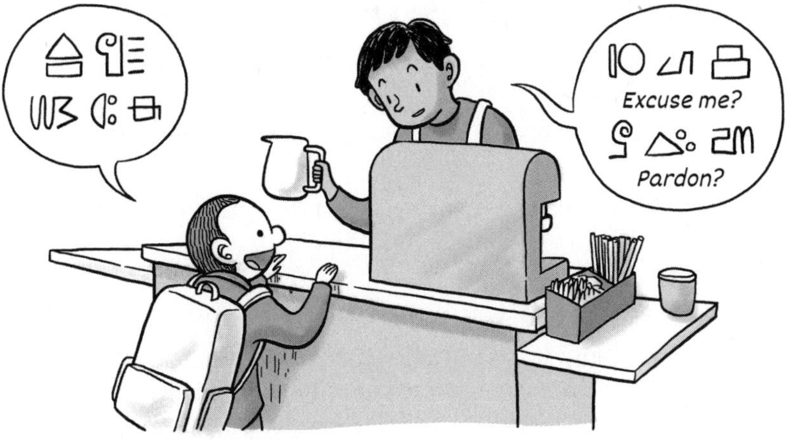
Excuse me?
Pardon?

Yanghao's English still sounds like our CR-V when it needed a tune-up, but he keeps repeating himself until the man gets it.

Today, only one rule is added. *Rules for Making Cakes number twenty-three: Yanghao is not to make poop-shaped cakes.*

> I said long strips, like fingers.

> That's why they're called ladyfinger sponge.

The coffee turns us into vampires.

Not really. Not the sleeping-in-a-coffin part. Or the blood-sucking part. Just the staying-up-at-night part.

I finally understand why the name "tiramisu" means "*pick-me-up,*" to cheer someone up or make someone more energetic, and why when Papa and I made tiramisu, he let Yanghao and me have only one slice each.

At about midnight I give up staring at the ceiling and stare at the TV instead. Yanghao joins me. It's nothing but infomercials for a bunch of weird home appliances. If we had credit cards, we'd have bought an all-in-one rowing, cycling, jogging, weight-lifting machine; an all-in-one chopping, julienning, dicing gadget; a cloth so absorbent that if you wrap it around a grape, it will suck out all the moisture and you'll get a raisin— all things to make your life awesome. I could have just told them to make cakes.

An infomercial comes on about a tree that has five different kinds of fruit growing on it, and I remember the tree I'm supposed to grow for Mrs. Lim.

"Yanghao, are any of those fruit on that tree a *family*? I need to bring a *family tree* tomorrow."

His eyebrows take turns going up and down, like a seesaw, and I know I must be way off in my guess. "*Family*" must not have anything to do with fruit. But it's too late. Yanghao falls off the sofa laughing and then rolls around on the floor cackling. He only shuts up when I warn that he'll wake all the ghosts.

"*Family*," Yanghao says, "is you, me, Mama, Papa, Ah-po, and Ah-gong. And Mango."

"Ah," I say. My homework is to make a chart that shows the people in my family, from the very old to the very young. I get up to go to the kitchen, where my backpack is, but Yanghao grabs my T-shirt.

"Where are you going?" His eyes are wide and darting left and right.

"I was only joking, dopey. There are no ghosts here."

"I know!" he says, but when I continue to the kitchen, he leaps off the sofa and sticks to me like a sweaty T-shirt.

I don't think there are ghosts in the house, but when Yanghao is scared, it gets me scared, so I let him be my shadow. I draw a family tree, which is easy because I did one in my old school some time ago. A time when Papa was still actually part of the tree. I cough to clear the lump in my throat and tell Yanghao to give me the Martian words to use.

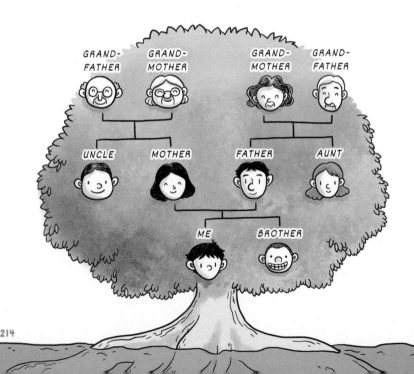

I stare at "*father*" on my family tree. There has never been a word this familiar and this strange at the same time.

When we finish, Yanghao and I go back to watching TV. It's the latest we have ever stayed up, and it is glorious. We are fools. Mama has been working this shift for two months, and we've only just thought of disobeying our bedtime.

At three in the morning, we shuffle back into bed because Mama gets off work in half an hour. I'm still awake when she comes home. She pads into the room, and I pretend to be asleep. I feel her kiss me on the forehead and tuck my hands under my blanket. I hear her do the same for Yanghao. She yawns a big yawn and shuffles away. I peek one eye open and get a heart attack; she hangs her head so low her silhouette looks headless.

If only I could tell her about the cake making, then she could have a slice of *pick-me-up*.

35

In the morning, I pay the price for last night's glory. I'm so sleepy I almost drown in my congee. Which doesn't worry me as much as the possibility of Mama asking why I'm so tired.

It's very hard keeping my eyes open during class. There's little difference in how much I learn when I'm asleep or awake, but I don't want the teachers to call on me. Besides, I have to be on my feet for social studies. I copy what Ben and all my other classmates-not-friends are doing and place my family tree on my desk. Then I join everyone else to roam around the classroom and study one another's projects. Everyone else's family trees are so much better than mine. They have color and photographs. Mine looks pitiful. Which is quite fitting, anyway, since my family tree is broken and forever missing an important branch.

But I'm too tired to dwell on this. While shuffling along like a zombie, I fall asleep and bump into someone in front of me.

Maybe I am a zombie. Or as scary as one. I'm definitely feeling as lifeless as one.

Thankfully, I don't have enough energy to worry about Joe, and I shuffle back toward my desk. That's when Ben's project catches my eye.

MY GRANDFATHER AND ME

Ben's and his grandfather's hands are all blurry, probably because they didn't stop working their dough for the camera. But their smiles are as clear as the tears that have somehow formed in my eyes.

I immediately rub my eyes while pretending to yawn.

For the rest of school, I wonder if Ben's grandfather, who looks even older than Ah-gong, is still actually on the family tree. Or has he been chopped off, too?

I also wish I had a photograph like Ben's, of Papa and me making a cake. In English, there are things called *past tense* and *present tense*. Miss Scrappell and Anna talked about these before, and even though I still get confused sometimes, I can say I wish I'd known when Papa was still an *is* that he'd soon be a *was*. I'd have taken so many photographs. If I'd known, maybe I wouldn't have been so ashamed of him and our cakes and done those terrible, shameful things. And now I wouldn't be so ashamed of being ashamed.

Thinking these thoughts makes me have to pretend to yawn again, but luckily Ben distracts me by passing a note that says *What is today's cake?*

I write back, *Blueberry cheesecake.*

Yummy!

Cool!

Yanghao also pays the price for last night's coffee glory. When I meet him at the gates after school, he has a big red splotch on his shirt. I almost die, thinking he's gotten hurt, but he says he nodded off during art class and spilled red watercolor paint on himself. I laugh and laugh because I'm too sleepy to differentiate funny from not funny.

"Jingwen, you're a booger," Yanghao says, running for the bus. "Hurry up, slow turtle. It's blueberry cheesecake time!"

But after Mama leaves for work, I end up being the only one making blueberry cheesecake.

Cakes ...

At least he's not breaking any *Rules for Making Cakes*.

I don't know how, but somehow, even though he isn't helping at all, Yanghao gets flour on his cheeks. Little brothers are simply magnets for messes and troubles that big brothers have to clean up. I huff and use a damp paper towel to wipe his face. He doesn't even stir. His flour face powder reminds me of that photograph of Ben and his grandfather.

All along I've been thinking Ben talks to me about cakes because he just likes eating them, like everyone else in the world, but maybe he likes making them just as much. Maybe cakes mean a lot to him because of his grandfather, just like with me and Papa.

· · ·

The oven timer rings, jolting Yanghao awake. "*Cakes!*" he yells. I tell him to wipe his drool as I open the oven. A puff of smoke billows out, and the top of the cheesecake is burnt to a crisp. Coughing, I look up at the smoke alarm in the living room, right above the coffee table. If the alarm goes off, I'll have to run over to Anna's for help or call the police. Either way, in the end I'll have to explain what caused the fire, and that'll be the end of cake-baking magic.

But there's no loud beeping. The only din comes from Yanghao.

My second blueberry cheesecake is perfect, but it turns out to be the kind of cake that's two slices maximum. Anything more, and Yanghao and I would have puked. He gives Anna the two slices he has left.

I decide to give my two leftover slices to Ben, partly because cakes also mean a lot to him, and partly because the button on my shorts is already screaming for mercy. It won't be nice if the cheesecake rots in my bag overnight and gives Ben the trots, so I pack the cakes into a plastic container and stash it next to the knob of butter behind the caramel-flavored milk boxes, to stuff into my bag in the morning when Mama isn't looking.

WHAT IS SUPPOSED TO HAPPEN ON FRIDAY MORNING:

But What Actually Happens on Friday Morning: I stop at *hi*.

Because what if he asks other questions? I won't have the replies ready, and I'll be staring at him like a frozen booger. I can't possibly prepare all the questions and all the answers. The number of questions he could ask is infinite. My English is very, very finite.

So the cheesecake stays in my bag, and Miss Scrappell

comes in to start the day with English. But when recess comes around, I'm still not brave enough to be an English-speaking booger, and I'm left alone in the classroom, with my lunch and the cheesecake. The cake doesn't smell sour, so it should be safe to eat. I take my first spoonful and open the cookbook. I've read this book front to back a couple of times, but it's better than staring at the empty room or looking out the window at the other happy students.

That's when Ben comes back in. He says he *forgot* something—he didn't say "*something*," but another word I didn't catch—and rummages in his bag. He glances at the cheesecake. "*Cakes?*" he asks.

I nod and pretend to be busy flipping pages. Offer him some, Jingwen. Come on! Come on!

Ben fishes out his wallet from his bag.

I get to the tiramisu page and remember how Yanghao spoke to the man behind the coffee cart. I cannot be lousier at speaking English than my little brother.

Doyouwantblueberrycheesecake?

Ben nods and drags his chair to my desk. I hand him my unused fork. He takes a bite and looks at the open cookbook, his eyes focused on the cake pictures, not the words that would be Martian to him. I flip it to the first page and pretend to read it again. When I think he's admired the pictures long enough, I flip the page. When we come to the page on Semolina Cake with Orange Syrup, Ben points to the picture and says, "*This was my grandfather's favorite cake.*"

Was. Past tense.

My family was as sad as I was when Papa became a past tense, but knowing that someone else in the world, someone outside of the family bubble, has gone through a similar experience somehow feels different. Grandfathers and fathers are different, and I really don't know much about Ben, but suddenly, in this vast universe, there's someone who is different but the same as me.

Just knowing that someone else understands is enough.

"*What is 'fa-favorite'?*" I ask.

"*It means my grandfather liked this cake the best.*"

After that, Ben and I finish the cheesecake without saying another word.

Chiffon cake isn't more difficult to make than all the cakes Yanghao and I have made, but I rank it the seventh-hardest *Pie in the Sky* cake because of caramel sauce. When Papa and I made it, it took us three tries. I wonder how many Yanghao and I will need.

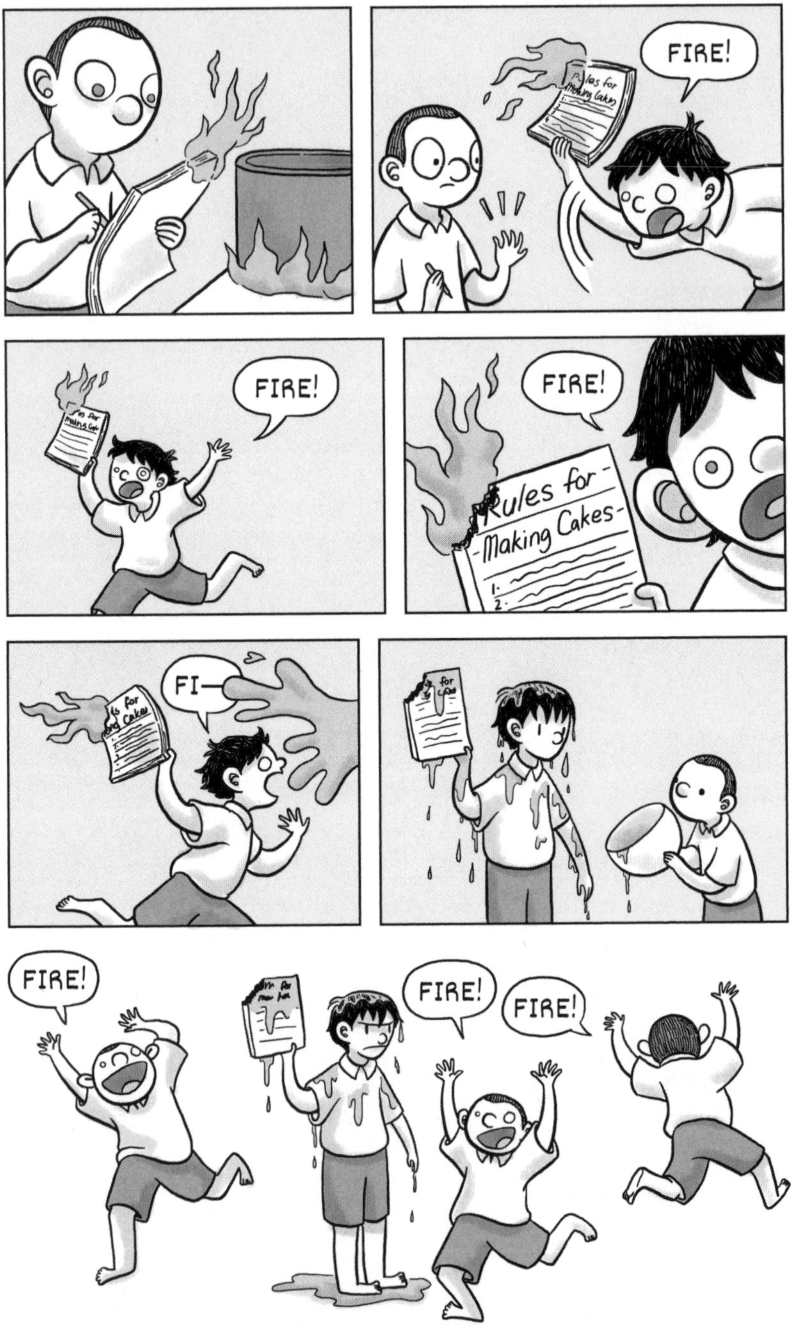
FIRE!
Rules for Making Cakes
FIRE!
FIRE!
Rules for Making Cakes
1.
2.
FI—
FIRE!
FIRE!
FIRE!

On the fourth try, we finally get the caramel sauce right, and Yanghao is in heaven. After the caramel has cooled, he keeps breaking rule number five and turning his fingers into caramel lollipops.

"Rule number five is for batter. This is not batter," he says between licks. "Jingwen, from now on, let's add caramel sauce to all the *Pie in the Sky* cakes. Imagine rainbow cake with caramel sauce."

I pour the caramel sauce over the chiffon cake. "I've told you. Rainbow cake is not a *Pie in the Sky* cake."

But he's not listening.

Saturday and Sunday pause everything.

Luckily, Mama's too tired to take Yanghao and me any-where. I've been dreading another outing like last Saturday's library trip.

So we stay in. Mama cooks and cleans. Yanghao reads *The Little Prince*. I flit between helping her, annoying him, and watching animal documentaries.

All the time, I wonder if the little prince and the pilot ever find their way home.

39

At the start of math class, Miss Scrappell says something that makes all my classmates-not-friends scuttle about. They chat excitedly as they drag their own chairs to other desks.

I'm the only one who's still, like a broken-down car in the middle of a big, busy road. Most of my classmates-not-friends are now gathered in twos and threes. I have no idea what we're doing, but I'm not supposed to do it alone.

Joe calls Ben and beckons him over. Max has already joined Joe at his table. Ben walks toward them, but he stops before he gets there and says something. I can't hear him over the din. Neither can Joe and Max because they shout, *"What?"*

I wish I had a phone to take a picture of Joe and Max, looking like they've had a bucket of ice poured on them.

Ben turns to me. "*Is that okay?*"

Yes! Yes! Yes! I clear my throat. "*Okay.*"

Miss Scrappell talks some more, walking up and down the rows of tables. As she passes my desk, she places an envelope on it. The envelope is the long white kind that you know contains important letters like the phone bill or something from the bank. On it is typed *Meixin Chen*.

A letter for Mama? What did Miss Scrappell write to Mama about? That I'm failing class?

I slip the envelope into my bag. Miss Scrappell catches my gaze, glances at Ben, back at me, then turns to the board.

Among the Martian words on the board, I recognize these: *Group, 2 to 3 students in a group, fractions and decimals, to be, math, in four weeks, you can make, or, whatever you want.*

When Miss Scrappell whirls around to face the class again, she looks at me. I get the feeling she's written all those detailed instructions just for me. I jot them down, even though I have no plan to look up those words. I don't have time, not until I've made all the cakes.

I'm still on the second *group* when Ben rips a page off his notepad and hands it to me. He has copied all the words for me.

With cakes, nothing can go wrong.

40

But something does go wrong with cake number eight.

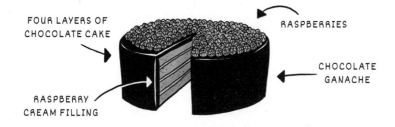

FOUR LAYERS OF
CHOCOLATE CAKE

RASPBERRIES

CHOCOLATE
GANACHE

RASPBERRY
CREAM FILLING

The chocolate raspberry torte looks perfect but ends up in the garbage because I used salt instead of sugar. And of all days, Yanghao chose today to not break rule number five: *No sticking dirty fingers in the batter.* By the time we cut the cake and take a bite and spit it out, it's almost eight o'clock, and we don't have enough raspberries to make another one.

Yanghao suggests we make a chocolate caramel torte.

"No, the *Pie in the Sky* torte is chocolate and raspberry."

"Why raspberry? It's sour. Caramel's better."

"Papa said the tartness of the raspberry cuts through the richness of all that chocolate, so you won't feel sick after a few bites." All of a sudden, the mention of Papa makes my nose burn. Maybe because my nose knows I haven't made a *Pie in the Sky* cake today. "Tomorrow, Yanghao. We'll make it tomorrow."

Yanghao trudges out of the kitchen. "Rule number

twenty-six," he shouts. "Jingwen is to remember *SUGAR* is sweet and *SALT* is salty."

I start washing the dishes. "Tomorrow, I promise."

There's no reply, so I check if Yanghao is sobbing somewhere. He's on the sofa, his nose in *The Little Prince*.

Missing out on making a *Pie in the Sky* cake matters much more to me than to him. Missing out on making the chocolate raspberry torte matters much more to me than to him.

Because he doesn't know.

That it was the last cake Papa and I made together.

That Sunday, as Papa and I assembled this torte, he suggested we make rainbow cake the Sunday after next for my birthday party at school. It was the big party that he and Mama had agreed to throw for me because I'd gotten all A's after years of mostly C's and some D's. In a way, I should have thanked Xirong and my other classmates for calling me Smell Like Cake and laughing at my family's broken-down CR-V. I'd only studied harder because I wanted to prove to them my family's cake shop wasn't that shabby, my family wasn't that poor, and we could afford a big birthday party.

But then there was Papa asking me if I wanted, for the most important thing in my big birthday party, a homemade cake. A cake that wouldn't make anyone go, "Wow!" at first sight.

I said all my other classmates who had birthday parties in school had colorful cakes with fancy shapes and edible figurines on top, and their party favors were colorful stationery or lollies.

He said his rainbow cake was colorful.

I said I wanted a SpongeBob SquarePants cake, and my classmate who had his birthday last month had bought one from a fancy cake shop in the city and everyone thought it was the most awesome cake ever.

Papa said how about a *Pie in the Sky* cake, then.

What other terrible things did I say to Papa?

41

Our cake shop's cakes are cheap.

Rainbow cake is fancier.

But still cheap.

Pie in the Sky cakes are definitely fancier and more expensive than both, but it wouldn't have mattered what Papa offered to make for my birthday party. Not even if it was ten-tiered with fireworks shooting out of it. I didn't want my old classmates to see anything he had made. I wanted a cake we purchased from another shop. Anything my classmates knew we spent money to buy.

I quickly finish Mr. Fart's homework, not bothering to check any words in the dictionary. I don't even double-check my math answers. Then I heat up dinner for Yanghao and me, take a shower, and go to bed.

I can't wait to make Papa's chocolate raspberry torte.

I can't wait for tomorrow to come.

Tomorrow comes, but the cookbook that has the recipe for chocolate raspberry torte is gone.

When I get to school, the book isn't in my backpack where I always keep it.

"*What did you forget?*" Ben whispers. He slides his pencil case toward me. "*Pen? Eraser?*"

I shake my head and stuff my things back into my bag.

At recess, Ben points to the door and asks, "*Want to come with me for lunch?*"

I shake my head and fish out my lunch box from my bag. He smiles that smile where instead of curving up, the corners of his lips curve inward. A disappointed smile that could also be a pitiful smile. Then he leaves me in peace.

I should have gone with him, but my mind is in a whirl. Which I know is silly because that booger Yanghao is probably the one who took the cookbook. Or maybe I've really forgotten it, and it's on the coffee table.

Without the cookbook, I have to watch the students in the courtyard for my lunchtime entertainment. As I munch on a fried prawn, I spot Yanghao below.

Then I spot Ben.

I shouldn't have turned down Ben's invitation.

Suddenly, despite the din, the crunch of the fried prawn seems very loud.

42

"I didn't take it! Ididn'ttakeitIdidn'ttakeitIdidn'ttakeit!" Yanghao doesn't let up all the way from the school gates to the grocery store to buy the ingredients, and along the whole walk home.

Mama gives us a kiss each. We smile widely and promise her we'll be good boys and we'll finish homework as well as dinner. We wave good-bye and wish her a great day at work. Once the door clicks shut, I scurry to the kitchen and sweep aside the homework I was pretending to do. I get ready to make chocolate raspberry torte, while Yanghao looks for the cookbook.

"It's the one with the chocolate cake on the cover," I say.

"It's not in the living room." He gallops toward the bedrooms. While I'm wondering how many grams of ground almonds are needed, he shouts, "I can't find it! I can't find any of the other cookbooks either."

"Did you look properly?" I huff and hurry to Mama's room.

Yanghao's on all fours. He has pulled out the suitcases under Mama's bed and is peering under the bed. "I did."

I toss Mama's blanket and pillows aside and check the drawers in her wardrobe before hurrying to my room. I toss my and Yanghao's blankets and pillows aside. I look under my bed. Just a suitcase. No cookbooks.

I storm to the living room.

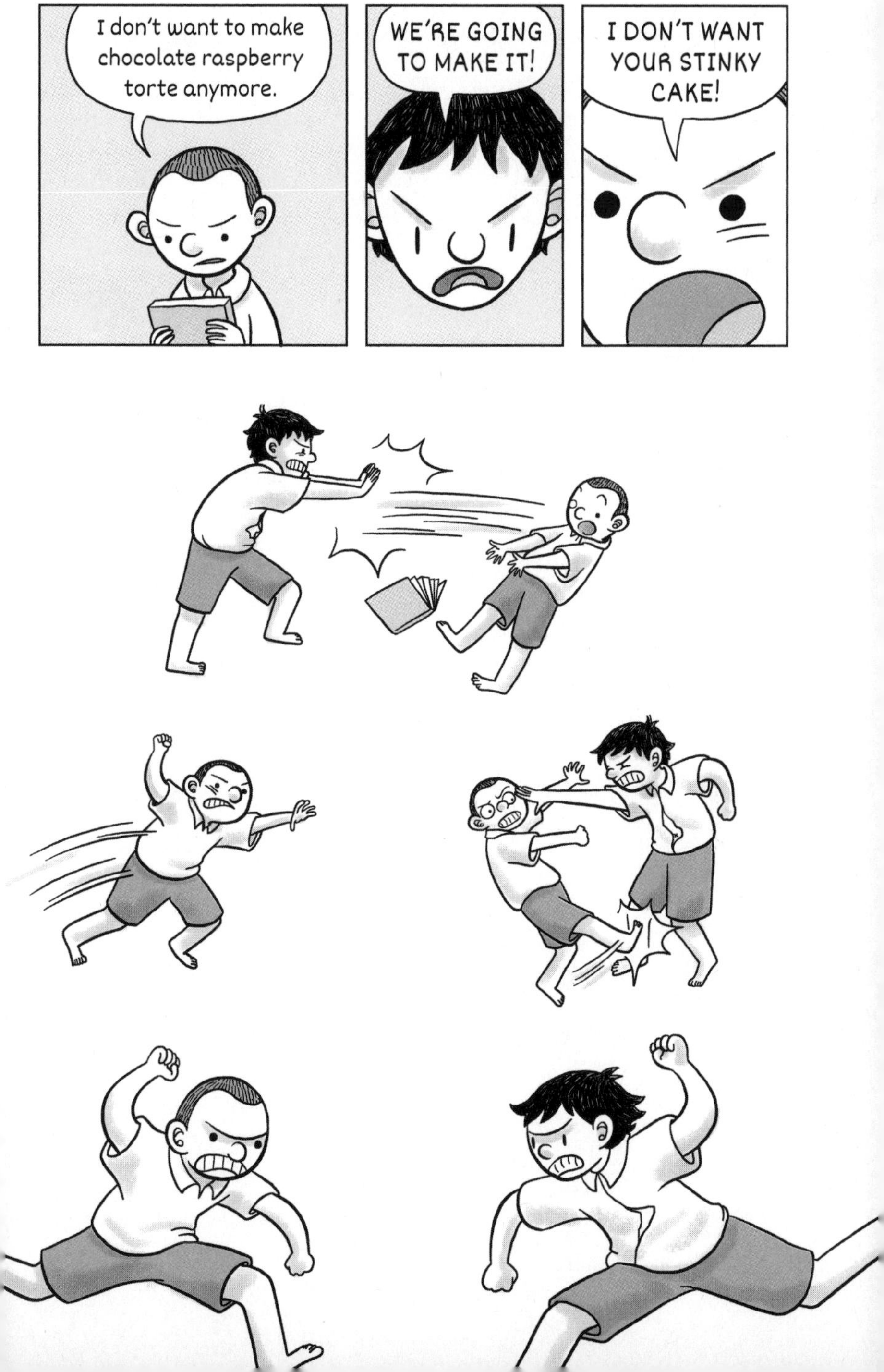
I don't want to make chocolate raspberry torte anymore.
WE'RE GOING TO MAKE IT!
I DON'T WANT YOUR STINKY CAKE!

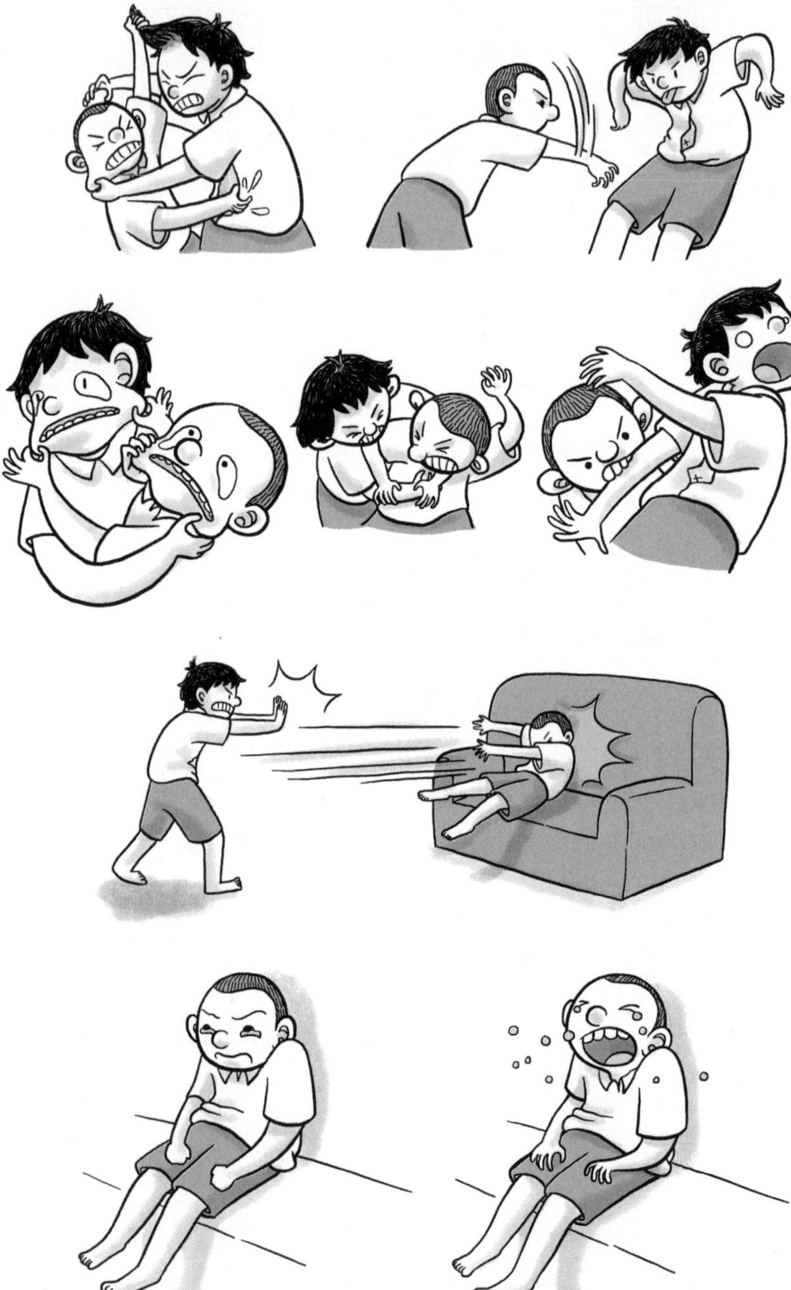

I win. "Stop crying. You started it."

That makes him cry louder. He sounds like a thousand cats caterwauling.

Someone knocks on the door, but before I can reach it, I hear keys jingling and then the door opens. Anna. When did Mama give her our keys?

"*Jingwen, what is happening—Oh, Yanghao!*" She rushes past me and plops down next to Yanghao. He doesn't resist when she pulls his head to her bosom. But still he cries and cries. Snot is everywhere.

Serves him right. He started it. I rub the spot where he bit my arm. It's wet with saliva, warm, and throbbing.

Anna asks me something, but in her panic, she forgets to speak to us like we're snails and, in the process, proves that I am, indeed, a snail because I don't understand her. But Yanghao wails, points to me, and says something to Anna. His words are so garbled I can't even tell if he's speaking Martian.

"*There, there, Yanghao.*" Anna speaks like we're snails again. She gets up, bringing Yanghao with her. "*Let's go to my house and have some cookies.*"

Without any hesitation at all, Yanghao leaves with Anna. Now that he has Anna's cookies, he doesn't care about the chocolate raspberry torte we won't be making today, the torte Papa and I made fifteen days before my tenth birthday. My nose tickles. I shouldn't think about Papa.

She holds the door open for me. *"Jingwen?   Come   on."*

Then it was fourteen days before my tenth birthday. Now my nose is on fire. So are my eyes.

"Come   over   later   if   you   want.   All   right,   Jingwen?" The door clicks shut.

Then it was thirteen, twelve, eleven days before my tenth birthday. Now my chest is on fire.

It was a nice afternoon.

Not rainy.

Not cloudy.

Papa wasn't home.

I was home.

Yanghao was home.

Mama was home.

Ah-po was home.

Ah-gong was home.

Even Mango was home.

Papa never came back.

A policeman came instead.

Ten days before

my

tenth birthday.

I rub my nose raw, but thoughts of Papa keep creeping back into my brain.

I race to my backpack under the dining table and throw open my dictionary. I pick random words. *"Avoid." "Deny." "Escape." "Hide."* But the words can't push out thoughts of how I was a terrible son to Papa just before he died.

The phone rings.

It's Mama. "What are you boys doing, Jingwen?"

"I'm doing homework." It no longer matters if I lie. "Mama, where are your cookbooks?"

"I'm keeping them in the cake shop."

"Why? We like to—uh—read them."

"I like to practice baking here whenever I have a break. *Barker Bakes* has the best baking equipment. Anyway, I found one of my cookbooks in your schoolbag. Why did you take a cookbook to school? You should read those books that I borrowed for you from the library instead."

I say nothing.

"What's your little brother doing?"

"Uh . . . he—"

The door opens, and Yanghao comes in. His eyes are swollen.

"He's not doing anything, Mama," I say, turning my back to him.

"Have you two had dinner?"

I spin around, but Yanghao has already escaped into our room.

"What's going on, Jingwen? You two aren't fighting, are you? You have to give in to Yanghao. You're the older one."

"We're not fighting now."

"Good. Make sure your brother finishes his dinner. I'll see you in the morning."

I hang up the phone and rub my back. Feels like a bruise. Maybe I deserve that punch, but did he have to hit so hard?

Yanghao doesn't say a word to me the rest of the night. After I heat up our dinner in the microwave, he finishes his dumpling noodles quietly. He watches SpongeBob without roaring with laughter or repeating English phrases he catches or asking me if I've finally finished my homework. He takes a shower without my needing to nag him. Then he disappears into our bedroom.

I don't say a word either.

When I get to bed, Yanghao is already asleep.

The space between our beds is only an arm's length, but it's as vast as the dark sky outside the window. He looks so, so small.

I get up and tiptoe the two steps over to his bed. As gently as I can, I untangle his blanket from where it's all scrunched up around his knees. I pull it up over his shoulders. His eyes move under the eyelids, but he doesn't make a peep.

Mama must know Yanghao and I fought. First, Yanghao's eyes are still swollen in the morning. Second, he and I don't talk as we eat breakfast, and not even as she walks us to the bus station. Third, we do everything she asks us to without question or complaint.

It isn't the first time—and I bet it won't be the last time—that Yanghao and I have fought. She doesn't press us about it, though. She must be enjoying our complete obedience while it lasts.

Even after all that wailing, Yanghao hasn't lost his voice. During recess, I spy on him from my usual window perch. He chatters away to Sarah. She replies without scratching her head, so his English must be getting pretty good.

I notice a smudge on the window. Here I am on one side of the glass, and everyone else is on the other.

I have to come up with a way to make that chocolate raspberry torte. But no matter how I squeeze my brain, I come up empty.

When the last bell rings, I wonder if he'll be waiting for me at the gates. Surely that crybaby wouldn't dare take the bus by himself.

As I pack my bag, Ben says, *"Want to go and have some cakes, Jingwen?"*

"*Ben*," Miss Scrappell says. I don't catch what she says next.

"*Is Jingwen in trouble, Miss Scrappell?*" Ben asks.

"*No. See you tomorrow, Ben.*"

Ben smiles at me and joins the rest of my classmates-not-friends trickling out of the room. Some of them glance at Yanghao and me, but Max holds my gaze, a look of either pity or mockery on his face, until he disappears out of view.

I don't want to lose the see-who-could-keep-quiet-the-longest contest, but I have no choice. I whisper to Yanghao, "What are you doing here? What did you do?"

He stomps his foot. "Not me. I was waiting for you at the gates when your teacher called me. She asked me to translate. She says you're supposed to stay back for an hour every day after school so she can tutor you in English, but you've never stayed behind. She thinks it's because you don't understand what she said."

What I'd give to be able to poof! into thin air.

"She said she'd been trying to call Mama. I think I spoke to her on the phone once when she called and Mama wasn't home. Anyway, she got hold of Mama at home this morning. She also said Mama said I have to wait for you. I think that's what your teacher said, anyway. She speaks a little too fast for me." He turns to Miss Scrappell. "*I told him, Miss Scrappell.*"

"*Thank you, Yanghao. Why don't you—*" I don't get anything else Miss Scrappell says, but Yanghao does, because he gives a King-Kong-sized sigh and trudges to a table at the back of the room.

"*Let's start, Jingwen,*" Miss Scrappell says, smiling and patting my desk as if we're about to play the funnest board game ever. I sigh. She's so truly excited about teaching me that I can't even hate her for putting me through this torture.

But maybe Yanghao hates her a little bit because waiting for my tutoring to end must be torture times infinity. Throughout the lesson, he keeps distracting me.

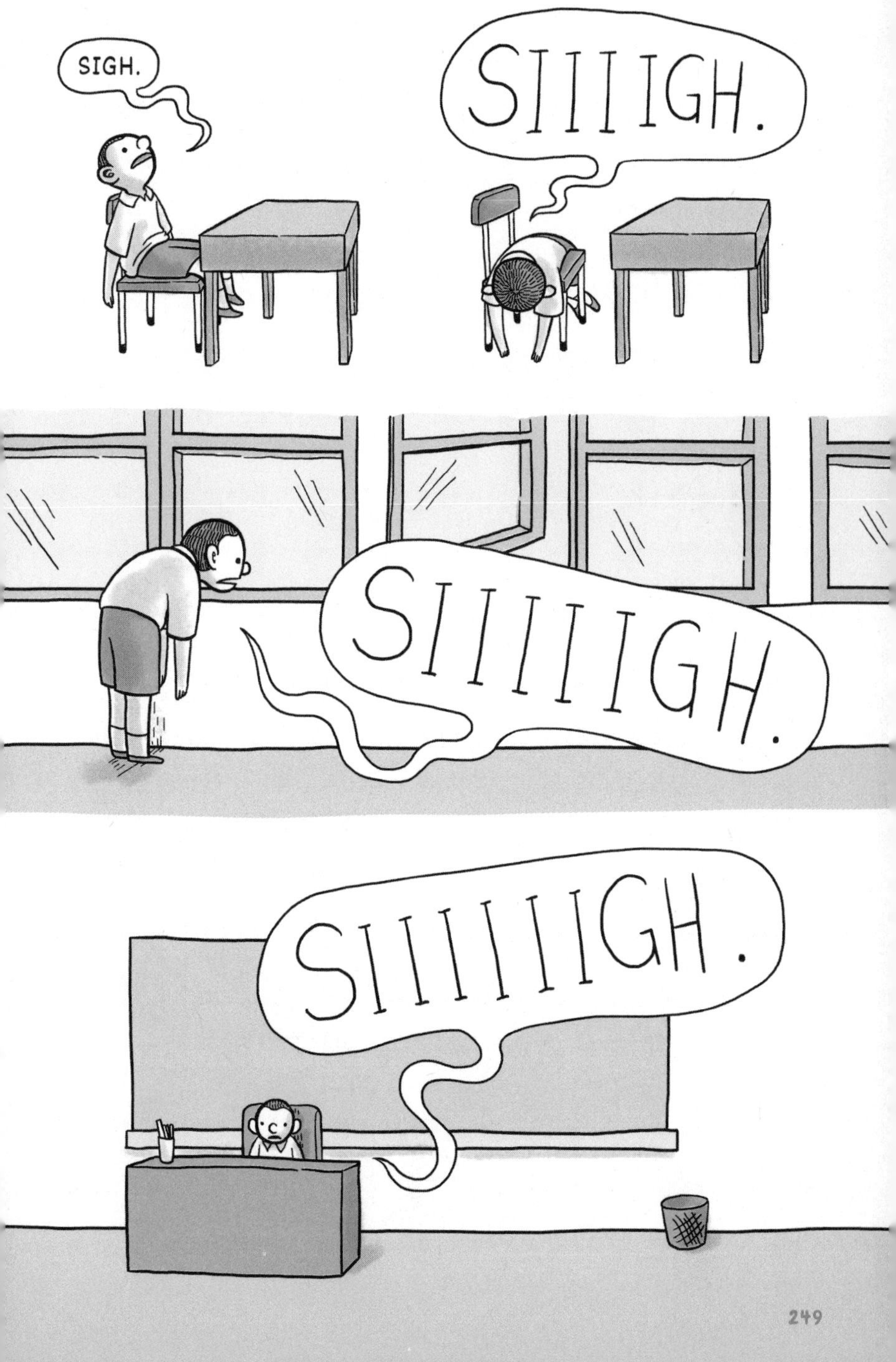
SIGH.
SIIIGH.
SIIIIGH.
SIIIIIGH.

Miss Scrappell isn't distracted at all and keeps correcting the sentences I write.

I going read book.
I going read a book.
I am going reading a book.
I am going read a book.
I am going to read a book.

I look up.

45

Now that he's won our see-who-could-keep-quiet-the-longest contest, Yanghao is once again a chatterbox. "It's so booooooor-ing! I have to wait for you like that every day," he says as we get off the bus at the station.

"Not every day." I pause. "There's no school on Saturdays and Sundays."

He rolls his eyes. I'd never tell him this, but he's too cute to pull off eye rolling.

"You don't have to wait for me. You can go home on your own, you know. Take the bus on your own."

"Ma-Mama would never allow that. I'm only nine."

"Almost ten," I say, and I realize he's now the same age I was when Papa died. That makes me a little grateful, that I had more time with Papa than Yanghao did, and then that makes me sad.

Suddenly, Yanghao guffaws and points to my arm.

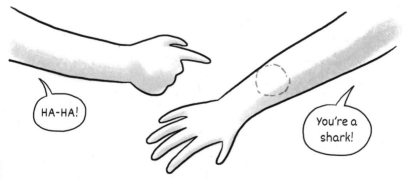

HA-HA!

You're a shark!

He chortles into my sleeve.

"Don't get snot on me," I say, and that sends him into another bout of giggles. Suddenly, as we pass by *Barker Bakes* on our walk home, he stops laughing and points into the window. "That's your classmate, right?"

On the other side of the glass, Ben stands by the display case. What a coincidence, that he asked me to get cakes from Mama's workplace. I ask Yanghao if he wants a cake.

"But we don't have the cookbooks anymore."

"No, I mean we can buy a cake—" That's when I see Ben is with someone else.

Are Ben and Joe good friends? Joe did ask Ben to join his math project group, but that doesn't mean they're good enough friends to hang out after school. I turn on my heels.

"What about the cake, Jingwen?" Yanghao asks, running beside me.

"Another day. Now, be quiet."

"Ten minutes, Jingwen." Yanghao tugs at my snotty sleeve

when we reach the playground. "Mama won't know since she already left for work by now, and we can't make cakes anymore anyway. Please?"

"No." I continue walking. I don't hear his running footsteps or his "Jingwen, wait!" but he must be right behind me, sulking.

But when I reach our apartment building, I don't see him in the reflection of the glass door. Oh no. Oh no. I dash back where I came from. We must have walked this route a million times. He can't possibly have gotten lost from the playground to home, can he? If anything happens to him, I'll be blamed for sure.

He's not at the playground. Oh no. Oh no. Oh no. Then, among the kids scrambling up and down like monkeys, I spot Sarah, she-whose-words-are-golden, whooshing out of the tube slide. Sure enough, Yanghao whooshes out after her. He sees me and gives me a pleading look.

"Ten min—" Before I finish, he's zoomed up the steps to the airplane-shaped tower. I crawl into the space under the tower and twirl the giant tic-tac-toe cubes. Yanghao can play for ten, fifteen minutes. Mama won't know. If Yanghao and I go straight home after my tutoring, the earliest we'll reach home is four thirty, and she'll have just left for work. As long as we're home when she calls around seven, we're safe.

"*No way, Joe.*" The familiar voice cuts through the din. It's Ben's voice.

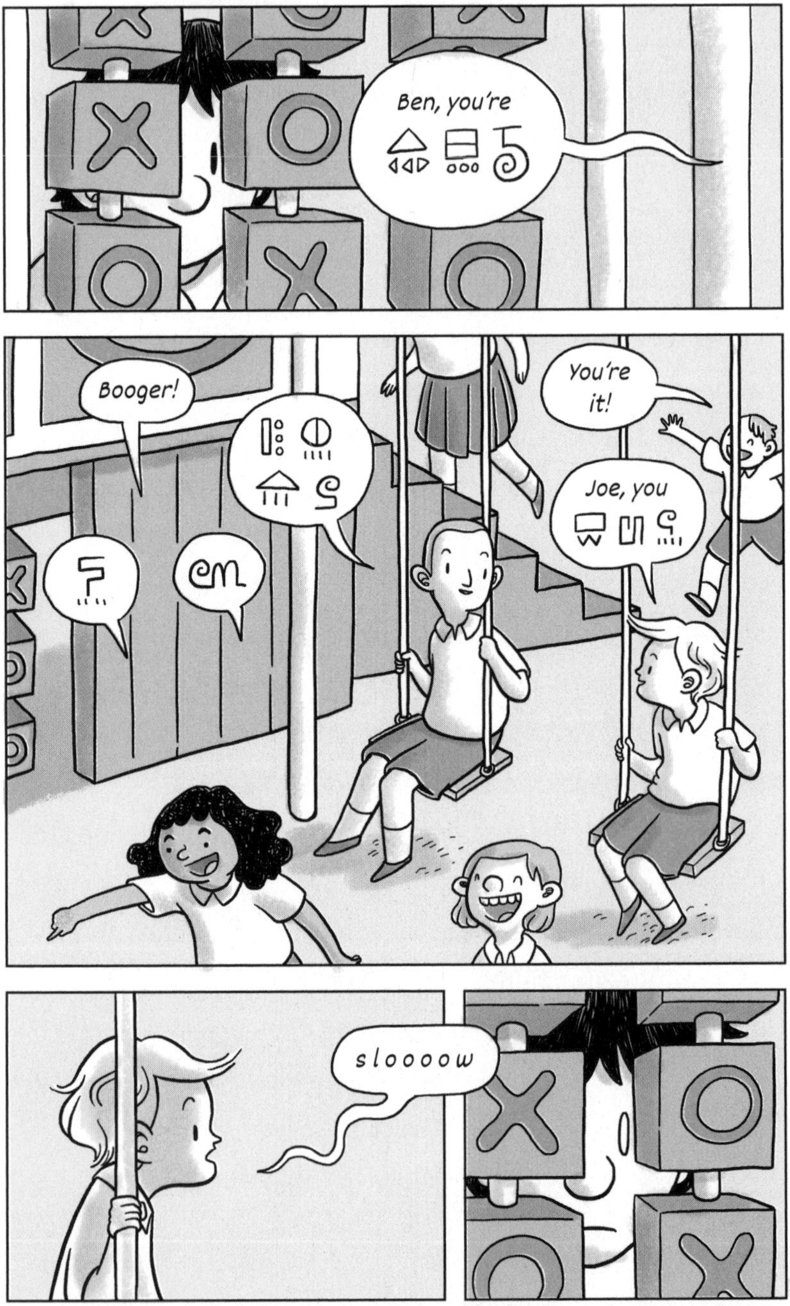
Ben, you're
Booger!
You're it!
Joe, you
sloooow

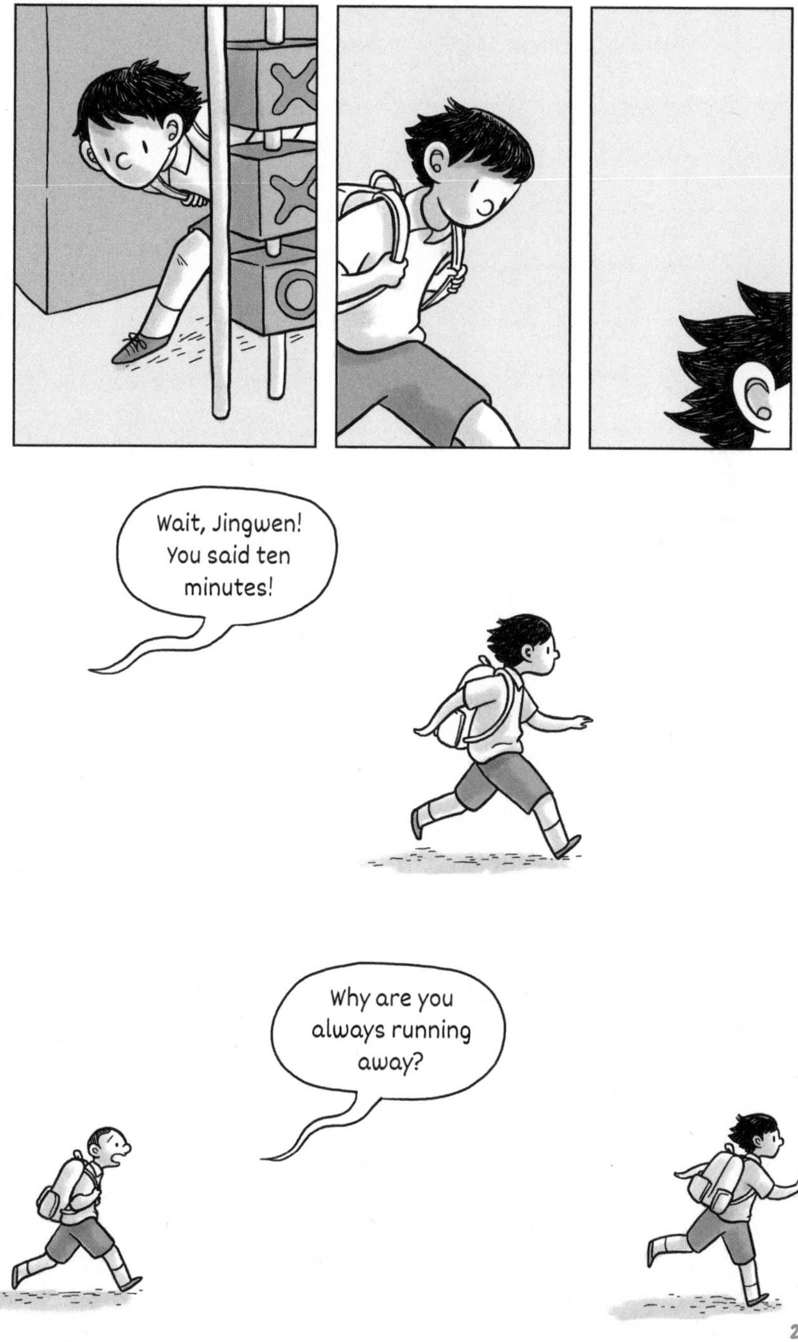

Wait, Jingwen! You said ten minutes!
Why are you always running away?

46

I need a distraction. "What happened to the prince?"

Yanghao squints at me. "The little prince? Why do YOU want to know?"

"Fine. Don't tell me."

"The little prince lives on an asteroid, but he got stranded in the desert, and he wants to go home. But he doesn't know how to."

"You told me that. What happens next? What happened to the elephant? And the very big snake?"

"They're drawings the author made. The author is the pilot who met the little prince in the desert. There are a sheep and a fox in the story, though."

"Does this desert have a zoo?" Stories with animals are the best.

Before I can find out if that desert did have a zoo, there's a flash of orange.

GINGER!

"You scared me," Yanghao says. "I didn't know you were here."

"Anna must have gone out and dropped Ginger off before we came home."

"How come she only came out now? We've been home almost an hour."

"Who knows. Cats are weird." I crumple up a piece of yellow notepaper and toss it. Ginger leaps off Yanghao's lap and chases after it. I pick it up and toss it again. After several rounds, I hear a creak and a bang. Anna's home.

Yanghao picks Ginger up. "I'll take her home."

I sigh. "That rule doesn't matter now. There's no cake making to hide."

Yanghao thinks for a moment, then continues toward the door. "I don't mind taking Ginger home." Off he goes. I hear Anna's door creak open again, then the muffled sounds of Yanghao and Anna talking, then the door bangs shut.

I want to march over and ask Yanghao what he's doing. Mama never gave him permission to hang out at Anna's house. I want him to annoy me. I want to not be alone with my thoughts.

There's no cake making to push out the hundreds of *s l o w* s swirling in my mind. I picture a chocolate raspberry torte dropping from above the *s l o w* s. But instead of dispersing the words, the cake smashes into bits. Then the *s l o w* s swarm around the bits like vultures.

I need to find a way to make that torte.

Yanghao leaves me alone for two hours.

Friday morning, there's a slice of cake in a plastic container on Joe's desk. It has three layers of puffy puffed pastry, like an apple mille-feuille has, except instead of little cubes of caramelized apples for filling, this one has cream and a thick slab of something brown.

Whatever it is, I hope it's overbaked and dry.

Ben says *hi* to me, but I pretend not to hear him, and then Miss Scrappell comes in for English class.

At recess, Ben places a plastic container on my desk. *"For you."*

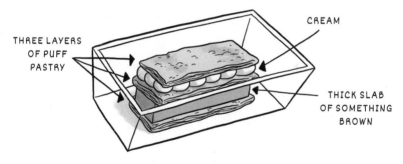

THREE LAYERS OF PUFF PASTRY

CREAM

THICK SLAB OF SOMETHING BROWN

I only nod, and Ben leaves.

What did Ben and Joe put in this cake? Laxatives? Did they spit in it? Is all of Ben's niceness a lie? Which kind of lie would it be? White, red, or colorless? If it's red, it'd all be a ploy: Pretend to be friends with the *s l o w* boy and then pull a prank on him.

Pretend to be interested in the *s l o w* boy's love of cakes, then use it to humiliate him. Ben and Joe would get away with it because the *s l o w* boy wouldn't figure out the cake made him sick. Even if I did, I couldn't tell anyone.

I march to the front of the class where the garbage can is, open the container, and flip it upside down. The puff pastry crackles as the layers break apart. I still have no idea what that thick slab of brown is. It looks like very hard jelly. Maybe Ben and Joe want me to break my teeth.

I turn around.

My first thought is to say *sorry*, even though Ben is the bad guy. But a very strange look is on his face. He continues to his desk and fishes out his wallet from his backpack. Then he leaves.

I march down the rows of tables back to my desk. There's something on Joe's desk: the container of cake.

I have so much I want to say to Ben.

But I don't have the English words.

During math class, Miss Scrappell has all of us sit in our groups and work on the project. Even though I'm still mad Ben called me *s l o w*, he's the closest thing I have to a friend, and I'm very relieved when he pulls his chair to my desk. But for that whole hour, he doesn't speak. He just writes numbers on pieces of colored paper.

At the end of school, he doesn't say *bye* to me, and I don't dare to be the first to say it to him. Surely he won't say it back.

During my after-school English tutoring, Miss Scrappell places an old-fashioned flip phone on my desk. No, wait. It's an electronic dictionary.

Booger. I got that. Which surprises me.

The first thing I do when I wake up on Saturday morning is tell Mama I have a craving for chocolate raspberry torte. I also want to ask if we could make one together, but I don't want her to suspect I'm still secretly making cakes, so I say something that sounds perfectly innocent.

Yanghao spends most of the day shuttling between our sofa and Anna's house, with his nose buried in *The Little Prince*.

Mama spends the whole day cooking a week's worth of lunch and dinner for Yanghao and me. She makes woks and woks of noodles with dumplings.

We are stuck.

In all different ways.

With nothing else to do, and nobody else to do anything with anyway, I have no more excuses not to do my homework. Since the little table in the kitchen is covered with onions, garlic, and Mama's other cooking stuff, I drop my schoolbooks on the coffee table and sit cross-legged on the floor.

When Yanghao comes back, he plops onto the sofa and buries his nose in *The Little Prince*. I'm about to comment he's taking forever to finish that book and if he returns that book late, he'll get a fine from the library, but then I think about the computers there.

I smack my own forehead. I can Google recipes! I need a library card for that, and mine hasn't arrived yet. Besides, I'm not speaking to a librarian to book a computer. Luckily, I have another idea.

"Yanghao," I whisper. "We can copy recipes from the cookbooks at the library. We can't ask Mama to take us now because copying cake recipes will look suspicious, and she'll interrogate us, then I'll have to lie. Really lie. We'll have to wait till Monday."

I'm about to call him a booger when he points to a white envelope on the table.

"What?" I ask. "Did Ah-po and Ah-gong reply already?"

No, the letter can't be from Ah-po and Ah-gong because there are kangaroos on the stamp and my name and address are all typed up. I rip the envelope open. The letter is written in Martian, but I recognize the first words: *Dear Jingwen.* Stuck to the bottom of the letter is a colorful card, like one of those cards Mama uses to withdraw money from the bank machine but won't let me use—a library card!

"I got mine, too. Mama checked the mail this morning," Yanghao whispers. "But how can we use the library's cookbooks? They're in English. Can you—"

"I can use a dictionary."

"Or if I know, I can just tell you."

I can't help but raise my voice. "*Booger.*"

"*Booger?*" Mama peeks her head into the living room. "I suppose I should be glad you're using English, Jingwen, even if it's not a very nice word."

Her eyes are red and teary from chopping onions, and I'm a little glad. It's better that she can't see me clearly.

Turns out, I don't have to wait forever. On Sunday, Mama surprises me. She takes Yanghao and me to *Barker Bakes*. She got permission from her boss for the three of us to use the fancy kitchen to make a cake together.

I say, "It's much, much bigger than it looks from outside."

Yanghao nods and wipes the drool off his face.

Mama chuckles. "The café part at the front is tiny in comparison because *Barker Bakes* is mainly a catering business. We supply cakes for events like birthdays and weddings, and also other cafés. Come on, let's bake a cake."

"A chocolate raspberry torte!" I say before Yanghao can make any suggestions.

She opens the cookbook she stole from my schoolbag. "Chocolate raspberry torte it is."

Mama measures the ingredients and handles everything to do with the hot oven or stove. She doesn't know I'm now a professional at doing those things, so she only tasks me with mixing the batter. Mama knows Yanghao can't even be trusted to remember to put on underwear in the morning, let alone help with baking, so he's only in charge of being a general nuisance, which includes sticking his fingers into the batter and picking at cake skin. All the rules broken.

We're about to assemble the four layers of chocolate sponge between raspberry cream when Mama's boss arrives.

"*Hello,*" she says. "*You two must be Jingwen and Yanghao.*"

"*Hello!*" Yanghao replies enthusiastically.

I force a smile and concentrate on stirring the bowl of chocolate ganache. Hopefully she won't ask me anything that forces me to reply in long sentences. *Yes* or *no* questions are all right, if I can understand the questions in the first place.

But I don't need to be nervous, because Yanghao hogs all the attention. "*I love your kitchen,*" he says.

What did she ask Yanghao and me to do? Does she want us to make a coffee cake? But Yanghao hops off the stool and follows Mama's boss out of the kitchen, with Mama close behind, so I guess not.

"Come on, Jingwen," Mama says. "We'll finish the cake later, together."

I sigh and do as I'm told. Mama's boss beckons us to sit at a table in the café before walking off.

"Are Yanghao and I going to drink coffee, Mama?" I ask.

"No," Yanghao answers. "You and I are going to have chocolate milk shakes. Mama and Heather are going to have coffee."

Heather? Like *weather*? Is that Mama's boss's name? When did she mention her name? When did she say *chocolate* milk shakes? What is "milk shake" in English? *Milk* something. I huff. Yanghao probably heard wrong.

But Heather does return with *chocolate milk* something and coffee. Yanghao almost-yells, *"Thank you, Heather!"* like she's given us a chest of gold coins.

"So, Jingwen and Yanghao." Heather sits down next to me. *"How do you like it here so far?"*

"I love chocolate milk shake." Yanghao slurps on his drink extra loudly.

Heather chuckles, then turns to me.

"Yes," I say, and slurp on my drink. *Milk shake*, I repeat in my head. *Shake* the *milk* to make a *milk shake*.

She fires off another question. *"How's school?"*

This isn't a *yes* or *no* question. I could lie and say *good*, but before I open my mouth, Yanghao saves me.

I can't tell if he's lying.

Mama beams like Yanghao has invented a vaccine for cooties, while I gnaw on my straw. But wait, Yanghao's not done turning her into a lightbulb.

So Yanghao has more than just one friend?

Yanghao is still the tiny bean sprout whose chin barely clears the table, but suddenly I don't recognize him. His voice sounds the same, but everything he says is unrecognizable. He's just across the table from me, so close I could kick him if I wanted to, but somehow the space between us feels as wide as the distance between Australia and our old home. Vast, vast oceans.

Mama and Heather make the oceans even wider when they speak to Yanghao in Martian.

My head hurts from all the translating, and I've been pretending to suck at my empty glass for way too long. I whisper to Mama that I'm going to pee, then I sneak off. She's so caught up in Yanghao's one-man show, she doesn't even tell me where the bathroom is.

I slip into the kitchen, then turn back and look through the little round glass window in the door. Once again, I'm stuck on the other side of the glass while Mama and Yanghao sail far, far away.

I stack the chocolate sponge layers, with raspberry cream in between. My tenth birthday cake had four layers with cream in between, too.

I pour the chocolate ganache over the stack. My tenth birthday cake had a layer of blue fondant, with little pink starfish all over.

On the top of the torte, I place a circle of raspberries. My tenth birthday cake had figurines of SpongeBob and his friends.

The cake that Mama, Yanghao, and I are supposed to make together, I build it up myself.

50

Starting at nine o'clock on Monday, I'm a ghost.

Not an awesome ghost with spooky powers.

But a ghost no one can hear or see.

At three in the afternoon, I become visible, but still a ghost who's neither dead nor alive. Miss Scrappell has all her attention on me as she teaches me all about *conjunctions*.

for

and

nor

or

but

yet

so

La-ti-do.

At least the electronic dictionary is much easier to use and doesn't cause paper cuts.

As soon as tutoring is over, I come to life again. I wish I were dead, though, because on our way to the library, Yanghao burps so loud that everyone nearby spins around to stare at us. He says his burp smells like the chocolate milk shake he had yesterday afternoon and would I like to smell it.

Once at the library, he says if I want to use the computer, he can talk to the librarian to make a booking. No, thanks. I don't need my little brother doing things for me. Also, I don't want to confirm that Xirong hasn't emailed me.

Yanghao returns fifteen of the sixteen books he's borrowed on his and my library accounts—he isn't done with *The Little Prince*—so we can borrow fifteen cookbooks.

The books I pick are those whose titles I understand, including *Short and Sweet*, *Sugar Rush*, *The Perfect Cake*. I also choose *Cakes and More Cakes* and flip through it until I reach a picture of a Neapolitan mousse cake.

Yanghao points to it. "That's the cake we're making today."

"I can see the picture, *booger*," I say.

Booger, booger, booger.

Is that the only English word you know?

Today Yanghao and I are free to break rule number four-teen, the one about packing the cake-making ingredients into our schoolbags, since Mama won't be home.

Carrying the shopping bag filled with flour and tubs of cream, I open the door of our apartment.

Heart. Uh. Tack.

I step back and shut the door, but I've only closed it half-way when Mama sees me. "You boys are home."

Behind me, Yanghao yips. I twist my arm and hold the bag of cake-making ingredients toward him. "Ma-Mama, doesn't your work start at four thirty?" The clock above the TV says it's a little after five. Yanghao takes the bag from me, and I hear his padded footsteps as he backs away from the door. Phew!

"No," Mama says. "I now work from eleven P.M. to nine A.M. Heather heard me calling you two during my break and asked if I wanted to change my shift. I won't be here to help you get ready for school, but overall, I'll have more time with you. And I've prepared a bath for you both. When you're done, you can have some of these prawn crackers." The crackers in the oil spit and crackle. "Come in, boys. What are you doing standing there?"

"Prawn crackers!" Yanghao jostles past me. He doesn't have the plastic bags. I step inside and close the door slowly, scanning the stairway. Where did he hide them?

"After-school tutoring went overtime, Jingwen?"

I nod. I'm telling the worst kind of lie. I can't think of how or who this lie would harm, but still I feel just like when I stuck my hand under the fridge to retrieve Yanghao's button and ended up bleeding.

Mama makes Yanghao and me take a bath. She sits on the rim of the tub and lathers his hair while he makes a plastic dinosaur waddle across the sea of foam. I scratch my palm. It's itchy even though the scab is long gone.

"How's school, Jingwen?" she asks. "When I spoke to Miss Scrappell, she said you're making progress. Although she says—and I agree—that you have to read and speak English more if you want to grasp it."

I ladle foam onto my head. "I can speak English. *Yanghao is a booger.*"

He looks up at Mama. "*Jingwen is a big booger.*"

"You boys—" she begins, but the phone rings, and she leaves.

"Yanghao," I whisper, "where did you hide the grocery bags?"

"On the stairs. Up on the fifth floor."

"I hope no one steals them. I'll get them once Mama's gone to work, but how are we going to make cakes now that she's home?"

He dunks the dinosaur into the foam. "Tomorrow?"

"Didn't you hear what Mama said? She'll be home every weekday until eleven o'clock."

The dinosaur peeks its head out of the foam. "We can ask Mama to make cakes for us on the weekend, then."

As he makes the dinosaur skip across the foam, he doesn't notice my shooting daggers at him, so I lean back and slide forward until the foam is up to my nose.

"Yanghao?" Mama peeks into the bathroom. "Sarah called. She asked if you wanted to meet her at the playground. I hope you don't mind, but I asked her if she wanted to come over and play instead. Her mama will bring her over here soon."

"Yes!" Yanghao jumps up, sending waves of sea and foam lapping against my face.

I think I'm drowning.

51

Yanghao and Sarah play their board games too loudly. Their squeals and shouts in Martian zoom all the way from the living room and pierce through the door of my room, where I sit on my bed trying to read *Cakes and More Cakes*. All that racket makes it hard to concentrate, especially when I have to use my dinosaur-age dictionary to look up many, many words in the many, many steps of making a *Neapolitan mousse cake*.

When Papa and I made this cake, I asked him why *Pie in the Sky* wasn't going to have the same cakes as our family's cake shop.

Hmm . . .

I asked if it was because the people in Australia wouldn't like our plain cakes.

I asked if it was because the cakes with lots of cream and chocolate would be much more expensive, which meant we'd get rich a lot quicker.

It was as if he hadn't thought about it at all. I asked if he'd chosen the cakes by eeny-meeny-miny-moe.

I was a little confused, but I had more important questions. I asked if we could get a new computer and a new car after we sold the expensive cakes of *Pie in the Sky*.

I never imagined Papa had thought so far ahead for me. I hadn't even turned ten.

I asked if he didn't have a good life.

I screwed up my face like I'd eaten one of those sour plums Ah-po gave us after we had to take bitter medicine. How old did Papa think I was?

"Jingwen," Papa continued, sounding very serious.

It's important you understand our cakes here aren't plain cakes.

They don't have cream or cocoa powder like this Neapolitan mousse cake.

They're made of more common, more affordable ingredients.

Like beans and flour and glutinous rice.

They don't have fancy designs or bright colors.

But they're delicious. And they fill up the tummies of people who are less well-off.

They're humble cakes.

Of course, by the time Papa and I made the last cake we'd ever bake together, chocolate raspberry torte, I'd tucked what he said in a locked suitcase in a corner of my brain, and I called all the cakes he made cheap cakes, even his *Pie in the Sky* cakes.

I never told him that I was sorry and that I didn't mean it. I don't even remember the last thing I said to him. Was it something nice? Did I make up for all the times I was a foolish kid and bad son?

I flip *Cakes and More Cakes* to the next page and search the dictionary for "*double-boiler.*"

Mama peeks into the room. "Jingwen? What are you doing? Why don't you play with Yanghao and Sarah?"

I say nothing, and she sits next to me.

"Remember when you and Yanghao and I made that cake at *Barker Bakes*?"

I nod. I won't forget the chocolate raspberry torte I put together alone.

"Well, Heather found the cake in the fridge. And she loved it! She gave me a promotion. I'm now in charge of finishing two of *Barker Bakes's* cakes instead of just prep work."

"That's good news, Mama," I say without looking up.

"What are you reading? A cookbook? An English one?"

Uh-oh. "I borrowed it from the library."

"When did you go to the library? Did you attend your tutoring?"

"I went after. With Yanghao."

"So tutoring didn't go overtime?"

"Only a little overtime. Like five minutes."

"Being a pastry chef is very hard work, Jingwen. You work with hot ovens and at odd hours. Life's better with a steady nine-to-five job in an office."

"I'm just reading for fun, Mama."

"*Neapolitan mousse cake*, huh? Let's see . . . What's this ingredient?" She points.

"Almonds."

She raises her eyebrows at me, but if I look into the mirror, I'll probably see my own eyebrows are raised, too. I know *almonds*? Since when? Mama points at another word. "What about this?"

"Cinnamon." Oh boy! Have I become a genius?

"And this?"

"*Double-boiler.* Used for melting chocolate." I'm Einstein!

Okay, I just looked up *"double-boiler"* a minute ago, but normally I'd have forgotten it. My brain remembers everything to do with cakes. Every subject in school should be taught in terms of cakes. *Describe the life cycle of a cake. Write an essay on Neapolitan mousse cake.*

"I do wish you'd borrow storybooks instead."

"But these cookbooks are in English, so it's the same. They taught me *'almonds,' 'cinnamon,' 'double-boiler.'*" Before she can be stubborn and tell me to return the cookbooks for storybooks, I get her to drop the subject by adding, "The cakes remind me of Papa."

Mama's lips squash together. It's evil of me to use Papa this way, but I really need the cookbooks. Cakes will fix everything, including my terrible English, and Mama will be happy about that.

She gets up. My evil tactic works. "I'm happy you're learning English, Jingwen." She goes to the door. "But these baking terms aren't very useful in everyday life or school."

And I'm alone again.

I lock the bedroom door and drag the suitcase from under my bed to check the leftover ingredients inside. Maybe some of them can be used for the *Neapolitan mousse cake*. I have *flour, vegetable oil, granulated sugar, icing sugar, cocoa powder, eggs, almonds—*

There's something stuck under the box of almonds.

The letter from the principal.

I've forgotten all about it.

I peel open the envelope.

Dear Mrs. Chen,

I am sorry to ⬡ Jingwen has not been ◻⬒ ⬡⬡ ⬡
His teachers ◻⬡ ⬡⬡ fifth-grade English is
too difficult for him ⬡ ⬡⬡⬡ ⬡⬡ ⬡⬡ ⬡⬡ ⬡⬡
⬡⬡ ⬡ ▷ If he has not ⬡⬡⬡ end of this term ⬡⬡
⬡ ⬡ next term ⬡⬡ move to fourth grade ⬡ ⬡

Please ⬡ me to ⬡ ⬡ ⬡

Christina Snider
Principal
Northbridge Primary School

I flip the dictionary so fast I get a thousand paper cuts. Turns out, my teachers think I'm not doing well in fifth grade at all, what with failing my homework and daydreaming during class. They figure it's all because my English is *poor*, so I should be given a better chance to catch up. The principal suggests that next term, which is in a month's time, I do not continue fifth grade but move down to fourth grade.

Fourth grade. The same as Yanghao. With my luck, I'll end up in the same class as him. With my nine-year-old brother. And his best friend, Sarah.

Cakes have made life better for everyone. Mama got her promotion, and Yanghao got new friends. I don't know how he became friends with Sarah, but he is pals with Anna only because he gives her cake. Things have gotten better for me too: I met Ben, even if he turned out to be evil, and my English has improved a little. But Mama and Yanghao are sprinting to the finish line, where the banner says "HAPPINESS." Meanwhile, I'm crawling. Now that I've stopped making cakes, I'm crawling backward. Crawling all the way back to another grade.

It's so unfair, and I don't care if that makes me sound like Yanghao.

Mama said it's easier for Yanghao to grasp English-that-sounds-like Martian because he's younger. But this, Mama and Yanghao sprinting while I crawl, can't have anything to do with age, since Mama's older than me and Yanghao's younger. What, then?

I gasp like I've been dunked into freezing water.

My crawling backward has everything to do with this: I was horrible to Papa.

Only I carry seashells filled with guilt in my pocket, and they're so heavy I can only crawl.

I don't know if I want to move on from Papa like Mama has done, but I know I'm sick of feeling like I'm feeling now.

After Papa was buried, I overheard Ah-gong, Ah-po, and Mama talking.

The period of mourning is supposed to be a hundred days.

No celebrations. No weddings. No birthdays.

Forty-nine days at least.

I don't want Jingwen to miss his birthday party. There's enough sadness as it is.

Yanghao cried himself to sleep again.

Yes, Wenyang wouldn't care about tradition, as long as his family is happy.

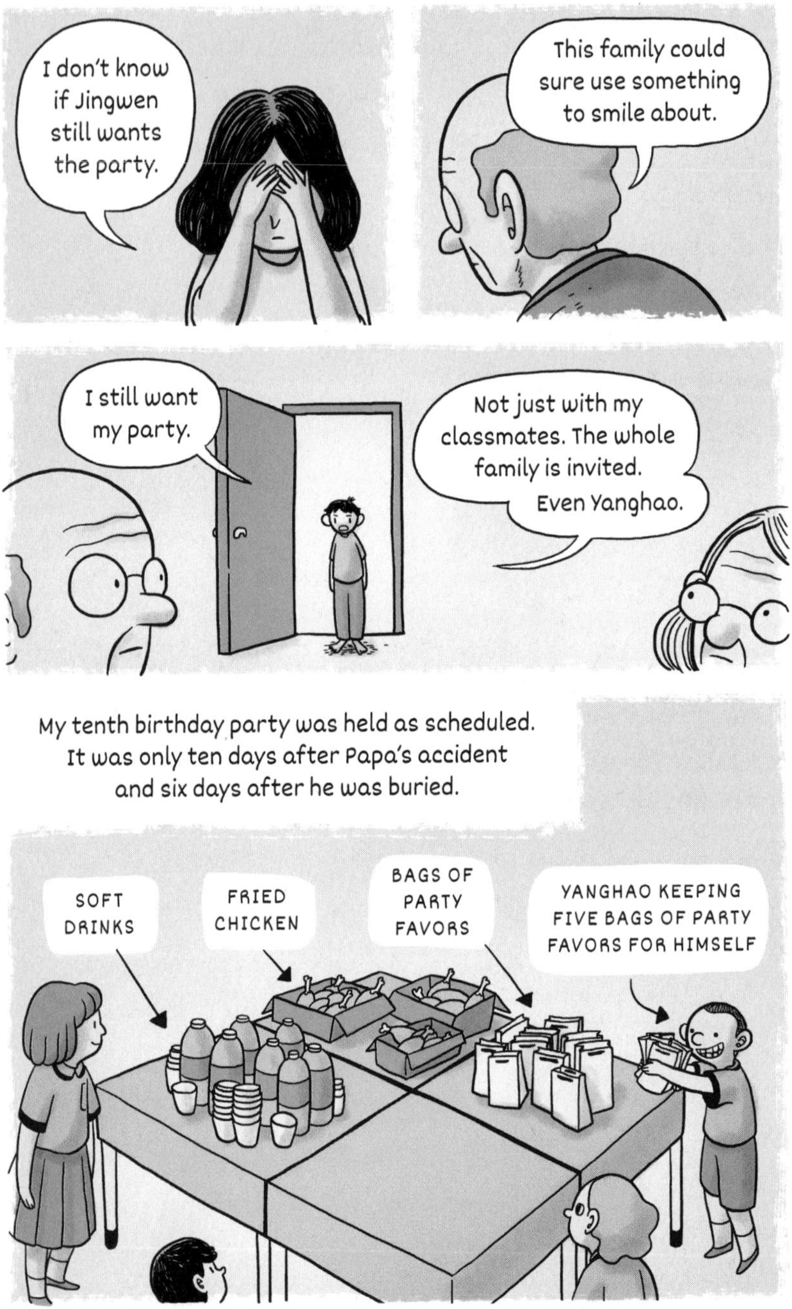
I don't know if Jingwen still wants the party.
This family could sure use something to smile about.
I still want my party.
Not just with my classmates. The whole family is invited. Even Yanghao.
My tenth birthday party was held as scheduled. It was only ten days after Papa's accident and six days after he was buried.
SOFT DRINKS
FRIED CHICKEN
BAGS OF PARTY FAVORS
YANGHAO KEEPING FIVE BAGS OF PARTY FAVORS FOR HIMSELF

I even got the fancy SpongeBob SquarePants cake, which I'd forgotten about.

Everyone was happy.

Jingwen, take a slice to Mama.

Where is she?

The school was deserted
save for my very noisy classroom.

Ma—

"I beg you," I heard her say. "I beg you . . ."

What I did next, I shouldn't have.

I never saw Mama cry again. I never heard Yanghao cry himself to sleep again. But even though my nose often burns, and sometimes my eyes, I never cried the way they did. Maybe I can't allow myself. The tears contain every memory I have of Papa, and if I cry them all out, what's left?

If I make all the cakes in *Pie in the Sky*, Papa will know I didn't forget him. He'll forgive everything I said and did. The seashells of guilt weighing me down will be gone from my pockets. My English will be perfect, I'll do okay in school, I'll have friends.

Only four more cakes left.

When will I get to make the next one, *Neapolitan mousse cake*? I decide: tonight.

53

Our bedtime is nine thirty. I have to keep myself awake while pretending to be asleep for about an hour, until Mama leaves for work.

Once I hear the front door click shut, I toss my blanket aside and jump out of bed. "Wake up, Yanghao! *Mousse* time!"

"It's still dark," Yanghao mumbles from his bed.

I shake him. "Mama's gone to work. We can make cakes now."

"Tomorrow."

"*Zzzzz?*" I ask. "What's that? A bee?"

"A sound in English that you make when you're sleeping. *Zzzzz.*"

This calls for a better tactic. I tickle the soles of his feet.

He tucks his legs under him, but my fingers follow his feet until he bursts out laughing. "Okay, okay! Let's make a cake."

The first night, we make *Neapolitan mousse cake*.

The second night, we make *red velvet crepe cake*. Well, mostly me.

Wednesday night, I make *pear tarte tatin*.

One last cake. Then all the *Pie in the Sky* cakes will be made. After tomorrow, after I've made the *apple mille-feuille*, I can finally be happy again.

"By the skin of your teeth, Jingwen," Mr. Fart says when I run into class two steps ahead of him. I think he's scolding me, but he's not my dentist, so I don't know.

This morning, Yanghao and I slept through the alarm clock, but we made it through the school gates just as the bell rang. Since the midnight cake making began, I've been nodding off in all my classes. I bet my teachers tattle to the principal, too. But I have no choice until all the cakes are made.

Mr. Fart makes me read. It's a short, easy question, and I know all the words. But snorts and giggles—most are muffled, but some aren't—come from my classmates-not-friends. The loudest ones are probably Joe and Max. I plop back onto my seat, my mind racing to figure out what it was about me that everyone found so funny.

Oh no. I've read *"mouse"* as *"mousse"* and *"desert"* as *"dessert."*

I wish I were a lone mouse in a vast desert, where I didn't have to utter a word of anything, much less English.

During math, Miss Scrappell has us work in our project groups again. Ben has brought a big, thick board, which I guess is for a display. Once again, he works without saying a word.

On a piece of colored paper, he writes: 0.38 = 3/10

Which is wrong. I slide the piece of colored paper toward me and write in pencil:

0.38 = 38/100 = 19/50

I push the paper back to him. He takes another piece of colored paper and writes out what I wrote but in pen.

But still he doesn't say anything. Not even when I take out an English cookbook.

Ben's cake looked like the one in *Cakes and More Cakes*. It was similar to the one in Mama's cookbook, save for the filling.

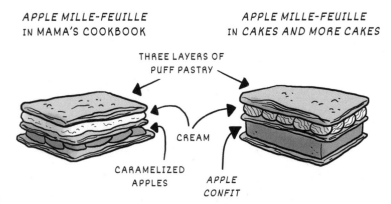

My heart goes THUMP!

I quickly key *"apple confit"* into the electronic dictionary. I've looked up so many words on this gadget, especially during Miss Scrappell's after-school help, that I should receive the Guinness World Record for fastest typist on an electronic dictionary. I have to look up six more words to finally get the meaning, but it's still a lot faster than using a dinosaur-age dictionary. Aha! *Apple confit* is made from thin layers of apples being stacked together and baked with sugar.

It has to be more than a coincidence that the last cake on the menu of *Pie in the Sky* is the same cake I've lost my friend over. It's the deities and the universe, and Ah-gong, telling me it's good to let things go. Ben might have been mean, but who knows if Joe somehow forced him to say it? And it was only that one time, which is nothing if I think about the many other times he was nice to me.

Once I've made this cake tonight, I'll keep a few slices and give them to Ben tomorrow. I won't have to say anything. He'll understand I'm saying sorry.

The cake will fix everything.

55

I bolt awake. The clock says one o'clock in the morning. How long was that nap I just took? Ten minutes earlier, I placed the apple confit in the fridge to cool and the puff pastry into the oven before joining Yanghao for a nap at the dining table.

"What's that?" Yanghao clasps his ears. "Make it stop!"

"It's the smoke alarm," I say, my voice as steady as an over-baked, hard-as-rock cookie, even though my heart is wobbly like a T-rex-is-stomping-closer jelly.

I quickly turn off the oven and open it. There's a slight smoky smell, but luckily, no dark clouds of smoke billow out. No fire. I'm so relieved I want to sink onto the floor like a cake taken out of the oven too soon. But Yanghao's still yelling for me to make the beeping stop.

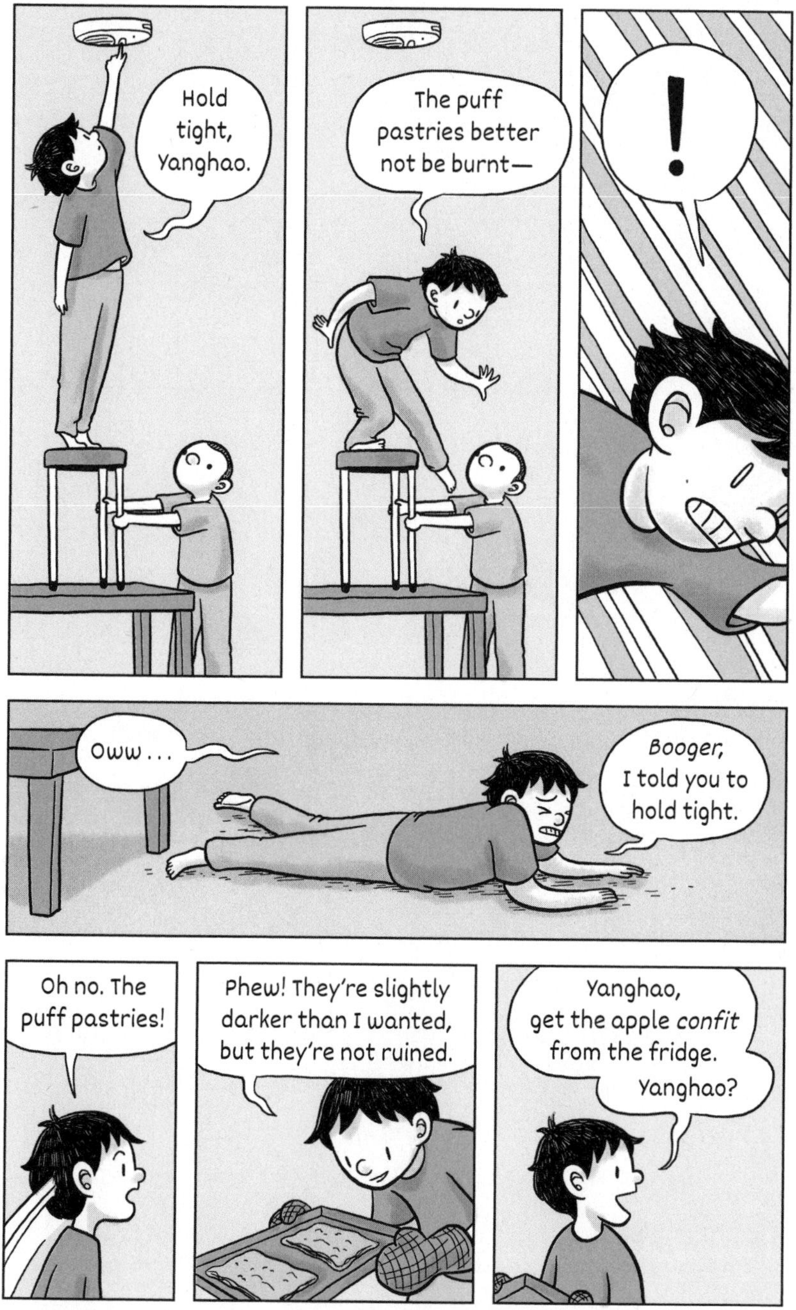
Hold tight, Yanghao.
The puff pastries better not be burnt—
!
Oww . . .
Booger, I told you to hold tight.
Oh no. The puff pastries!
Phew! They're slightly darker than I wanted, but they're not ruined.
Yanghao, get the apple *confit* from the fridge. Yanghao?

I press a clean tea towel against his temple. "Hold it there."

He does as told but cries even louder at the same time. I dance around the living room like I've gone to the beach on a very warm day and the sand is scorching. Should I call an ambulance? What should I say? Would I even know all the right English words?

my little brother

pain

fell (but he didn't fall)

chair

crying

not dead

Maybe I should call Mama. She can speak English to the police and have the ambulance sent here.

But before I can pick up the phone, I hear keys jingling, and then the front door is thrown open.

Anna sees Yanghao and the bloody gash and spits out, *"Fudge!"* From her tone, she's clearly using that delicious sweet treat as a swear word, so I must have heard wrongly. And that is all I can think about, helpless as Yanghao continues wailing and Anna makes a phone call. *"May I speak with Meixin, please? Hi, it's Anna. Now, don't be—"*

I don't catch anything else she says to Mama after that, but Mama rushes into the apartment five minutes later, and a second later Mama jostles Yanghao out of the house.

56

Anna tells me to *go to bed*. She actually looks a bit sorry for me. She's probably thinking about the horrible sentence Mama will hand down to me later.

I go to my room, but of course I can't fall asleep. Ten seconds later Anna's snores thrum through the apartment. I don't want to think, so I find something to do.

I assemble the apple mille-feuille, making as little noise as I can, though I could have banged pots and pans, and it still wouldn't have been louder than Anna's snores.

I set aside two slices for Ben.

I eat three slices.

The rest of the apple mille-feuille, I leave it on the table. Yanghao surely must have spilled everything to Mama at the hospital, so there's no need for me to follow *Rules for Making Cakes* and get rid of the evidence.

. . .

I don't know what time it is when Mama and Yanghao come home, but it's still dark outside. Mama and Anna talk in hushed voices, then Mama comes into my bedroom, carrying Yanghao. She lays him down on his bed. In the dark, I make out a long dark line crisscrossed with little ones across his temple. Since he doesn't have to stay in the hospital, it shouldn't be as bad as the time he had a bruise on his brain.

Mama tucks his hands under his blanket and kisses him on the forehead. When she turns, I shut my eyes. And wait.

It's silent for a while, like she's standing still. Then I hear her footsteps as she walks away. She didn't kiss me or make sure my hands aren't cold.

Then there's nothing to do but think.

Cakes bring smiles. Cakes are magic. Cakes fix everything. So why did a cake break Yanghao? I must have done something wrong. Maybe I shouldn't have made smaller cakes, but the same-sized ones Papa and I made. Maybe I had to use the same exact recipes Papa and I used, which are the ones in Mama's cookbooks. Not the recipes from the library cookbooks. I thought it'd be okay. Papa and I were just practicing.

Maybe I was wrong. Or it's just too little too late. I'll never be forgiven.

I wake up before the alarm clock rings. Yanghao is surely stay-ing home from school today, but I'm not sure if I have to go. I don't know which I'd prefer. In case Mama wants me to go to school, I get up and creep into the kitchen. On the dining table are one bowl of congee and one glass of milk. That means I have to go to school.

I give the *apple mille-feuille* to Ben.

He looks surprised, then he says, *"Thank you."*

When Mr. Fart calls on me, Ben helps me with the word *"chrysalis."*

Cakes are fixing things again. Which makes me very, very confused.

If cakes truly are magic, where did I go wrong?

· · ·

But Ben doesn't write me any notes. At recess, he doesn't ask me to go to lunch with him. After last bell, he doesn't say *bye*.

He must have said *"thank you"* and *"chrysalis"* just because he's a nice person, even if he was mean that one time, not because he's a friend.

When I get home, I'll say sorry to Mama and explain to her that I didn't go behind her back and make cakes and lie and accidentally hurt Yanghao because I was naughty and had to have my way. It was because they were not just any cakes, but *Pie in the Sky* ones, and I made them for Papa. Then at least she won't be so mad at me. I hope.

58

But before any words can make their way through my lips, Mama's spatula makes its swift, hard way onto my left palm.

It's the very same spatula I used to commit my baking crime. Mama interrogates me, even though when I got home, Yanghao gave me his best-ever puppy-dog eyes and whispered, "I broke rule number one."

I give up everything: blowing our pocket money on ingredients, the burn on the kitchen table, the midnight cake making, and that we've made twelve cakes in total. Well, I give up almost everything. I don't tell her about my theft from the emergency stash. She's so angry she can't do math and doesn't realize how much those twelve cakes cost to make. If she asks, I'll confess. If she doesn't, I can't. She'll hate me.

She moves on to scolding me.

That's when I start to get mad.

Half of my brain knows the secret cake making is wrong, but a quarter of my brain says the accident with Yanghao wasn't actually caused by a hot cake-making oven. The last quarter is angry at Mama for dragging me to Mars. And for being happy while I'm the opposite of that.

I don't apologize.

I don't tell her about *Rules for Making Cakes*.

I don't tell her about *Pie in the Sky*.

When Mama finally gets tired of lecturing me, she makes me do my homework. Even when angry, all she can think about is my grades and my English. If only I'd thrown my dictionary into the oven and let it burn to a crisp. I slip the notepad with *Rules for Making Cakes* under my homework book just as Mama walks down the hallway and into the kitchen, wheeling my suitcase behind her.

She opens the suitcase and tosses the packet of flour, bag of sugar, bottle of vanilla extract, and everything else into the garbage, until there's only one item left in the suitcase: an envelope. The envelope.

My hands tremble as she reads the letter from the principal.

She asks, without looking up, "Why didn't you give this to me?"

"I—I forgot."

She stands up and wheels the suitcase away. I hear her tossing things in my room. A while later she comes back with a paper bag. She goes to the coffee table and dumps books—my cookbooks—into the bag.

"I'll be back soon," she says, still not looking at me. "Yanghao's sleeping, but give him his dinner when he wakes up."

"Where are you going with those books?" I ask.

"Library. To return them. I've also confiscated your library cards."

It no longer matters because I've made all the *Pie in the Sky* cakes, but for some reason, I can't let it go. "You said that my English has improved since reading those cookbooks—"

"From now on, you and Yanghao will only go to the library with me. You can only borrow storybooks." Without casting one glance at me, she straightens up and heads toward the door. "No more cookbooks."

NO MORE MAKING CAKES!

There is a wail. Yanghao stands in the hallway. The skin near the black thread stitched across his right temple is red. That will surely leave a scar.

"Let us make cakes, Mama!" he cries.

I want to tell him it doesn't matter. We've made all the *Pie in the Sky* cakes. If things haven't gotten better, there is nothing more I can do. My life on Mars will simply be stuck on stinky. But this time my lips don't obey me and I swear at them—only in my mind, since they're not doing what I want them to.

Mama tells him to go back to bed. He walks away, but continues wailing. She bends down to slip on her shoes. "You're the older brother, and you should've known better, Jingwen."

I stare at *Rules for Making Cakes*.

"These cookbooks can't help much with your English. Because what use are *almond* and *double-boiler* outside of a kitchen? The reason why you find English so hard is because you refuse to use it. You need to be more like Yanghao."

She wants me to use English? Fine.

hate

you.

At last, she turns to look at me.

It's the same look she had when I asked her why we came to Australia without Papa, maybe more miserable. I know I've hurt her, but I just can't say sorry. All that's in my head is a gif of a volcano spewing lava. Mama takes a deep breath and walks out.

For some bizarre reason, now it's not only my lips, but also the rest of my body that is acting beyond my control. I shoot to my feet, pick up the dictionary, and hurl it so hard into the trash can that the garbage topples over. The dictionary rolls out and flops open to show me double pages full of English words. Mocking me.

I don't care about those words printed on the pages, but only those words I said.

Those English words I said, I didn't mean them.

I said what I didn't mean.

I meant what I didn't say: *I'm sorry.*

It must have been thirty seconds later.

My heart beats so hard, so fast, so loud.

What if those words are the last words I ever say to Mama? If something happens to her on her way to the library, my brain will surely remember *I hate you*.

No matter how hard I beg my brain, I can't remember the last thing I said to Papa or the last thing we did together. What was he doing? Where was he going? What was he thinking? My memories of him are like a swarm of monsters locked in that suitcase under my bed. Every day I let a few go. Just a few. Because one more than that will kill me.

But I have let go and let go and let go, and now there is only one monster left.

On the day of my tenth birthday party, I left Mama where she was, crying and begging. I went back to the classroom, where everyone was happy.

I placed the fancy cake back in the fancy box.

At the very bottom was Papa's signature.

Underneath it, the date, ten days before my birthday.

The day of the crash.

The monster that has escaped from my suitcase is raking its claws all over me. All those cakes I made are not luring it away. I play that morphing game Yanghao and I used to play. Metal shields materialize all round my legs, arms, torso, head.

Mama comes home safely from the library. Seeing her walk in allows me to throw some of the seashells in my pocket back into the sea.

But the next day, the tide washes them all back up onto the beach.

Saturday begins with Mama's announcement that Anna will babysit Yanghao and me from 4 to 8 P.M., Monday to Friday. Mama has changed her shift so she'll be gone from 9 A.M. to 8 P.M. There will be zero chance for cake making. Which is very ha-ha-ha, since I've made all the cakes I needed to make, and I've gotten into all this trouble and hurt Mama and Yanghao for nothing. Only the thought of listening to Anna talk like a robot for four hours every day stops me from laughing. There is nothing I can do. So I put myself into automatic mode, like a robot (though not an annoying one like Anna).

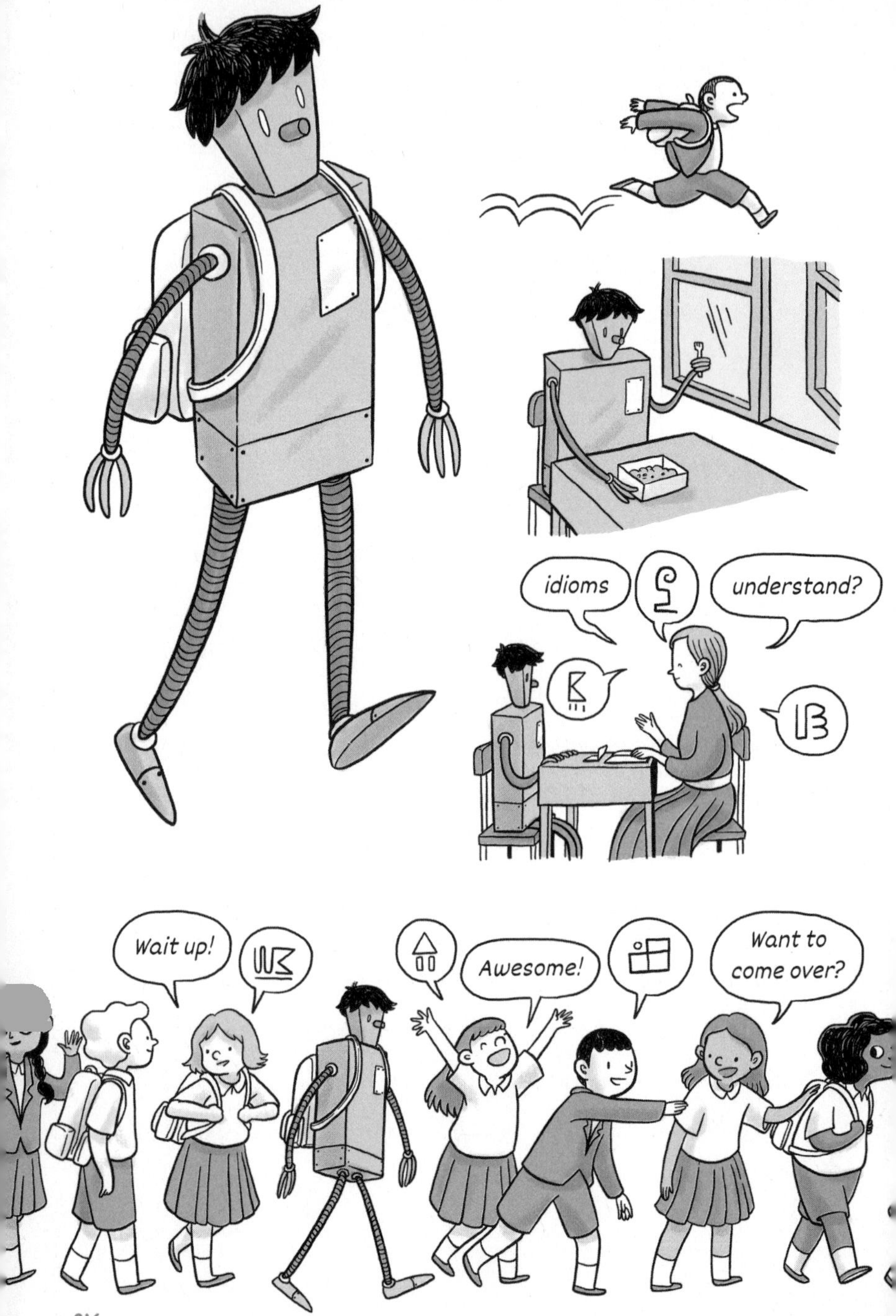
idioms
understand?
Wait up!
Awesome!
Want to come over?

It's a relief to have a heart made of metal and nuts and bolts that feels nothing. But my smart robot brain knows that even machines break down.

On Thursday night, two weeks later, my robot heart short-circuits.

Anna is slowly reading *The Little Prince* with Yanghao, and I'm at the dining table trying to do my homework when Mama comes home.

Anna finally leaves, and Mama fishes out a letter from her handbag. "It's from Ah-po and Ah-gong. There are no individual letters. It's addressed to the three of us." She hands me three whole pages of the letter and a torn page with three lines of Ah-po's handwriting.

I say, "What happened here?"

"I tore away the recipe for rainbow cake."

Yanghao says, "Oh!"

Mama continues. "Ah-po thought I asked for the rainbow cake recipe for your birthday, Jingwen."

My twelfth birthday. In four weeks' time. Which means that in four weeks minus ten days, we will have been without Papa for two whole years.

"Are you going to make rainbow cake for Jingwen's birthday, Mama?" Yanghao asks.

Mama tidies up Yanghao's storybooks that are scattered all over the coffee table. She says nothing.

Yanghao looks at me for an answer.

I lower my head and stare at my homework. Sparks are flying inside my robot heart.

I was wrong all along.

Rainbow cake is supposed to be on the menu of *Pie in the Sky*.

Everything has not become all right because I haven't finished making all the *Pie in the Sky* cakes.

Everything has not become all right because I haven't made rainbow cake.

Everything will be all right once I make this last cake.

Papa's cake.

62

While Mama is in the shower, I search for the recipe. It isn't in her handbag or anywhere in her room. She must have put it in that cubbyhole at *Barker Bakes*, the same place where she keeps all her cookbooks.

And that's where I go on Friday after English tutoring.

"Because she's mad at me, so she won't," I say.

"She's not mad anymore."

"Not at you. Never at you. Because I'm the older one, and I'm supposed to know better. You'll never understand because you'll always be a little brother."

"Let's go to the library and book a computer and Google the recipe."

"No."

He places a hand on my shoulder. "Don't worry, I'll do all the talking."

I shrug his hand off me. "*Booger.* It's not that. For the other cakes we could use any recipe because Papa and I were just practicing, but the rainbow cake recipe is special. It's been passed down from our great-great-great-great-grandparents. The ones on the internet won't be the same."

"Ooooh." He's caving. Convincing him will be *a piece of cake.* Which is an idiom I just learned from Miss Scrappell.

"Do this one thing for me. For my birthday."

"It's still weeks away."

"As my brother."

He lets out a sigh that's too big for someone so little. "Okay, okay."

Piece of cake! There are probably two more times in our whole lives that I can play that brother card.

"But Mama's in there. She'll see me. Even if she doesn't, someone else will, and they'll ask me what I'm doing in the staff-only area. What if they think I'm a thief and call the police?"

I pace around in tighter circles. "Help me think of a better idea, then."

Yanghao peers into the café. "Maybe we can ask your friend."

I don't have a friend. But I look up anyway.

Ben's sitting at a table. He isn't eating. Instead, there's a big cardboard poster and pieces of colorful paper in front of him. He's doing the math project I'm supposed to be doing with him, the one that's supposed to be exhibited this Monday, which is three days away.

"Your friend really likes cakes too, huh?" Yanghao says. "This is the second time we've seen him here."

"Ben's not my friend."

Yanghao squints at Ben. "He's not the one who you think said something mean about you, is he? That was the tall boy, wasn't it?"

"Ben, too. I heard him and the tall boy talking at the playground the other day. Ben also said I was *s l o w*."

I smack his hand down. "What are you talking about?"

He points to Ben. "That boy in there, the one that likes cake a lot. Ben? I heard him at the playground. He said whipping egg whites by hand was s l o w. He wasn't talking about you at all!"

"But—But—" There is nothing more to that sentence.

I've horribly misunderstood Ben. I didn't hear my name mentioned at the playground, but because he was with Joe, and because of what happened with Joe and the word s l o w, I assumed they were talking about me. I was a booger for thinking that just because Ben hangs out with Joe sometimes that Ben is as evil as Joe. After all, I hang out with Yanghao a lot, but I sure hope I'm not as annoying as him. I smack my forehead.

"Look," Yanghao says, peering into the café again. "He knows Mama's boss."

Ben is indeed talking to Heather. She ruffles his hair and gives him a hug. Heather then disappears into the staff-only area. I turn back to look at Ben. He's staring at Yanghao and me. I yip and duck. But Yanghao waves and beckons for him to come out.

"What are you doing?" I hiss.

"He knows Heather. Maybe we can ask him to get the recipe for us."

"You booger—" I say, but then think it could be a good idea. If Ben is willing to help me even though I've been such a jerk lately.

Ben steps outside, looking bewildered.

"Tell him, Jingwen," Yanghao says.

Yanghao pipes up. "He said what for?"

"I know that, *booger*," I say, but then I don't have the next English words. "Yanghao, translate for me. Tell Ben how Joe called me s l o w in school, and then tell him about the playground thing where I thought he called me s l o w."

As I talk to Yanghao, a look of total confusion spreads

across Ben's face. That must be how I look to everyone when they speak to me in English.

Yanghao turns to Ben and prattles off English-that-sounds-like-Martian, but I catch *Joe, slow, playground*. He also says *booger*, which 100 percent refers to me, and I'm about to tell him not to add personal comments, but Ben is looking less confused.

"Yanghao, tell Ben I'm sorry I threw away his cake, but it was because I thought he and Joe were playing a trick on me."

"He gave you cake, and you threw it away?" Yanghao almost-yells. "You said we can't throw away food!" He utters another bunch of Martian words, and Ben looks at me.

"Joe is Ben's cousin," Yanghao says to me before turning back to Ben. "*Do you know Heather?*"

"*How do you know my mom?*" Ben asks.

Yanghao then says a lot more things to him. *Rainbow cake, our mom, recipe, please.*

Ben's expression is like that of a mime's, changing from are-they-cuckoo to are-they-really-doing-this to that's-strange-but-somewhat-curious to that's-cool.

"*Okay.*" He chuckles. That's all he says before marching into the café.

Two minutes later, he scuttles back out with one hand in his pocket.

"Yanghao," I say, "ask Ben what I can do for the math project."

Yanghao translates for me, and Ben's eyes light up. "*Meet me here tomorrow morning. We'll finish the project. Nine o'clock?*"

I haven't paid much attention to the project this past two weeks because Ben wasn't talking to me, and because I was sure I'd be sent down to fourth grade next term—just thinking about it makes me grimace. But now that I know there's still one last cake to make before everything is fixed, there may be a miracle. So I'd better buck up.

I hatch a plan: On Sunday, Yanghao will ask Mama to take him to the zoo or the pineapple under the sea or wherever he wants. I'll say I can't go because I have a lot of homework to do. Which isn't a lie. While they're away for a few hours, I'll make a rainbow cake and keep a slice for Yanghao to enjoy in secret. Mama has no reason to suspect I'll be making cakes, since I don't have any cookbooks.

"What if Mama asks Anna to babysit you?" Yanghao asks.

Sometimes, maybe once or twice in his whole life, he's not such a clueless booger, but I'd never tell him that. "You have to ask Anna to go with you to the zoo or wherever. You're already best friends with her anyway."

Fine.

But only if you add caramel sauce to the cake.

"That'd be too sweet," I say.

"Then too bad—"

"But I can make caramel sauce and keep it on the side. You can pour it on your slice of cake."

. . .

But early Saturday morning, I'm woken up by the ring of the telephone.

I get to the living room as Mama is hanging up the phone. "I have to go to work," she says. "A colleague called in sick. I'll get Anna to babysit." She goes next door, but when she comes back, Anna isn't with her; Ginger is. "Anna's on her way out, so she can't babysit. I should be back around four." She looks me dead in the eyes. "Jingwen, will you look after your brother?"

I nod.

"No making cakes. Or I'm going to be furious. Promise?"

I have to make one more cake. This is the perfect chance. If I don't lie today, I'll have to lie tomorrow according to the plan anyway. This chance has been gifted to me by the deities or the universe, which is being nice for once.

Rainbow cake doesn't look too complicated to make. The frosting is simple whipped cream. The cake bit is basically the same sponge cake recipe for all seven layers, except a different food coloring is added to each. In the whipped cream filling between the layers, there's fresh fruit: kiwi, mango, and strawberry.

Yanghao and I have plenty of time to bake and wipe clean evidence of illegal cake making before Mama comes home.

Later, at the grocery store, as we search through the aisles for ingredients, he starts singing another made-up song. "Rainbow caaaake!"

I shush him, but he continues as we wait on line to pay. After Yanghao's smoke alarm accident, every time I got my allowance, I stuck it into the can, so I had to take some back out before we left home. Yanghao has no idea. And it's still just borrowing.

When we're stepping out of the store, Yanghao shuts up. But only for one second.

Sarah!

"What did you say yes to?" I ask.

"Sarah asked me to play at the playground. We can go once her mum comes out of the store."

Inside my head, something goes pop! "What about our rainbow cake?"

"Ah," he says.

How could he have forgotten about it when it's the very reason we are here at the store in the first place?

He tugs at my sleeve. "Can I play for ten minutes? It's not even nine o'clock now. We have a lot of time before Mama comes back at four."

I yank my sleeve free. "No."

"Pleasepleasepleasepleaseplease—"

"No."

He huffs, then turns to Sarah.

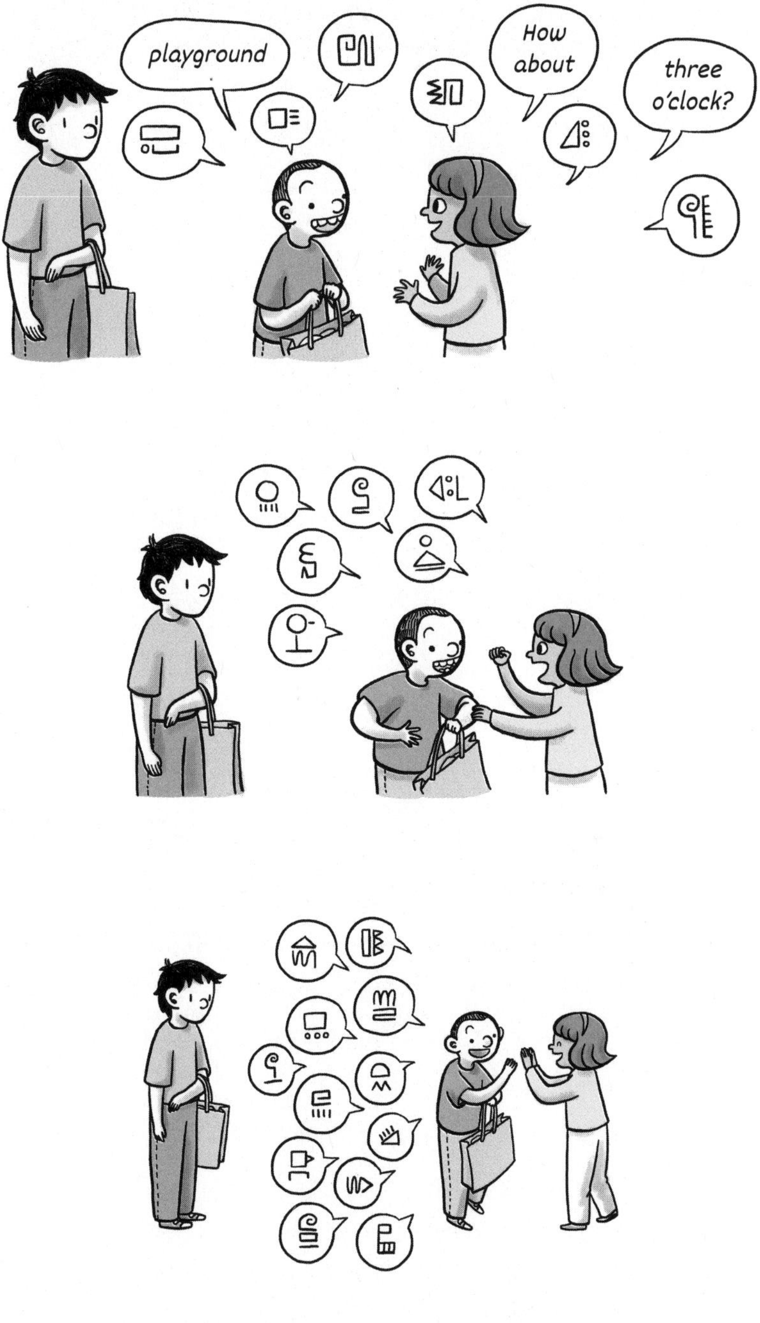
playground
How about
three o'clock?

Several seconds later, I hear Yanghao. "Jingwen! Wait!"

I don't slow down. He catches up with me as I cut through the bus station. At least he chose me over Sarah.

"I told Sarah I'll meet her later, after the rainbow cake is done. I'm meeting her at the playground at three o'clock. I'll call Mama and ask."

He doesn't get it. It is not just about the cake. "We're not making the caramel sauce," I say.

"But you said you'd make it for me."

"You can't combine caramel with rainbow cake. Too sweet. Makes everyone vomit."

Yanghao stops. His face scrunches up. Tears glisten in his eyes, but he doesn't wail.

"Don't be a crybaby."

"*I. Am. Not. A. Cry. Baby.*"

Each English word lands with a plop! Plop! Plop! It feels like the moment when he dropped the rainbow cake on the plane all over again. I snatch his grocery bag from him. "I'm sick of you showing off your English. Add this one last rule to *Rules for Making Cakes . . .*"

Yanghao is never allowed to make cakes with Jingwen EVER again.

NEVER. FOREVER.

Translate that to English yourself.

I stomp home.

I don't look back.

Yanghao doesn't run after me or shout, "Jingwen! Wait!"

I only slow down when I pass by *Barker Bakes* and spot Ben inside. Oh no! I'm supposed to meet him for our project. I turn to step inside to ask him if we could work on our project tomorrow instead. But I stop at the door. The only English words I have are *I can't*.

Ben doesn't notice me. He's laying out the big cardboard poster on a table.

Yanghao doesn't appear. He must be in snail mode. He can't give me the words to give to Ben.

I back away from the door and hurry past the café. I need to bake the rainbow cake today. Right now. Who knows when Mama will be called in for work on a weekend again? Once I make this cake, everything will be all right. Everything. I don't dare peek from the corner of my eye to see if Ben saw me.

When I get to our apartment building, I'm still lost in my thoughts about what a terrible friend I am to Ben, and I crash face-first into the glass main door. "*Fudge!*" I hiss, cursing whoever wiped the glass so spotless I didn't see it was there. But as I walk up the steps, I can't help but think about how I thought lies of omission are invisible and so I could tell as many of them as I wanted. But what if they're like glass? I might not see it when I'm not paying attention, but it's there, and I might walk into it and hurt myself. Or someone else might.

At our apartment, I lay out the ingredients slowly. But Yanghao doesn't come back. That *booger*. He must have run off to the playground again.

Ginger is nowhere to be seen, so Anna must have used her keys to take Ginger back home while Yanghao and I were at the grocery store. *Crap*. If Anna tells Mama we weren't home, what should I say?

I've got it. I'll say we were at the library. To read story-books. Mama might get mad that we went out, but not as mad as if we made cakes by ourselves.

I sit at the table and watch the clock for ten minutes, then I get up to march to the playground and drag Yanghao back home. But before I step out of the kitchen, there's a creak, followed by a few moments of silence, and then a bang. That *booger*. He went straight to Anna's apartment instead of coming home.

Pfft. I don't need him anyway.

66

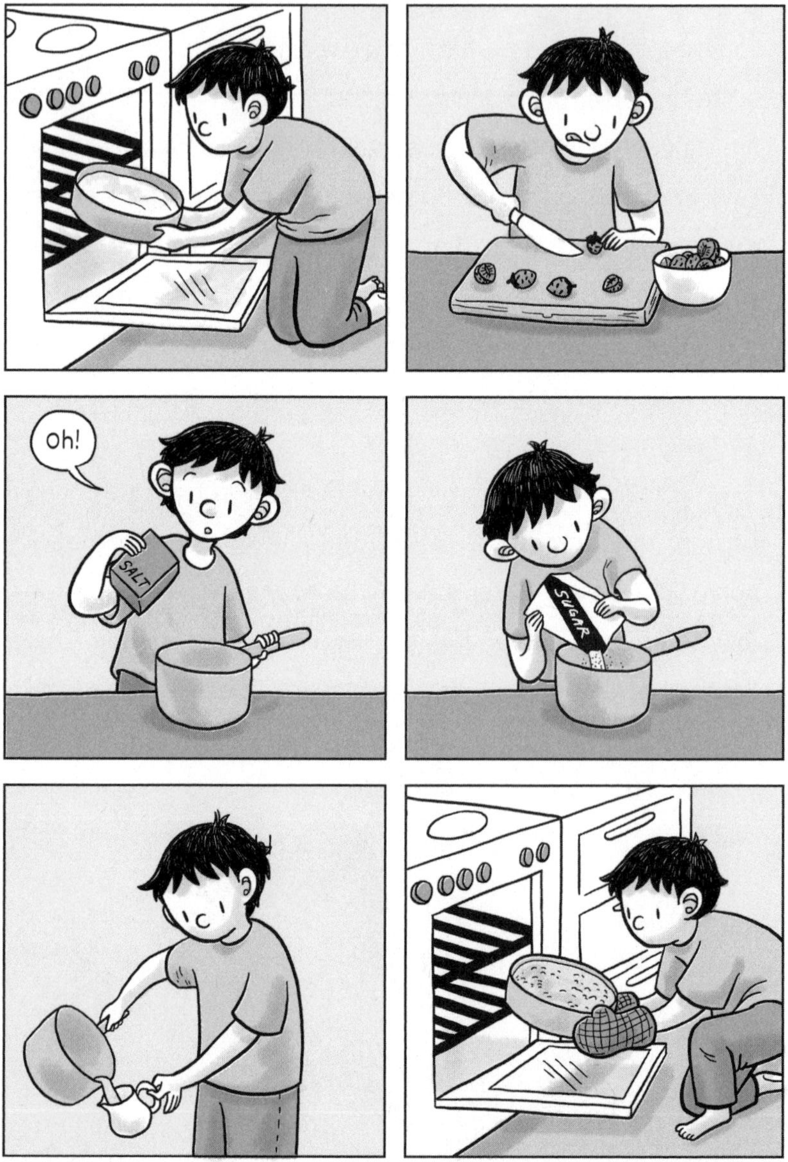
Oh!
SALT
SUGAR

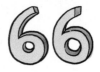

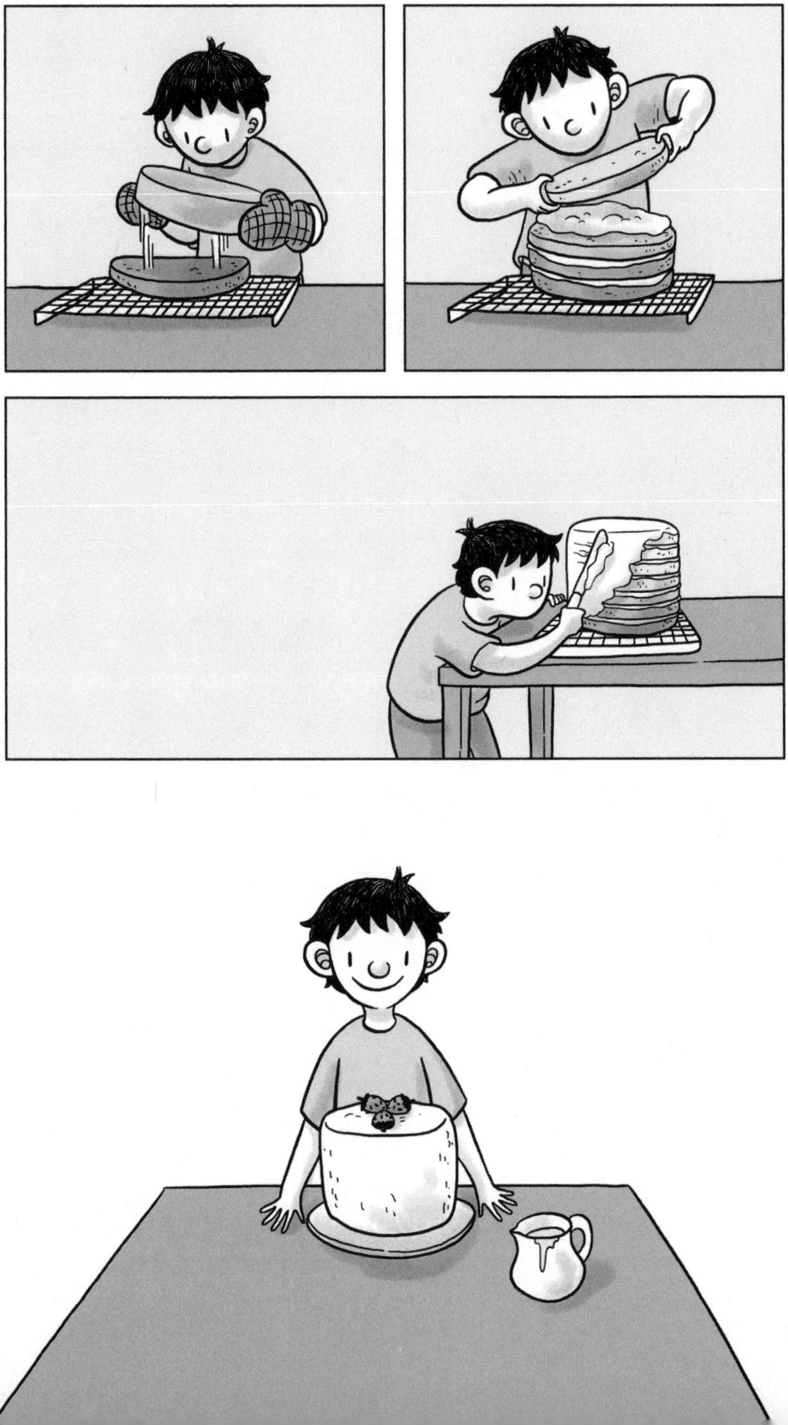

I made Papa's rainbow cake, just like I wanted.

I made all the *Pie in the Sky* cakes, just like I wanted.

Just like I wanted.

So why am I the exact opposite of happy?

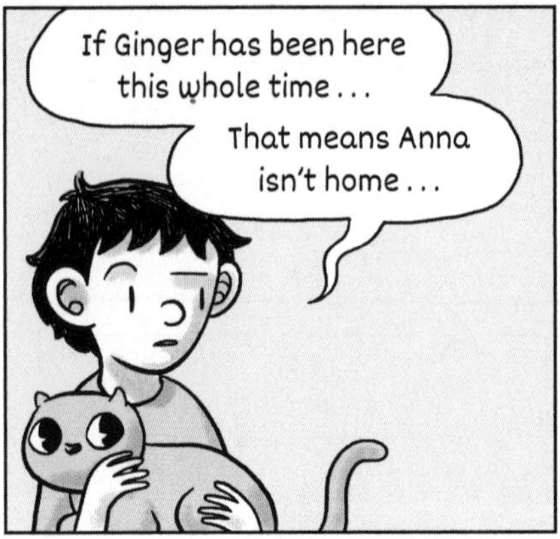
If Ginger has been here this whole time . . .
That means Anna isn't home . . .

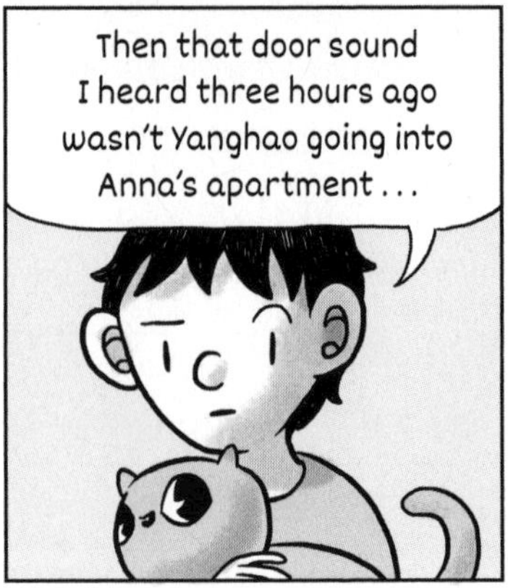
Then that door sound I heard three hours ago wasn't Yanghao going into Anna's apartment . . .

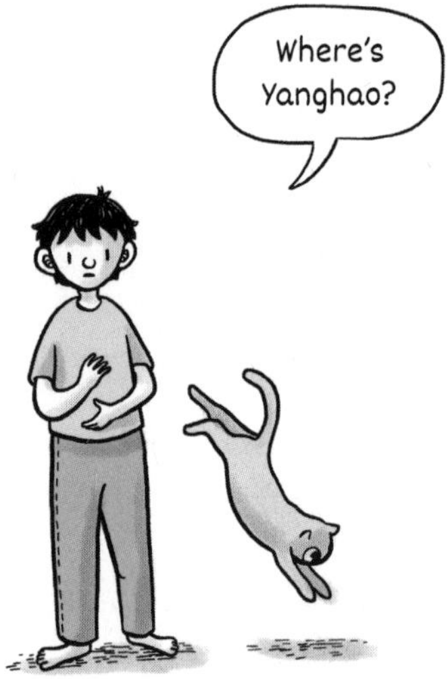
Where's Yanghao?

67

I bang on Anna's door. "Anna! Yanghao! Anna! Yanghao!"

No one answers. He must be at the playground. But can he really climb up and down like a monkey for three whole hours?

I scurry down the steps, almost slipping and getting a bruise on the brain or a gash on the temple. Which I deserve.

I almost crash into Anna.

For the first time, I'm glad Anna speaks to me like I'm a snail. The creak and bang I heard three hours ago must have been Anna coming back to get her wallet.

I zip past Anna. She shouts, "*Jingwen, where are you*—" I'm out of the building before she finishes.

There's only one kid at the playground, and it's not Yanghao. I search under the tower and inside the slide. No Yanghao.

He can't still be at the bus station, can he?

I run pell-mell to the bus station. I circle it once, twice, detour to the grocery store, zoom up and down the aisles once, twice, return to the bus station, and circle it again. No Yanghao.

I sprint back toward the playground. When I zoom past *Barker Bakes*, I glance inside. Ben isn't there. How long did he wait for me before he gave up? Will he still want to be friends with me after I stood him up like that?

Back at the playground, Yanghao is still nowhere in sight.

I lost Papa. I lost Yanghao. I lost Ben.

When Mama finds out, I'll lose her too.

. . .

I hurry home as fast as I can with my exploding lungs. I need to call Mama and tell her what happened. I'm so terrified about how angry, how disappointed she will be that I tremble.

But when I get home, Mama's already there. Anna must have called her and told her I went out.

"Jingwen." Mama's voice is ice. I am an ice cube at the door. "I told you no more making cakes." Her eyes dart to the left and right of me. "Is Yanghao hiding behind you? Get inside, Yanghao."

I tell Mama all my lies. My red, bleeding lies.

She says nothing to me, but speaks in Martian to Anna. I catch the word "*doctor*."

Anna propels Mama out the door, saying, "*It's all right. I've been eating too much. I'll go later.*" With that, Mama disappears.

I'm surprised I caught everything Anna said, even though she spoke like a normal person to Mama. And then I'm horrified. Yanghao once said Anna said the doctor told her to eat healthily. We gave her cakes. Technically, it was Yanghao, but I was the one forcing Yanghao to make cakes. Did I make Anna sick? Or make her have to get her toe amputated because of too much sugar in the blood like Ah-gong?

Anna looks at me and sighs. "*Jingwen, those cakes Yanghao gave me . . . You made them. What were you thinking?*"

I go into my room. My and Yanghao's room.

I lie down on Yanghao's bed. It smells just like me, because we use the same shampoo and the same soap and the same toothpaste. Our clothes smell of the same detergent. Under his pillow I find an empty gummy wrapper and a book. *The Little Prince.*

Scribbled all over the pages, in pencil, are meanings. Meanings of words Yanghao didn't know. Meanings in the margins, meanings in the spaces between sentences, from the first page with the drawing of an elephant in a boa constrictor right till the end. His big, fat alphabets all squished into the blank spaces.

I wish and wish for that boa constrictor to swallow me up.

I flip the book to the later pages. Did the little prince make it home?

I read much faster than I expected because of Yanghao's words. They're written in pencil. He must have planned to erase them all before returning the book to the library. I wonder if he did this in all the other storybooks he read. It's no wonder his English is much better than mine.

I wish and wish for that boa constrictor to swallow him up too. He could have told me instead of making everything look so darn easy for him.

The little prince dies. He gets a poisonous snake to bite him, and he dies.

That is where Yanghao's words ended. He hasn't finished reading the book. Forty percent of me wants to hurl the book across the room, ten percent wants to curl into a ball and cry, but fifty percent of me needs to find out what the rest of the Martian words in the remaining pages say.

I grab my dictionary from my backpack and plop myself back on Yanghao's bed. And I read.

The little prince's body disappears. The book doesn't say for sure, but it hints that his body can't be found because he has returned to his home. I don't know what to feel.

It's like that time Papa happened to see a live sea turtle for sale at a fish market. He bought it, we kept it in our bathtub and fed it shrimp until the weekend, then he took Yanghao and me on a tiny rented motorboat out to sea. Yanghao and I lowered the sea turtle back into the water and watched it fly in the ocean. When it was out of our view, I turned to see that Yanghao had a ridiculous look on his face.

I laughed and laughed, not understanding why he had that look on his face, but maybe now I finally know what it meant.

Sadness mixed with happiness. The author of *The Little Prince* could have ended the story differently, with a happily ever after, but this is how it happened.

Gently, I close the book and slip it back under Yanghao's pillow. I lie there, imagining myself as the little prince lying alone, possibly dead, in the desert. But Yanghao's face keeps replacing mine, and that makes me want to cry, so I go to the kitchen. Anna says nothing and doesn't move from the sofa.

My salty tears mix with the sweet caramel.

Even though I have no idea how to make everything bet-ter, I have to try to make one thing better.

I quickly slip on my shoes and wave good-bye to Anna.

Jingwen?
Where are you—

I'll help Mama look for Yanghao.

They aren't at the playground, but when I reach the bus station, I see Mama. She stands at the other end, some distance away from me. She stops passerby after passerby and talks to them. I can't hear her, but she's making a motion with her hand to indicate Yanghao's puny height. He is so tiny.

I step in front of a man.

So many buses pulling in and out of the station.

So many buses taking so many people so many places.

But none of these buses can take me where I want to go.

Or bring me the people I want to see.

Have you seen my little brother?

I can't catch any of the Martian words the police officers say after *yes!* I wave my hands frantically and run toward Mama. I keep glancing behind to make sure the police officers are following me.

When Mama spots me, she's shocked, then angry, then she sees the police officers. They speak, but the words are too fast, and my brain is too excited and nervous and hopeful and terrified to translate.

Mama grabs my hand, and we follow the police officers to their patrol car, which still looks like a taxi to me, parked next to the bus station.

"They're taking us to the police station," Mama says as she helps me buckle my seat belt.

She tells me what the police officers told her. Yanghao didn't move from where I left him at the bus station. Someone noticed the little boy standing all alone. When the little boy didn't move for a good half an hour, that someone asked him what his name was, where he lived, and what he was doing there all alone. He never replied. That someone called the police to report a lost boy.

Two police officers responded. They asked Yanghao what his name was, where he lived, and what he was doing there all alone. He never replied. Not a word. So they dragged him, kicking and screaming, in a language the police officers neither understood nor recognized, into their patrol car and drove him to the police station. He lost his fight and his tongue somewhere in the car.

It was a challenge trying to get information from him.

The police officers guessed he didn't understand English, so they gathered colleagues who could speak languages other than English to ask him what his name was, where he lived, and what he was doing there all alone. They spoke Irish, Korean, Mandarin, Cantonese, Indonesian, and Tamil. But he said nothing. He just sat there at a detective's table, looking small and glum.

Then the detective had the bright idea of placing a telephone in front of Yanghao. Without saying anything, Yanghao picked up the phone and punched the buttons, with the detective frantically jotting down the number. The detective then took the receiver from Yanghao but found that the number didn't connect. The detective tried the number again, to the same effect. Then another policeman said the number Yanghao punched in had eleven digits, but Australian telephone numbers only had ten. The detective pointed to the telephone, and Yanghao dialed again. Still eleven digits.

All the police officers were at a loss. It was at that moment that a cake was brought out. A carrot cake with cream cheese topping. Apparently it was the detective's birthday. The detective cut a piece for Yanghao and placed a slice on a paper plate on his lap, not expecting him to eat it.

But he took a big mouthful. Then he placed the cake on the table. He picked up the phone. The detective and the other police officers scrambled to memorize the number he punched. It was a different number. This time, there were only ten digits.

This time, he called our new home, instead of our old home, which he'd forgotten couldn't be reached without dialing the international code first.

The detective grabbed the phone from Yanghao and found Anna on the other end. She told him Mama was out looking for Yanghao, but she'd tell Mama to go to the station as soon as Mama got back, and would the police please look out for Yanghao's older brother too.

While the detective was on the phone with Anna, Yanghao suddenly burst into tears. A concert of tears, wails, snot, and cake crumbs.

・　・　・

"So he's okay?" I ask.

Mama nods.

The car isn't going very fast at all, but the other cars, the buildings, and the trees are a blur.

I'm sorry about Yanghao.

All the words I couldn't say.

All the words I needed to say.

Then I bawl. A concert of tears, wails, snot, and cake crumbs.

71

By the time Mama and I reach the police station, Yanghao and I have stopped crying. Mama talks with the detective while I'm left in an office with Yanghao.

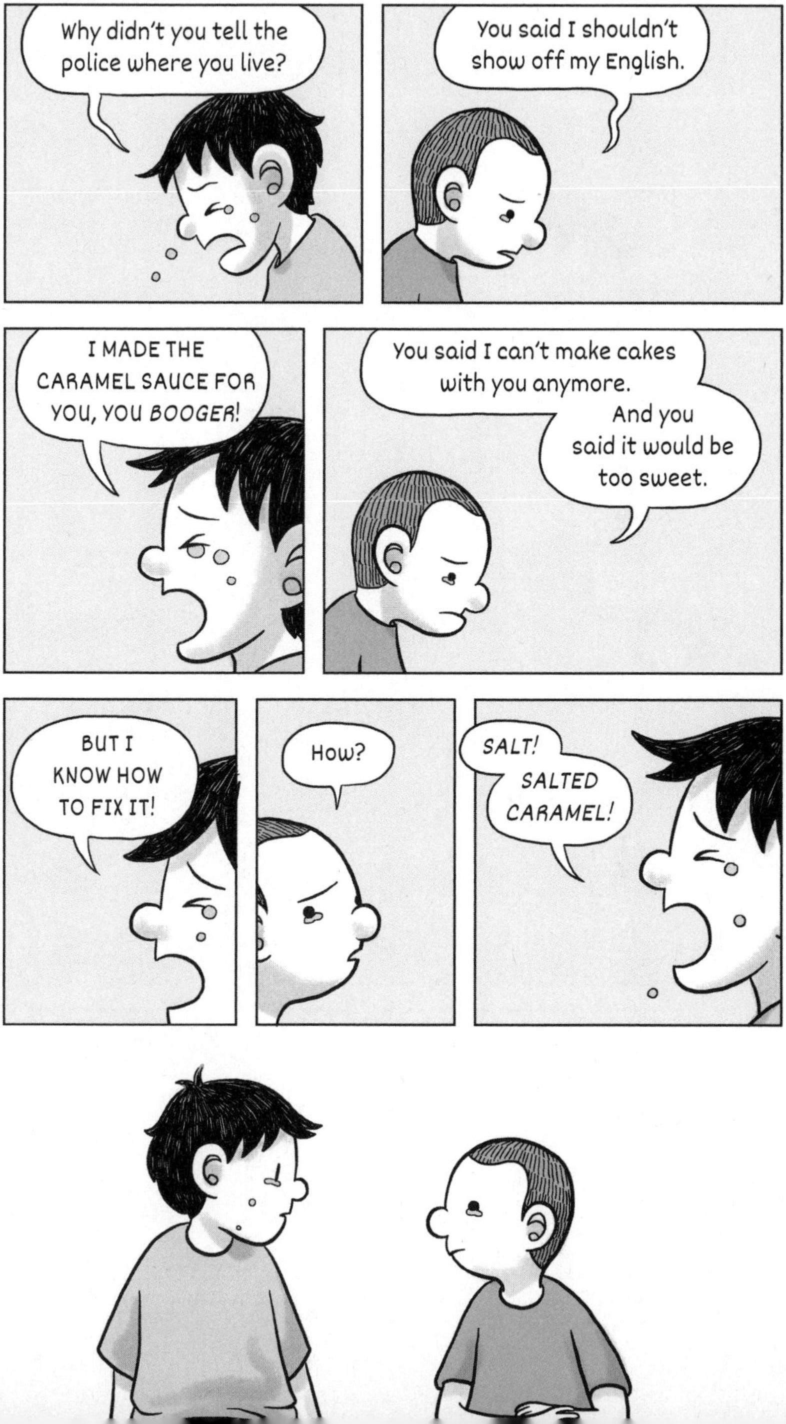

Why didn't you tell the police where you live?
You said I shouldn't show off my English.
I MADE THE CARAMEL SAUCE FOR YOU, YOU *BOOGER*!
You said I can't make cakes with you anymore.
And you said it would be too sweet.
BUT I KNOW HOW TO FIX IT!
How?
SALT!
SALTED CARAMEL!

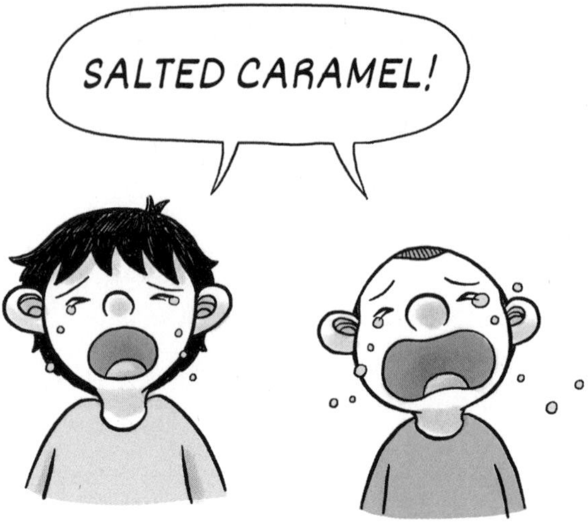
SALTED CARAMEL!
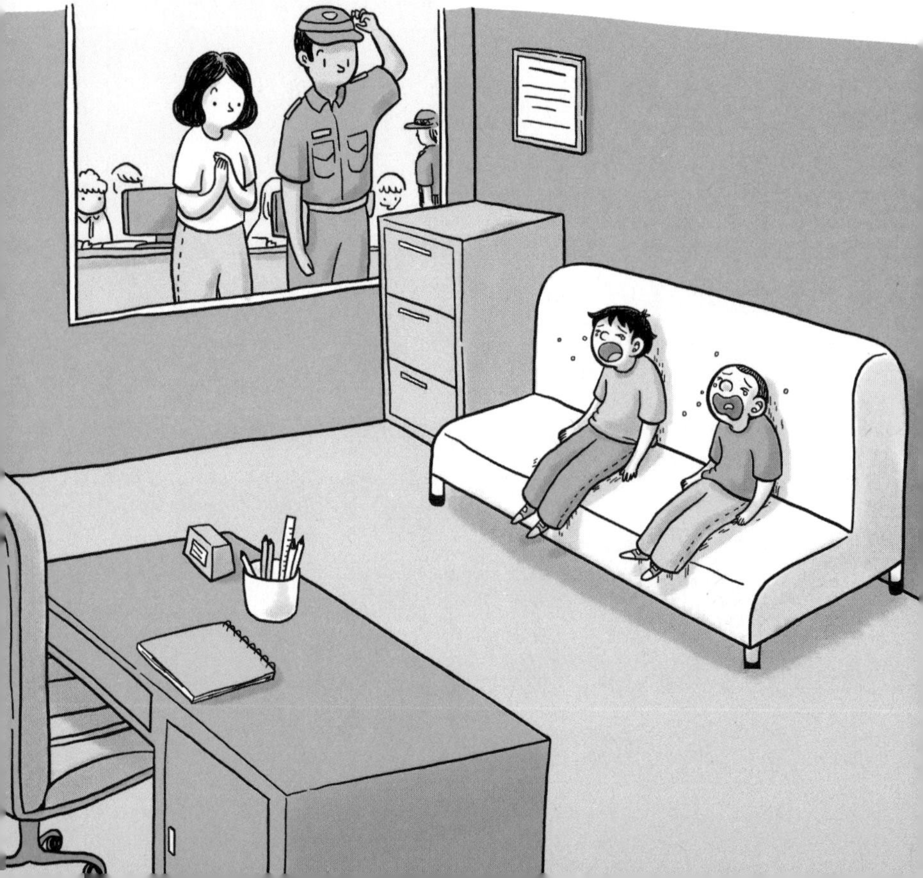

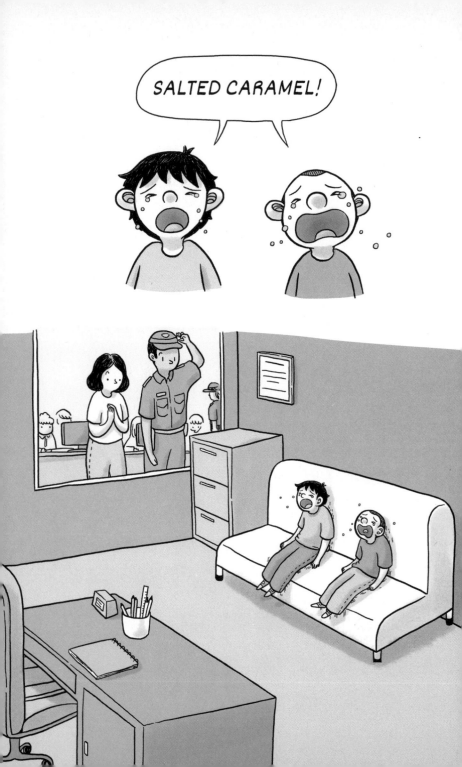

Mama doesn't scold me for the rainbow cake, or for leaving Yanghao. She even lets Yanghao eat the too-sweet rainbow cake with caramel sauce. But I will have my allowance halved until the emergency money is returned.

"Jingwen, you said you two were making *Pie in the Sky* cakes," she says. "Do you know why Papa chose those cakes for the menu?"

Yanghao quips, "Because they're delicious?"

She chuckles. "They are, but . . . For a long time, Papa had the idea of opening a cake shop called *Pie in the Sky* in Australia, but he never really thought about what would be on the menu."

It seemed that way when I asked him about it.

"It was only when he and Jingwen started making cakes on Sundays that Papa knew the *Pie in the Sky* cakes had to be different from the ones at our family's cake shop," Mama says.

"How come?" Yanghao and I ask at the same time.

"Do you remember, Jingwen? That you and Papa started making *Pie in the Sky* cakes together after you'd stopped hanging out in the kitchen?"

I nod. Mama had told Papa I'd stopped following her around and I wasn't little anymore.

"He realized that he'd been so busy with work he'd hardly spent any time with you and had missed you growing up. Soon you'd be a teenager who'd rather die than spend time with his parents. So Papa thought making cakes was a good way to spend time with you while he could, but he knew you weren't interested in our shop's cakes anymore. That's why the *Pie in the Sky* cakes had to be different."

That is all I can say. All this time, I've been making *Pie in the Sky* cakes for Papa. But it was Papa who first made *Pie in the Sky* cakes for me.

73

That evening, Mama dials the international code, followed by the eleven digits Yanghao punched in at the police station. Yanghao speaks first. He prattles on about being "arrested" by the police, as if it's something to be proud of. After he's done, I thank Ah-po for the rainbow cake recipe. She keeps asking me about what really happened because she doesn't believe the police would arrest a kid, and like me, she knows Yanghao's tales have to be taken with a giant heap of salt. I hear Ah-gong in the background, pestering her for answers, so I pass the telephone to Mama.

Ha-ha. Yes. The two of them were sitting in the police station...

Crying about something sweet and salty... I guess Jingwen is salt and Yanghao is sweet.

I want to say Yanghao isn't all sweet. He is often very, very annoying.

That's true, the secret to a good cake is a balance of sweet and salty.

. . .

In the middle of the night, I'm woken up by a series of knocks.

Yanghao is fast asleep, drooling onto his pillow. The light streaming through the doorway of our room is brighter than usual, so I know the light in Mama's bedroom must be on. I tiptoe out.

In her room, Mama's suitcase is open on the floor next to her bed. Next to the suitcase is a hammer.

Mama stands on her bed, facing the wall. Her head is down, like she's looking at something in her hands, but I can't see what it is. She lifts her arms. Something golden gleams.

She hooks it onto the nail in the wall.

She takes a few steps back, the bed creaking with each step, then looks up at the photograph.

"Maybe now," she says softly. "Maybe now I can see your face and not cry."

I go back to my room. I lie in bed thinking about how I can fix one other thing.

On Sunday morning, I get up early.

I shake Yanghao awake and ask if he'll help me with a cake.

I find Mama in the kitchen and ask her if she'll help me with the cake.

I go next door and ask Anna if she'll help me with the words.

In the kitchen of *Barker Bakes*, I lay out on the counter the cake-making ingredients that Mama helped me buy. Then I wait.

Maybe I'll end up looking like a humongous *booger*. But the twenty-fifth rule in *Rules for Making Cakes* is *never give up*.

Ben shows up. "*My mom told me you need my help,*" he says, not looking angry at all. But because he doesn't smile like he used to when he sees me, I know he's at least a little upset. That's just how nice he is, willing to help someone he probably wants to call a nincompoop.

Even though next term, we won't be in the same class,

he's been nothing but kind to me, and I shouldn't be a jerk. I say the words Anna helped me with.

"*I'm sorry I didn't show up for our meeting. Please make cakes with me.*"

His eyes pop. He's probably surprised about the cake making, or the fact that I spoke so many English words, or both of those things. But it doesn't matter, because he grins and says, "*Okay.*"

$\frac{1}{5} = \frac{20}{100} = 0.2$

$\frac{1}{10} = 0.1$

$\frac{1}{15} = 0.067$

$\frac{1}{2} = \frac{50}{100} = 0.5$

$\frac{1}{4} = \frac{25}{100} = 0.25$

$\frac{1}{8} = 0.125$

$\frac{1}{3} = 0.333$

$\frac{1}{6} = 0.16$

$\frac{1}{20} = \frac{5}{100} = 0.05$

$\frac{1}{7} = 0.$

$\frac{3}{5} = \frac{6}{10} = 0.6$

$\frac{2}{5} = \frac{4}{10} = 0.4$

I don't have English tutoring on Monday because of Math Fair, which runs from four to eight. When the dismissal bell rings at three, all my classmates rearrange the desks and chairs for the fair.

Yanghao says he's staying behind to help Ben and me set up our display, but I know it's really because he doesn't want to take the bus alone. I don't say that, though.

Mama and Heather take time off from the café to come to the Math Fair. Even Anna drops by after her doctor's appointment, where she was told to eat less cake.

The principal and Miss Scrappell come to see our display. For some reason, Miss Scrappell looks nervous. She wrings her hands and keeps looking at the principal's face as the principal inspects every inch of every cake as if she's picking one out to eat.

Finally, the principal straightens her back and says, *"All right, Miss Scrappell."*

"Yessss!" Miss Scrappell clasps her hands together and turns to Mama and says a bunch of English-that-sounds-like-Martian.

WHAT??

JINGWEN, WERE YOU REALLY SUPPOSED TO COME TO MY CLASS NEXT TERM?!?

"Su-Supposed to?" I ask.

Mama looks at me. "Miss Scrappell told the principal you've been improving slowly but surely. The principal, after seeing your excellent math project, agreed to let you stay in fifth grade one more term. If you continue to improve, you won't be sent down a grade."

"*Good job, boys*," Miss Scrappell says to Ben and me before disappearing into the crowd of students and parents.

I hesitate for a second, then I run after her, pushing my way through. "*Miss Scrappell.*"

"*May I help you, Jingwen?*"

See you tomorrow . . .

"*See you tomorrow, Jingwen,*" Miss Scrappell says, her eyes twinkling. When she turns to leave, her skirt twirls like an umbrella again, and I think about how umbrellas shelter me from the rain.

I take the long way back to my display so that I can have a look at my classmates' projects. I stop by a display about the division of fractions. The students sitting next to this stand turn out to be Joe and Max. They have their noses buried in comic books and haven't seen me yet. But then Max looks up. He elbows Joe.

I'm about to run away, but Joe is so startled by the sight of me that he falls off his chair. He hops to his feet and lunges to leave, but the crowd hems him in. For several seconds, all he can do is shuffle on the spot, looking like he needs the bathroom. I blink, not understanding what I'm seeing, and the next time I open my eyes, he has disappeared into the sea of people.

I look at Max, waiting for him to escape from me, but he stays put, and says, "*Jingwen, I'm sorry Joe and I said what we said. We're giant boogers.*"

Max seems truly sorry, but what's going on with Joe? Maybe Joe is like English, very confusing at first, but slowly, over time, I'll come to understand him. Unless he's like the word "*fudge.*" I'll probably never understand how it could be a swear word. But I don't know yet how to say all that to Max, so I rack my brain for the words I have now.

Max laughs. So do I.

When I return to my display, Yanghao is poking Ben in the arm like a woodpecker and saying, *"Letmeeatthecakes. Letmeeatthecakes."*

Ben turns to me. *"Your brother is very annoying,"* he says.

. . .

Once Math Fair is over, we pack all the cakes up and take the bus to *Barker Bakes*. Me, Yanghao, Mama, Anna, Ben, and Heather.

At the café, Heather brings out tea or coffee for the adults and caramel chocolate milk shakes for the lucky little people. "*On the house*," she says. Which is strange since she's placing all the cups and mugs on the tables.

I distribute the already-portioned cakes from Math Fair to everyone. Anna gets only the small sliver that stands for 5 percent. Mama has brought the salted caramel sauce Yanghao loves, and he drizzles it over the cakes.

As everyone is laughing and talking, I think about Papa and wish he were here. I guess this is what it will be like from now on, me missing him whenever I'm happy. Salty and sweet.

I take pictures with our camera so I can print them for Ah-po and Ah-gong. I'll mail them the same time I mail the postcard I bought yesterday for Xirong. It has kangaroos and koalas. If he doesn't reply, that's okay.

In their last letter, along with the rainbow cake recipe, Ah-po and Ah-gong also asked to be sent pictures of my twelfth birthday celebration. I've dreaded birthdays since that tenth year, but maybe my twelfth, in a few weeks' time, won't be so bad. We can have a small party like this one we're having, maybe even Ben and Sarah can come. We'll have a proper rainbow cake with all the layers atop one another, all the colors together in one cake.

When I mail the pictures to Ah-po and Ah-gong, I'll tell them I'm doing fine, and it won't be a lie. Today Australia feels a little bit less like Mars. It's not exactly like my old home, and I think they will always be the same but different. But they can both be good.

I'm ready to eat my cake, but first, I turn to my little brother.

Yanghao, what time is it?

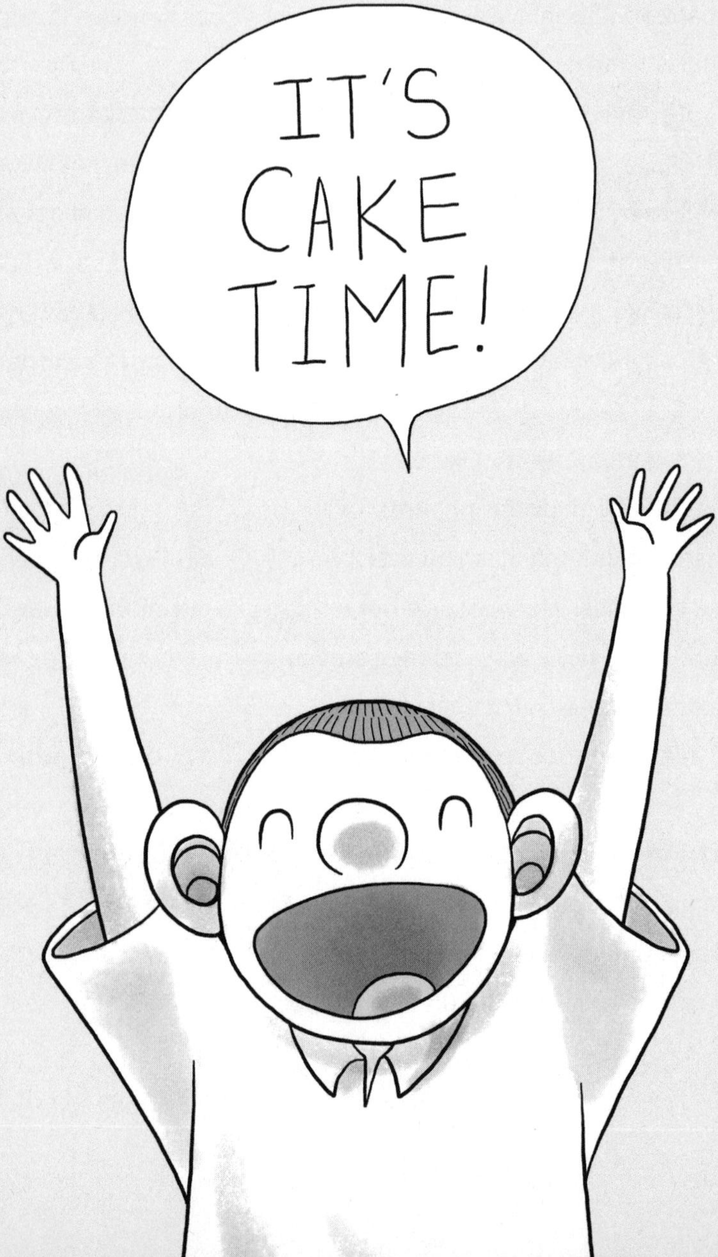
IT'S CAKE TIME!

Acknowledgments

Thank you, thank you, thank you to:

My agent, Jim McCarthy The Beard. For your guidance on how to make my book shine, for squealing with me over every piece of good news, for your boundless patience, for knowing just what to say when I freak out, and for everything and everything. I love you, Jim!

My editor, Brian Geffen. For getting this book and my jokes, for reading this book over and over, for guiding me to make it the best it can be, for all your kind words, and for being so awesome in every way. You're the best, Brian!

The rest of the Henry Holt/Macmillan team: Christian Trimmer, Jean Feiwel, Carol Ly (you made my book oh-so-gorgeous!), Patrick Collins, Melinda Ackell, Molly Ellis, Kelsey Marrujo, Lucy Del Priore, Allegra Green, Melissa Zar, Mariel Dawson, and Kristin Dulaney. MJ Robinson for the fantastic colors, and Ana Deboo.

I'm very, very lucky. My book couldn't be in better hands.

Amanda Rawson Hill and Cindy Baldwin, for seeing the heart of my story when it was still in shambles, for believing in it (and me) when I couldn't.

Bronwyn Clark, Reese E., and Jennifer Bee, for your critiques, for reading crappy drafts, for trusting me with your own stories, and for all the cheerleading.

Jin Gan, Liping, Christina, Onglye, and Yuan Yee, for never once saying that I shouldn't or couldn't.

The PitchWars team: Brenda Drake and Heather Cashman, my fellow '17 mentees for giving me a writing family that understands my neuroses. Extra love to Kit Rosewater, Karen Chow, and PITA Rajani Larocca.

My four siblings, for giving me a lifetime of tears of anger, frustration, plain incredulity, and, most of all, of joy and laughter.

My dogs: Poop-roller and Bossy Boots!

And to my papa, who told me I could be anything I wanted to be.

Rainbow Cake Recipe

1.

14 egg yolks   2 cups sugar

3-1/2 cups cake flour

5-1/4 tsps baking powder

Whisk until pale yellow.

1 cup water

7/8 cup vegetable oil

BOWL A

7/8 tsp salt

7 tsps vanilla extract

2.

14 egg whites

7/8 tsp cream of tartar

BOWL B

Whisk until stiff peaks form.

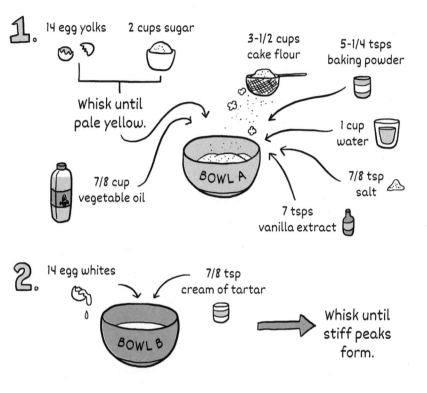

3. Gently fold the mixture in BOWL B into BOWL A until mixed.

4. Divide the mixture into seven equal portions and mix one to two drops of food coloring into each portion. Colors: yellow, red, blue, green, purple, orange, and pink. Pour each batter into separate cake pans.

7 x

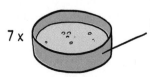

8" round cake pans lined ONLY at the bottom

(Do not grease or line the sides)

5. Bake at 350°F for 18 minutes.

6. Remove from oven. Let cool for 10 minutes before removing from pans (run a knife around the sides if needed) and leave until completely cool.

7. Prepare the filling and frosting.

6 cups
whipping cream

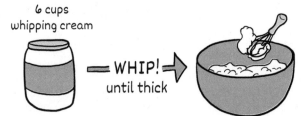

WHIP!
until thick

8. Stack the seven layers of cake together.

whipped cream filling
with cut-up fruits
(mango, kiwi, strawberries)
between each layer of cake

9. Frost all around with the remaining whipped cream!